REPLAY

Marc Levy

REPLAY

*Translated from the French
by Kate Bignold and Lakshmi Ramakrishnan Iyer*

Europa
editions

Europa Editions
214 West 29th Street
New York, N.Y. 10001
www.europaeditions.com
info@europaeditions.com

Copyright © 2012 by Marc Levy/Versilio
First Publication 2014 by Europa Editions

Translation by Kate Bignold and Lakshmi Ramakrishnan Iyer
Original title: *Si c'était à refaire*
Translation copyright © 2012 by Susanna Lea Associates

Library of Congress Cataloging in Publication Data is available
ISBN 978-1-60945-202-5

www.marclevy.info

Levy, Marc
Replay

Book design by Emanuele Ragnisco
www.mekkanografici.com

Cover photo © ClarkandCompany/iStock

Prepress by Grafica Punto Print – Rome

Printed in the USA

"How happy one would be if one could throw off one's self as one throws off others."
—MADAME DU DEFFAND

REPLAY

Melt into the crowd. Carry out your task without any-one realizing what's happening or even noticing you at all.

You're wearing sweats so you'll go unnoticed. At 7 A.M. in Hudson River Park, everybody's out for a run. In a city where schedules are tight and nerves are constantly tested, people go running—to keep in shape, to clear a hangover, and to cope with the stress of the day ahead.

Find a bench. Put your foot on the seat and retie your shoelaces as you wait for the target to come closer. The hood pulled down over your forehead narrows your field of vision, but it helps hide your face. Give yourself a chance to catch your breath, and make sure your hands aren't shaking. You're sweat-ing, but that's okay, it won't attract attention or give you away. Everyone else is sweating too.

When you spot him, let him go past. Wait for a few seconds before you start jogging along again. Keep a good distance behind him until the moment is right.

You've rehearsed this scene every morning at the same time for a week. The temptation to act has grown stronger each time. But your success depends on careful preparation. There's no room for error.

The target comes down Charles Street, following his usual route. He waits for the lights to turn red so he can cross the first four lanes of the West Side Highway. The cars are speeding north, people heading to work.

He reaches the median. The little illuminated figure on the traffic light is already flashing. Toward Tribeca and the Financial District the cars are bumper to bumper, but he moves forward anyway. He responds to the blaring horns the way he always does: by lifting his fist, his middle finger pointing to the sky. He veers left and onto the pedestrian walkway along the Hudson River.

He's running his twenty blocks amid all the other joggers, pleased when he overtakes the ones who aren't as fit as him, cursing those who leave him behind. They have youth on their side. Back when he was eighteen, this used to be an unsavory part of town. He'd been one of the first to come out here and run till he was short of breath. Hardly anything remains of the docks that once jutted out over the water on stilts, stinking of fish and rust mingled with the smell of sewage. How much his city has changed in twenty years; it's grown fresher and more attractive. And in the meantime the years have begun to show on his face.

Across the river, the lights of Hoboken go out as dawn breaks, followed soon afterwards by Jersey City's.

Don't lose sight of him. When he gets to the intersection with Greenwich Street, he'll leave the pedestrian walkway. You'll have to act before then. On this particular morning, he won't make it to Starbucks to order his daily mochaccino.

When he passes Pier 4, he won't notice, but the shadow following him will have caught up to him.

One more block to go. Step up your pace. Blend into the gaggle that always forms in this spot because the footpath narrows and the slower runners hold up the faster ones. The long needle shifts under your sleeve. You hold it in place with a firm hand.

Aim between the top of the sacrum and the lowest rib. A quick strike, in and out quickly and deeply in order to perforate the kid-

ney and reach the abdominal artery. As it's pulled out, the needle will leave behind internal tears. They'll be beyond repair by the time anyone realizes what has happened, the ambulance will arrive and he'll be rushed to the hospital. It won't be easy getting to the hospital at this hour — even with the sirens wailing, in such dense traffic, the best the driver can do is curse his powerlessness.

Two years earlier he might have had a chance. But they closed St. Vincent's Hospital, and the nearest emergency unit is now on the east side, across the island from Hudson River Park. He'll hemorrhage too heavily; all the blood will drain from his body by the time he gets there.

He won't suffer, at least not too much. He'll just feel cold, then colder still. He'll shiver and gradually lose all feeling in his limbs, and his teeth will chatter so much he won't be able to talk. What would he say anyway? That he'd felt a sharp pinch in his back? So what? The police won't be able to deduce anything from that.

There is *such a thing as a perfect crime. Don't all the finest police officers confess at the end of their careers that they have their fair share of unresolved cases hanging over them, burdening their consciences?*

You've drawn level with him now. You've simulated the gesture many times on a bag of sand, but the feeling will be different when the needle pierces human flesh. The most important thing is to not hit a bone. Hitting a lumbar vertebra would mean failure. The needle must be plunged in and immediately drawn back inside the sleeve.

After it's done, continue running at the same speed. Resist the temptation to turn around. Remain anonymous, invisible, in the crowd of joggers.

Hours and hours of preparation for an act that will take you only a few seconds.

It will take him some time to die, probably a quarter of an hour. But by 7:30 this morning, he'll be dead.

1.
MAY 2011

A ndrew Stilman had started out as a freelancer at twenty-three and made his way up the ladder one rung at a time, becoming a staff writer by thirty. Since he was a kid, he'd dreamed of carrying a press pass from one of the world's best-known papers, and every morning, upon entering the double doors of 620 Eighth Avenue, he glanced at the newspaper's name on the façade: *The New York Times*. It never failed to give him a thrill. Thousands of hacks would give their right arm just to visit.

Andrew had spent four years working in the research department before taking over as Deputy Obituaries Editor. The previous editor had been run over by a bus as she was leaving work one day and ended up featured in the very section she used to write for. She'd been rushing home so as not to miss the delivery of some sexy underwear she'd ordered online. Life really does hang by a thread sometimes.

Andrew spent another five years toiling away anonymously. Obituaries don't carry their author's name—the deceased get all the credit. Five years writing about men and women who were now only memories, whether good or bad. One thousand eight hundred and twenty-five days, and nearly six thousand dry martinis consumed every evening after work between 7:30 P.M. and 8:15 P.M. at the bar of the Marriott Hotel on 40th Street.

Every glass came garnished with three olives. With each pit he spat into an overflowing ashtray, Andrew would chase away the memory of yet another extinguished life he'd summed up that day. Living in the company of the dead was driving him to the bottle. By Andrew's fourth year on obits, the barman at the Marriott was refilling his glass six times a night. He'd often show up at the office ashen-faced and sleepy-eyed, his shirt collar askew and his jacket crumpled. Luckily a suit and tie weren't de rigueur in the newspaper's open-plan offices, least of all in the department where he worked.

Either because of his elegant, precise prose, or because of the devastating effects of a particularly hot summer, the column he was in charge of had expanded to two full pages. When the quarterly results were being prepared, a statistics-mad analyst in the financial department observed that the revenue per obituary was soaring; families in mourning were taking out more lines to express the extent of their grief. Good news travels fast within large companies, and at its fall meeting the management committee discussed the results and decided to promote the no-longer-nameless person behind them. Andrew had been made Editor. He was still on the births, deaths and marriages beat, but now he'd been put in charge of the highly unprofitable wedding pages as well.

Andrew was never short of ideas. For a time, he'd abandoned his usual watering hole and started hanging out in the upscale bars frequented by the city's various gay communities. Striking up conversations between countless dry martinis, he'd handed out business cards left and right, explaining to anyone who would listen that his column was only too happy to publish announcements of *any* nuptials, including the kind most other newspapers refused to accept. Same-sex marriage was still nowhere near legal in the state of New York, but the *Times* was free to mention any exchange of vows between consenting adults. At the end of the day, it was the thought that counted.

Within three months, births, deaths, and marriages had

spread to four pages in the Sunday edition, and Andrew was given a substantial raise.

That was when he'd decided to cut down on the booze—not out of concern for his liver, but because he'd just bought himself a Datsun 240Z, a car he'd been dreaming of since he was a kid and which had been beautifully restored in his best friend's auto shop. The police had begun taking a hard line on motorists under the influence and he was left with a choice: drinking or driving? Andrew, who was crazy about his vintage car, made his choice. And though he'd started frequenting the Marriott again, he never had more than two drinks, except on Thursdays.

As it happened, it was on a Thursday a few years later that Andrew bumped into Valerie Ramsay as he was coming out of the bar. She was as drunk as he was, and giggling uncontrollably after tripping against a newspaper vending machine and landing on her backside in the middle of the sidewalk.

Andrew recognized Valerie immediately. Not her face—she looked nothing like the girl he'd known twenty years earlier—but her laugh. An unforgettable laugh that set her breasts bouncing. Valerie Ramsay's breasts had occupied Andrew's thoughts throughout his adolescence.

They'd met in junior high. Valerie had been kicked off the school's cheerleading squad for a stupid locker room fight with a notorious drama queen, and she'd joined the choir instead. Andrew had a knee cartilage injury (which he didn't get fixed until years later, when he started dating a girl who loved to dance), and couldn't play sports. He didn't have too many other options, so he'd also signed up for choir.

He'd flirted with Valerie all through high school. No actual sex, but enough wandering hands and tongues to give him an introduction to the world of romance and an intimate acquaintance with Valerie's generous curves.

Of course, he did have Valerie to thank for his first orgasm in somebody else's hands. One match evening while everyone else was at the basketball game, when the two lovebirds were cooing away in the empty locker room, Valerie finally agreed to slip her hand inside Andrew's jeans. Fifteen giddy seconds later, he was listening to Valerie's peals of laughter, her bouncing breasts prolonging the fleeting pleasure. You never forget the first time.

"Valerie?" Andrew said, amazed.

"Ben?" Valerie replied, equally surprised.

Everyone had called him Ben in junior high. He couldn't remember why, and he hadn't heard the nickname for twenty years.

Valerie attempted to justify her sorry state by pretending she'd been on a girls' night out of the kind she hadn't experienced since college. Andrew, who was in only marginally better shape, cited a promotion. He failed to mention he'd gotten it two years earlier.

"What are you doing in New York?" Andrew asked.

"I live here," came the reply as he helped Valerie up off the ground.

"Have you been living here long?"

"Quite some time, but don't ask me how long—I'm in no state to count. So what are you doing these days?"

"What I always wanted to do. How about you?"

"Twenty years of life makes for a long story, you know," Valerie answered, dusting off her skirt.

"I'll give you nine lines," Andrew sighed.

"What do you mean, nine lines?"

"You tell me about twenty years of your life and I'll sum them up in nine lines for you."

"Yeah, right."

"Wanna bet?"

"Maybe. How much?"

"Dinner."

"I'm seeing someone, Andrew," Valerie replied.

"I wasn't suggesting a night in a hotel. How about dumpling soup at Joe's Shanghai? Are you still crazy about dumplings?"

"Absolutely."

"Just tell your boyfriend I'm an old girlfriend."

"First let's see if you can condense the last twenty years of my life into nine lines."

Valerie looked at Andrew with the sly grin he remembered from high school, right before she'd suggest he come meet her in the shed behind the science wing. That grin hadn't changed one bit.

"Okay," she said. "One for the road and I'll tell you my life story."

"Not in this bar—it's too noisy."

"If you think you're taking me to your place tonight, you've got the wrong girl."

"Didn't even cross my mind, Valerie. I just think that in the state we're both in, we should grab a bite or our bet won't stand a chance."

Andrew was right. Although Valerie's heels were now planted firmly on the dirty sidewalk of West 40th, she was swaying gently, as if she were on the deck of a boat. She could do with something to eat. Andrew hailed a taxi and gave the driver the address of his favorite late-night spot in SoHo. A quarter of an hour later, Valerie was sitting down opposite him at a table and began to tell him her story.

She'd gotten a scholarship from the University of Indianapolis, the first of all the colleges she'd applied to that had accepted her. The Midwest had never been a part of her childhood dreams, but she couldn't afford to wait for a reply from a more prestigious institution. Without this scholarship, she'd have wound up waiting tables in Poughkeepsie, the podunk town in upstate New York where they'd both grown up.

Eight years later, Valerie left Indiana with a degree in veterinary sciences under her belt, and followed in the footsteps of many ambitious young women by coming to try her luck in Manhattan.

"You did your whole vet degree in Indiana only to end up in New York?"

"What's wrong with that?" Valerie asked.

"Sticking a thermometer up poodles' asses? Was that really what you aspired to?"

"You're such a jerk!"

"Sorry, I didn't mean to offend you. But you have to admit Manhattan isn't exactly rich in wildlife. Apart from Upper East Side pooches.

"In a city with two million single people, you'd be surprised how important pets can be."

"Oh, I see. You also treat hamsters, cats, and goldfish?"

"I'm a vet for the NYPD, actually. I look after their horses as well as police dogs. Definitely no poodles—just Labradors trained to find corpses, a few aging German Shepherds, and some drug-detecting Retrievers and bomb-sniffing Beagles."

Andrew raised one eyebrow and then the other. It was a trick he'd learned in journalism school. It always disconcerted whomever he was talking to. When he was interviewing someone and doubted the sincerity of their account, he would launch into this eyebrow dance and judge by the other's reaction if they were lying to him or not. But Valerie's face remained expressionless.

"I wasn't expecting that answer at all," he said, amazed. "So are you in the police or just a vet? I mean, do you carry a badge and a weapon?"

Valerie gaped at him, then shrieked with laughter.

"I can tell you're much more grown-up than the last time I saw you, dear Ben."

"Were you pulling my leg?"

"No, but that funny face you made reminded me of the way you looked back when we were in school."

"I'm not surprised you became a vet," Andrew went on. "You've always loved animals. Do you remember that night you called me at my parents' house, begging me to sneak out straight away and come meet you? I thought you had something romantic in mind, but it was nothing of the sort. You made me carry an old, foul-smelling dog with a broken leg that you'd found on the side of the road all the way to the vet in the middle of the night."

"You remember that, Andrew Stilman?"

"I remember everything we did together, Valerie Ramsay. Now will you tell me a bit more about what happened between that afternoon when I waited in vain for you at the Poughkeepsie movie theater and your reappearance this evening?"

"I'd received the admission letter from the University of Indianapolis in the mail that morning, so I packed my bag. I left Poughkeepsie that same evening with the money I'd been saving from my summer jobs and babysitting. I was so glad I'd never have to watch my parents arguing again. They didn't even want to take me to the bus station, can you believe it? But, seeing as you can only devote nine lines to your ex-girlfriend, I'll spare you the details of my university studies. Anyway, when I moved to New York, I had a string of part-time jobs in various vet surgeries, until one day I answered a police ad and landed a position. I've been on the permanent staff for two years."

Andrew asked a passing waitress to bring them two more coffees.

"I like the idea of you being a vet in the police. I've written more obituaries and wedding announcements than you could imagine, but I've never heard of that particular profession. I wouldn't even have imagined it existed."

"Of course it exists."

"I was angry with you, you know."

"What about?"

"About running off without saying goodbye."

"You were the only person I confided in about wanting to leave the second I could."

"I hadn't realized your secret was a warning."

"Are you still mad at me?" Valerie asked, teasingly.

"I should be. But hey, it's ancient history."

"And you? You actually became a journalist?"

"How do you know?"

"I asked you earlier about what you were doing with your life and you answered, 'What I always wanted to do.' And you always wanted to be a journalist."

"You remember that?"

"I remember everything, Andrew Stilman."

"So who's this guy you're seeing?"

"It's late," Valerie sighed. "I have to get home. Anyway, if I tell you too much you'll never manage to put it all into nine lines."

Andrew smiled mischievously. "Does that mean we're having dinner at Joe's Shanghai?"

"If you win your bet. I'm a woman of my word."

They walked through the deserted SoHo streets to Sixth Avenue without saying a word to each other, Andrew holding Valerie's arm to help her cross the uneven cobblestones.

He hailed a taxi and held the door open for Valerie as she slid into the back seat.

"It was a great surprise to see you again, Valerie."

"For me too, Ben."

"Where can I send you my nine-line masterpiece?"

Valerie rummaged in her bag, pulled out her eye pencil and asked Andrew to open the palm of his hand. She wrote her phone number on it.

"If it's nine lines, you should be able to text them to me. Goodnight."

Andrew watched the cab drive off. When he'd lost sight of it, he continued on to his apartment, a fifteen-minute walk away. He needed the fresh air. Although he'd memorized the number on his hand as soon as he'd seen it, he kept his palm open, glancing at the number every few seconds to be sure it hadn't disappeared, all the way home.

2

I t had been a long time since Andrew had summed up someone's life in a few lines. For the past two years, he'd been working on the paper's foreign desk. He'd always had a strong interest in current events and world affairs.

Now that computer screens had replaced the banks of Linotype machines and typesetters, the entire editorial staff had access to the articles that would be appearing in the next day's edition. On several occasions, Andrew had noticed flawed analyses and factual errors in the International News section. Each time, he'd flagged them at the daily editorial meeting, which all the journalists attended, saving the newspaper from having to publish corrections in the wake of readers' complaints. It didn't take long for his keen eye to get noticed and when it came to choosing between an end-of-year bonus and a new position, he had no difficulty deciding.

He found the idea of having to write another "life chronicle," as he liked to call his past pieces, very stimulating. He even felt a tad nostalgic for his old job as he began work on Valerie's obit.

Two hours and eight and a half lines later, he texted the interested party.

He spent the rest of the day attempting, in vain, to write an article on the likelihood of a Syrian uprising. His colleagues reckoned it was improbable, if not impossible.

He couldn't concentrate. His eyes wandered from his computer screen to his cell phone, which remained hopelessly silent. When it finally lit up around 5 P.M., Andrew lunged for it. False alarm—it was the dry cleaner informing him his shirts were ready.

It wasn't until around noon the next day that he received the following text: *Next Thursday, 7.30 P.M. Valerie.*

He replied immediately: *Do you have the address?*

And he regretted his haste when a few seconds later he read a laconic: *Yes.*

* * *

Andrew continued working and stayed sober for seven whole days. Not a single drop of alcohol. (Well, except for a beer, but that didn't count.)

On Wednesday he popped into his dry cleaner's to collect the suit he'd left the previous day, and then went to buy a white shirt. He took the opportunity to go to a barber's to have his neck and face tidied up as well. As he did every Wednesday, he met up with his best friend, Simon, at around 9 P.M. in an unassuming little café that served the best fish in the West Village. Andrew lived nearby and Mary's Fish Camp was his canteen on the many evenings he worked late at the office. While Simon ranted, like he did every time they had a meal together, about the Republicans preventing the President from implementing the program he'd been elected on, Andrew stared dreamily through the window at the passersby and tourists strolling through his neighborhood.

"And I heard—from a very reliable source—that it looks like Obama's fallen big time for Angela Merkel."

"She *is* quite pretty," Andrew answered distractedly.

"Andrew, either you're working on a mammoth scoop, in which case I forgive you, or you've met someone, in which case talk right now!"

"Neither," Andrew replied. "Sorry, I'm just tired."

"I haven't seen you this clean shaven since you went out with that brunette who was a head taller than you. Sally, if my memory serves me right."

"Sophie. But how could you be expected to remember? I only went out with her for a year and a half! It just proves you find my conversation as interesting as I find yours. Why would I mind you forgetting her name?"

"She was mind-numbingly boring. I didn't once hear her laugh," Simon continued.

"That's because she never found your jokes funny. Are you done eating? I want to go to bed," Andrew said with a sigh.

"If you don't tell me what's eating *you*, I'll keep ordering desserts until I explode."

Andrew looked his friend in the eye.

"Do you have one particular girl who you remember from when you were a teenager?" he asked, waving to the waitress to bring him the check.

"I knew it wasn't work making you act like this!"

"It's not what you think. As a matter of fact, I'm working on a horrifying story at the moment—stomach-churning."

"What's it about?"

"Sorry, confidential, I can't talk about it yet."

Simon paid in cash and stood up.

"Let's go for a stroll. I need some fresh air."

Andrew got his raincoat from the rack and went outside to join his friend on the sidewalk.

"Kathy Steinbeck," Simon muttered.

"Who's Kathy Steinbeck?"

"The girl I remember from when I was a teenager."

"Valerie Ramsay," Andrew declared.

"You don't give a damn about why Kathy Steinbeck had an effect on me when I was young, do you? You only asked me so you could tell me about your Valerie."

Andrew took Simon by the shoulder and led him a short

way up the street, down three steps leading to the basement of a small brick building, and into Fedora, a bar where Count Basie, Nat King Cole, John Coltrane, Miles Davis, Billie Holiday and Sarah Vaughan had once performed as young musicians.

"Do you think I'm too self-centered?" Andrew asked.

Simon didn't answer.

"You're probably right. I've written summaries of strangers' lives for so long, I've ended up believing that the only time anyone might take an interest in me is when I appear in my own goddamn obituary."

Andrew raised his glass and proclaimed: "'Andrew Stilman, born in 1975, worked for most of his life at the famous *New York Times* . . . ' See, Simon? It's like with doctors—they can treat anyone but themselves. The basic tenet of my trade is: only use adjectives to describe the deceased. I'll start again. 'Andrew Stilman, born in 1975, worked for many years at *The New York Times*. His meteoric rise led to him becoming executive editor in 2020. With Stilman at the helm, the newspaper enjoyed a boom and once again became the most respected paper in the world.' Am I going a bit overboard?"

"You're not going to start again, are you?"

"Hang in there. Let me get to the end. Then I'll do yours."

"At what age are you planning to die? Just so I know how long this nightmare's going to last."

"With all the progress in medicine, who knows? Where was I? Oh yes, 'With Stilman at the helm, blah blah blah, the newspaper rediscovered its former glory. In 2021, he won the Pulitzer Prize for his visionary article on . . . ' Hmmm, not quite sure yet—I'll figure that out later. ' . . . a subject that led to him writing his first, award-winning book, which is on reading lists at all the top universities.'"

"And the title of this magnum opus was *A Treatise on*

Journalistic Modesty," Simon jibed. "How old will you be when they give you the Nobel Peace Prize?"

"Seventy-two. I was getting to that. 'He retired from his position as Editor-in-Chief at the age of seventy-one after a remarkable career, and the following year he was . . . '"

" . . . arrested for first-degree murder after he'd bored his best friend to death."

"You're not being very sympathetic."

"Why do you need sympathy?"

"I'm having a weird moment, Simon. Loneliness is getting to me, which isn't normal, because I've never loved life more than when I'm single."

"You're approaching forty."

"I still have a few years before I turn forty, thank you. The atmosphere at work is asphyxiating," Andrew continued. "It's like there's a sword hanging over our heads. I just wanted to cheer myself up. So who was this Kathy Steinbeck of yours?"

"My philosophy teacher."

"Really? I wouldn't have imagined that the girl who marked your adolescence was a grown woman."

"Life's strange. When I was twenty, I fantasized about women fifteen years older than me; now I'm thirty-seven, it's girls fifteen years younger who catch my eye. Tell me more about this Valerie Ramsay of yours."

"I bumped into her last week on my way out of the Marriott's bar."

"I see."

"No, you don't see. I was crazy about her in high school. When she left our hometown without a word, it took me years to forget her. To be honest, I wonder if I ever totally did."

"Big disappointment seeing her again?"

"No, quite the opposite. There's something different about her that gets to me even more now."

"She's become a woman—I'll explain the mechanics to you

one day! So are you telling me you've fallen in love again? 'Andrew Stilman falls head over heels on West 40th Street.' What a headline!"

"I'm trying to tell you I'm confused, and that hasn't happened to me for a long time."

"Do you know how to get hold of her?"

"I'm having dinner with her tomorrow evening. I'm as nervous as a teenager."

"I don't think you ever get over those nerves. Ten years after mom died, my dad met a woman in a supermarket. He was sixty-eight at the time. The day before his first date with her, I had to drive him into town because he was absolutely set on buying a new suit. In the tailor's fitting room, he told me word for word what he was going to say to her during dinner, and asked me what I thought. It was pathetic. Moral of the story: you'll always lose your cool around a woman you're attracted to, whatever your age."

"Very reassuring. Thanks."

"I'm just warning you that you're going to say one wrong thing after another, you'll think your conversation is boring—which it probably will be—and when you get home you'll curse yourself for being so pathetic the whole damn evening."

"Please don't stop, Simon. It's so good to have real friends."

"Hey, stop complaining. I just want you to remember one thing for tomorrow: sit back and enjoy the evening. After all, it's a date you never thought you'd have. Be yourself. If she likes you, she likes you."

"Are we that powerless in the matter?"

"Just look around this bar and you can see for yourself. I'll tell you about my philosophy teacher another day. We're having lunch on Friday—you can give me the rundown on your reunion then. Oh, and try not make it as detailed as your obit."

The coolness of the night air took them by surprise when

they left Fedora. Simon jumped into a taxi, leaving Andrew to walk home.

On Friday, Andrew told Simon that his evening had gone as he'd predicted, maybe even worse. It had started off disastrously—on the way to the restaurant, Andrew suddenly realized he hadn't specified whether they were to meet at the Midtown location or the one in Chinatown. He panicked for half an hour thinking that Valerie might go to the wrong location and think him a fool for not being more specific. But she showed up in Chinatown smiling, and Andrew did his best to hide his relief. Andrew thought he'd probably fallen back in love with Valerie Ramsay, which was inconvenient because she'd mentioned once again that she was seeing someone, though she hadn't offered any details.

She didn't phone him the following day, or the following week, and Andrew was starting to feel pretty low. He spent all day Saturday at the office. On Sunday he met Simon at the basketball court on Sixth Avenue and West Houston, where they exchanged a few passes, but not many words.

His Sunday evening was as gloomy as Sunday evenings get: he'd ordered Chinese takeout, then sat flicking between a movie he'd seen before, a hockey game, and yet another TV series in which police scientists were getting to the bottom of grisly murders. Basically, a depressing evening in. Until around 9 P.M., when his cell phone lit up. It wasn't Simon texting him though, but Valerie, who wanted to meet up ASAP.

Andrew texted back immediately to say he'd love to and ask when.

Now, the next message told him. *9th and A, across from Tompkins Square Park.*

Andrew glanced in his living room mirror. How long would it take to get himself looking halfway decent? The shorts and old polo he'd kept on since his basketball game with Simon weren't exactly stylish, and he really needed to shower. But the urgent tone he'd detected in Valerie's message worried him, so he slipped on a pair of jeans and a clean shirt, grabbed his keys out of the dish in the hall and raced down the three floors of his apartment building.

The neighborhood was quiet: not a taxi in sight. He began running towards Seventh Avenue, spotted a cab at the light at Charles Street and caught up with it just before it drove off. He promised the driver a generous tip if he could get him to his destination in under ten minutes.

Tossed around in the back seat, Andrew regretted his offer. But the driver earned his tip, and he arrived sooner than planned.

Valerie was waiting for him in front of a shuttered café called the Pick Me Up. The name made him smile briefly. Only briefly, when he saw how haggard Valerie was looking.

He walked up to her. She slapped him hard across the face.

"You made me come across town to slap me?" he asked, rubbing his cheek. "What did I do to deserve that?"

"My life was just about perfect until I bumped into you outside that damn bar, and now I don't know what the hell is going on."

Feeling a wave of warmth wash over him, Andrew thought to himself that he'd just received the most delightful slap of his life.

"I'm a nice guy, so I'm not going to hit you back. But you took the words right out of my mouth," he whispered, not taking his eyes off her.

"I haven't stopped thinking about you since we had dinner, Andrew Stilman."

"When you ran away from Poughkeepsie, I thought about you day and night, for three, four years . . . If not longer."

"That was then. I'm not talking about when we were teenagers, I'm talking about now."

"It's the same, Valerie. Nothing's changed—not you, and not the way I felt when I saw you again."

"What if you're just saying that? Maybe you just want to get back at me for what I put you through."

"Where do you get such warped ideas from? You can't be all that happy in your almost perfect life to be thinking that way."

Before Andrew realized what was happening, Valerie had put her arms around his neck and kissed him. Hesitant at first, her kiss soon became bolder.

She broke off and looked at him with tears in her eyes.

"I'm screwed," she said. "What are we going to do, Ben?"

"Be together. For now, maybe for a while longer. If you promise never to call me Ben again."

3.

To be together, all that remained for Valerie to do was leave her boyfriend. Breaking up after two years of living together wasn't something she could do in one evening. Andrew waited eagerly, but knew that if he hurried things she wouldn't stay.

Twenty days later, in the middle of the night, he received an almost identical message to the one that had turned his life upside down that other Sunday. When his taxi stopped in front of Café Pick Me Up, Valerie was waiting for him, a black smear down each cheek and a suitcase at her feet.

Back at his place, Andrew set down the baggage in his room and left Valerie to unpack her things. When he returned, she'd slipped under the sheets without turning the light on. He sat down by her, kissed her, then walked back to the door, guessing she needed to be alone to mourn the relationship that had just ended. He wished her goodnight and asked if she still liked hot chocolate. Valerie nodded and Andrew left the room.

That night, from the sofa in the living room, where Andrew had trouble sleeping, he heard her crying and ached to go and comfort her, but stopped himself. Only she could help herself get over that kind of grief.

In the morning, Valerie found a breakfast tray on the coffee table in the living room. On it was a bowl containing cocoa powder and a note:

I'm taking you to dinner tonight.

It'll be our first time.
I've left you a spare set of keys in the hall.
Love,
Andrew

Valerie promised Andrew she'd only stay as long as it took her ex to move his things out of her apartment. If her best friend Colette didn't live in New Orleans, she'd have gone to stay with her. Ten days later—much to Andrew's regret, as having her around was making him happier every day—she packed her suitcase and went back to her place in the East Village. Seeing Andrew's saddened face, she reminded him they'd only be fifteen blocks away from each other.

Summer arrived. During the weekends, when the heat in the city became unbearable, they took the subway to Coney Island and spent hours on the beach.

In September, Andrew left the States for a ten-day trip, refusing to give Valerie the slightest bit of information about it. He used the word "confidential" and swore she had no reason to doubt him.

In October, when he went on another trip, he promised to take her on vacation as soon as he could so she'd forgive him. But Valerie didn't like consolation prizes and told him he could screw his vacation.

As fall drew to a close, Andrew was rewarded for the work that had taken up all his time and energy. Weeks and weeks of research and two trips to China to gather evidence and verify the credibility of his sources had allowed him to uncover the details of a child trafficking racket in Hunan Province and put together an investigation demonstrating just how corrupt and horrific human behavior can be. His article was published in the Sunday paper, the most-read edition of the week, and caused a real stir.

Sixty-five thousand Chinese babies had been adopted by

American families over the previous ten years. The scandal was that hundreds of them hadn't been abandoned, as their official papers claimed, but forcibly taken away from their birth parents and placed in an orphanage that was paid five thousand dollars per adoption. The lucrative trade had greased the pockets of corrupt police officers and civil servants who had set up the trafficking ring. The Chinese authorities moved quickly to cover up the scandal, but the damage was done. Andrew's article forced a large number of American adoptive parents to grapple with the tragic implications of his investigation.

Andrew was the buzz of the *Times'* editorial offices, and even got mentioned on the evening news. He was congratulated by his peers, though some of them were clearly jealous, and received a personal email from editor-in-chief as well as numerous letters from readers who'd been deeply moved by his investigation. Three anonymous death threats were sent to the newspaper, though such threats were nothing new.

Andrew was on his own for the holidays. Valerie had gone to visit Colette in New Orleans. The day after she left, Andrew was attacked in a parking lot by someone with a baseball bat. It could have turned nasty if the tow truck guy he'd had an appointment with hadn't arrived just in time.

Simon had gone skiing in Beaver Creek, Colorado, to celebrate the New Year with a group of friends. Andrew spent Christmas and New Year's Eve sitting at the bar of Mary's Fish Camp with a plate of oysters and a few glasses of dry white wine.

2012 got off to a promising start, apart from a minor accident in early January, in which Andrew was hit by a car as he was passing in front of the Charles Street police station. The driver, a retired cop revisiting his old workplace while on vacation, was mortified that he'd hit Andrew and relieved to see him get back up unhurt. He insisted on treating Andrew to dinner at the restaurant of his choice. Andrew wasn't busy that evening, and a good steak sounded better than filling out an insurance claim form. Besides, no journalist can refuse a meal with a garrulous old New York cop. The inspector told him his life story and the highlights of his career.

Valerie had kept her apartment, which Andrew nicknamed her "safe house," but from February on she slept at his place every night, and they started thinking seriously about finding a bigger place and moving in together. The only hitch was that Andrew refused to leave the West Village: he'd sworn to himself he'd live there till the end of his days. He knew the stories associated with those charming streets by heart and took pleasure in retelling them when they went for walks. Like the Greenwich Avenue intersection where the diner that had inspired Edward Hopper's famous painting *Nighthawks* once stood, or the house where John Lennon had lived before moving to The Dakota. The West Village had played a role in nearly every American cultural revolution and was home to the country's most famous cafés, cabarets and nightclubs.

"I mean, Joan Baez got her start here," Andrew told Valerie.

"Who?"

Andrew was indignant. How could someone not know who Joan Baez is? But when he turned he saw in Valerie's face that she was teasing him. He smiled. "That's reason enough to live here, right?"

"Oh, sure," said Valerie.

One afternoon, he came home early from the office, emptied out his closets and transferred most of his belongings to a storage unit. That evening, he opened the wardrobe doors for Valerie and announced that there was no longer any hurry to find a new place; she now had all the space she needed to move in properly.

In March, Andrew was commissioned by his editor to undertake a new investigation, in the same vein as the previous one. It was an important special report and he got to work immediately, thrilled at the prospect of going to Argentina.

In early May, back from Buenos Aires and knowing he'd have to return there soon, Andrew couldn't think of any other way of getting Valerie to forgive him for his travels than to announce to her when they were at an Italian restaurant one evening that he wanted to marry her.

She stared at him suspiciously, then burst out laughing. Valerie's laughter upset him. He looked at her, unsettled to realize that though he'd popped the question without really thinking about it, the idea of marrying her actually made him very happy.

"You're not serious, are you?" Valerie asked, wiping the tears from the corners of her eyes.

"Why wouldn't I be?"

"Come on, Andrew. We've only been together a few months. Don't you think that's too soon to be making that sort of decision?"

"We've been together for a year and we've known each other since we were teenagers. Don't you think we've had plenty of time?"

"With a short interlude of twenty years!"

"I think the fact that we met in our teens, lost touch, then bumped into each other again by chance on a New York sidewalk is a sign."

"I thought you were a fact-obsessed, rational journalist. Since when do you believe in signs?"

"Since I saw you."

Valerie looked him straight in the eye without saying a word, then smiled.

"Ask me again."

Andrew stared at Valerie. She was no longer the rebellious

girl he'd known twenty years earlier. The Valerie sitting opposite him at the dinner table had swapped her patched jeans for
a flattering skirt, her sneakers painted with nail polish for
patent high heels, the shapeless army jacket she used to practically live in for a cashmere V-neck sweater that hugged her
beautiful breasts. She no longer overdid the eye makeup—a
light dusting of eyeshadow and a touch of mascara was all she
wore. Valerie Ramsay was by far the most beautiful woman
he'd ever met, and he'd never felt this close to anyone.

Andrew felt his palms turn clammy, which was a first for
him. He pushed back his chair, walked around the table and
knelt on one knee.

"Valerie Ramsay, I don't have a ring on me because my
intention is as spontaneous as it is sincere, but if you would like
to be my wife, we'll go and choose one together this weekend,
and I intend to do all I can to be the best husband ever so that
you wear it your whole life through. Or let's say my whole life
through, in case you decide to remarry after I die."

"You can't help adding a touch of black humor even when
you're asking me to marry you!"

"I promise you that kneeling like this, with all these people
watching me, the last thing I was trying to be was funny."

"Andrew," Valerie whispered in his ear, "I'm going to
answer 'yes' because I want to. And because I want to stop you
looking like an idiot in front of the whole restaurant. But when
you get back in your chair, I'll tell you the one condition I'm
setting for our marriage. The 'yes' I'm going to say out loud
now will remain provisional for the next few minutes, all
right?"

"Okay," Andrew murmured back.

Valerie planted a kiss on his lips and said yes for all to hear.
The other diners in the restaurant, who had been holding their
breath, applauded enthusiastically.

The owner of the trattoria came out from behind the bar to

congratulate his loyal customers. He took Andrew in his arms, squeezed him tight and, in his thick New York Italian accent, said softly into his ear: "I hope you know what you've just done!"

Then he took Valerie's hand and kissed it.

"I'm allowed to kiss you now that you'll be a Mrs.! I'll get some champagne brought over to you to celebrate. On the house. Yes, yes, I insist!"

Maurizio returned to the bar and signaled to his only waiter to serve them immediately.

"I'm all ears," Andrew said quietly as the champagne cork popped.

The waiter filled their glasses and Maurizio came over with his own glass to drink to the future married couple.

"Just give us a second please, Maurizio," Andrew said, holding his arm.

"You want me to set out my condition in front of him?" Valerie asked, surprised.

"He's an old friend. We have no secrets," Andrew answered dryly.

"Fine! So, Mr. Stilman, you can take me to become your lawfully wedded wife if you give your word of honor never to lie, be unfaithful to me or intentionally make me suffer. If one day you don't love me anyone, I want to be the first to know. I've had my fill of affairs that end in nights of sorrow. If you can make me this promise, then yes, I will marry you."

"I swear, Valerie Ramsay-Stilman."

"On your life?"

"On my life!"

"If you betray me, I'll kill you!"

Maurizio glanced at Andrew and crossed himself.

"Can we drink to you now?" inquired the restaurant owner. "I do have other customers . . ."

They made love all night long, stopping every so often to

watch old black and white shows on the TV at the end of the bed. In the early hours of the morning, they crossed the city and went and sat on a bench overlooking the East River to watch daybreak.

"You must remember this night forever," Andrew whispered in Valerie's ear.

4.

Andrew spent the first ten days of June in Buenos Aires. On his return from this second trip to Argentina, he found Valerie more radiant than ever. A dinner together with their maid of honor, Valerie's old friend Colette, and best man turned out to be one of the more pleasant evenings he'd ever spent. Colette thought Andrew was very charming.

In the weeks before the wedding, which was planned for the end of the month, Andrew spent every day and many evenings fine-tuning his article, fantasizing from time to time that he'd win the Pulitzer Prize for it.

The air-conditioning in his apartment had finally given up the ghost and the couple moved into Valerie's one-bedroom in the East Village. Some nights, Andrew would stay at the paper until the early hours, on others he'd work at Valerie's, keeping her awake with the sound of his typing.

The heat in the city was unbearable. Violent storms struck Manhattan almost daily. Andrew heard them described as "apocalyptic." Little did he realize that his own life was about to take an apocalyptic turn of its own.

* * *

He'd sworn to Valerie that there'd be no strip joint or night-club full of bachelorettes; just an evening with friends.

For his stag night, Simon invited Andrew to a trendy new

restaurant. In New York, trendy restaurants open and close as fast as the seasons change.

"Are you sure about your decision?" Simon asked, reading the menu.

"I'm still hesitating between the chateaubriand and the pork tenderloin," Andrew answered distantly.

"I was talking about your life."

"I got that."

"Well?"

"What do you want me to say, Simon?"

"Each time I broach the subject of your marriage, you dodge the issue. I'm your best friend, okay? I just want to know how you're feeling."

"Liar. You're scrutinizing me like I'm some lab rat. You want to know what's going through my mind in case this kind of thing happens to you one day."

"No risk of that!"

"I could've told you that months ago."

"Okay, you're my lab rat. So what really made you take the leap?" Simon quizzed, leaning closer to his friend. "Tell me: do you feel any different since you made this decision?"

"Look, we're both in our late thirties. The way I see it, we've only got two options. Either we keep screwing around . . . "

"That's an attractive prospect!" Simon exclaimed.

" . . . and turn into one of those aging Lotharios who think fooling around with girls thirty years their junior will help them recapture their lost youth. Or we settle down."

"I'm not asking you to give me your theory of life. I'm asking if you love Valerie enough to want to spend the rest of your life with her."

"If I hadn't asked you to be my best man, I'd probably say that's none of your business."

"But I *am* your best man!"

"The rest of my life? I've no idea, and anyway that doesn't only depend on me. What I do know is that I can't imagine my life without her anymore. I'm happy. I miss her when she's not there. I'm never bored in her company. I love the way she laughs, and she laughs a lot. I think that's what I find most attractive in a woman. As for our sex life . . . "

"Okay, okay," Simon interrupted, "you've convinced me! The rest of it is definitely none of my business."

"But are you the best man?"

"Yes, but I'm not responsible for what the two of you get up to in bed when the lights are off."

"Who said anything about turning off the lights?"

"Okay, stop. Too much information. Can we change subjects?"

"I'm going to go for the pork tenderloin," Andrew said. "You know what'd make me really happy?"

"Me writing a great speech for your wedding?"

"No, I won't ask for the impossible. What I'd really like is to wind up this evening at my new favorite bar."

"That Cuban place in SoHo?"

"Argentinian."

"I'd had something else in mind, but it's your night. Your wish is my command."

Novecento was jam-packed. Simon and Andrew managed to elbow their way through to the bar. Andrew ordered a Fernet topped up with Coke. Simon tasted it, made a face, and ordered a glass of red wine instead.

"How on earth can you drink that stuff? It's bitter as hell."

"I've knocked back a lot of these in Buenos Aires lately. You get used to it, believe me. Even end up liking it."

"Speak for yourself."

Simon spotted a Bond girl lookalike with a lot of leg, and peeled off with barely an apology. Andrew smiled as he watched his friend walk away. There was no doubt which of the two options he'd mentioned earlier Simon had chosen.

A woman sat down on the bar stool Simon had just vacated and flashed Andrew a smile as he ordered a second Fernet and Coke. They exchanged some small talk. The young woman said she was surprised to see an American liking that drink; it was pretty unusual. Andrew replied that he was an unusual kind of guy. She smiled some more and asked him what made him so different. The question caught him off guard, as did the depth of the woman's gaze.

"What do you do?"

"Uh, I'm a journalist," Andrew stammered.

"That's an interesting job."

"Some days, yeah," he answered.

"Financial?"

"Oh no. What made you think that?"

"We're not far from Wall Street."

"If I was having a drink in the Meatpacking District, would you think I was a butcher?"

The young woman burst out laughing. Andrew liked the way she laughed.

"Political?" she asked.

"Not that either."

"Okay. I like guessing games," she said. "You've got tanned skin, so I'm guessing you travel."

"It's summer. And you've got a tan too. But you're right, my job does take me abroad."

"I've got olive skin, but that's genetic. Got it: you're an investigative reporter!"

"You could say that."

"What are you investigating at the moment?"

"Nothing I can tell you about in a bar."

"How about somewhere other than a bar?" she whispered.

"Only in my office," Andrew replied, feeling a sudden wave

of heat surge through him. He took a paper napkin off the bar and wiped the back of his neck.

He was dying to question her too, but the mere fact of entering into conversation with her was igniting something a lot less innocent than guessing games.

"What about you?" he said hesitantly, glancing frantically around for Simon.

The young woman looked at her watch and got off her stool.

"I'm sorry," she said. "I'd lost track of the time. I have to go. It was nice to meet you. What's your name, by the way?"

"Andrew Stilman," he answered, standing up.

"Maybe I'll see you around sometime."

She said goodbye. He didn't take his eyes off her. He even hoped she'd turn around as she walked out the door, but he never found out if she did. He felt Simon's hand on his shoulder and jumped.

"What are you staring at?"

"Can we get out of here?" Andrew asked in a subdued voice.

"What, already?"

"I need some fresh air."

Simon shrugged and steered Andrew outside.

"What's the matter? You've gone white as a sheet. Is it that stuff you were drinking?"

"I just want to go home."

"First tell me what happened. You should see your face! You want to keep your work secrets from me, fine, but I hardly think you were working in there."

"You wouldn't understand."

"Is there anything about you I haven't understood in the past ten years?"

Andrew started walking up West Broadway without replying. Simon caught up with him.

"I think I've just experienced love at first sight," Andrew murmured.

Simon roared with laughter. Andrew quickened his pace.

"Are you serious?" Simon asked, catching him up.

"Very serious."

"You fell for a stranger while I was in the restroom?"

"You weren't in the restroom."

"You fell head over heels in love in five minutes?"

"You left me all alone at the bar for over a quarter of an hour!"

"Not all that alone, apparently. Explain what happened."

"There's nothing to explain. I don't even know her first name."

"And?"

"I think I just met the love of my life. I've never felt anything like it, Simon."

Simon grabbed Andrew's arm and forced him to stop.

"You didn't meet anyone of the kind. You drank a bit too much and your wedding day's looming. The combination is lethal."

"I'm one hundred percent serious, Simon. I'm not in the mood for joking."

"Neither am I! It's your nerves talking. You'd use any excuse—you've got cold feet."

"I'm not nervous, Simon. At least I wasn't before I went into that bar."

"What did you do when this dream girl talked to you?"

"I said some boring stuff to her and felt pathetic when she left."

"My lab rat is discovering the side effects of the marriage potion, which is quite strange considering he hasn't even been fed it yet."

"Exactly!"

"Look, you won't even remember what this woman looks

like tomorrow morning. Here's what we're going to do: we'll just forget all about this evening at Novecento, and everything will go back to normal."

"I wish it was as simple as that."

"Do you want us to go back there tomorrow night? With any luck your stranger will be there, and maybe when you see her again you'll be able to think straight."

"I won't do that to Valerie." Simon was probably right; he had drunk far too much to be thinking straight, and fear was making him go off the rails. Valerie was an exceptional woman and one of life's unexpected strokes of luck, as her best friend, Colette, kept telling him.

Andrew made Simon swear he'd never tell anyone what had happened that night, and thanked him for making him see reason.

They climbed into the same taxi. Simon dropped Andrew off in the West Village and promised to call him the next day to find out how he was doing.

* * *

Andrew woke up the next day feeling the exact opposite of what Simon had predicted. The face of the stranger he'd met in Novecento and the smell of her perfume were crystal clear in his memory. He shut his eyes again and the sight of her long hands toying with her glass of wine, her penetrating gaze and the sound of her voice came flooding back. As he made himself a coffee, he felt an emptiness, or rather an absence, and the urgent need to see the woman whom he imagined could fill it.

His telephone rang. Valerie brought him back to a reality that wrenched his heart, asking if his evening had been up to expectations. He told her he'd had dinner with Simon in a good restaurant and a drink in a bar in SoHo. Nothing special.

He hung up, feeling guilty about lying for the first time to the woman he was about to marry.

Then he remembered the little white lie he'd told when he'd come back from Buenos Aires and sworn to Valerie he'd already taken his wedding suit to be altered. As if to right his wrong, he called the tailor immediately and arranged to take it in during his lunch break.

Perhaps that was the reason for the unfortunate episode in the bar. In life, every little thing had meaning, and that incident had only happened to remind him he needed to get his wedding suit pants rehemmed and jacket sleeves shortened, so his future wife wouldn't be bitterly disappointed when he showed up for their wedding looking like he'd borrowed his big brother's suit.

You don't even have a big brother, you jerk, Andrew mumbled to himself. *And, as jerks go, you're hard to beat.*

Andrew left the office at noon. As the tailor chalked the alterations on the jacket sleeves and darts on the back that he said were vital if his client wanted to look stylish, and complained for the umpteenth time that this really was leaving it till the last minute, Andrew felt a deep sense of unease. Once the fitting session was over, he took off the suit and hurriedly got dressed again. Everything would be ready the following Friday, the tailor assured him; Andrew could drop by at the end of the morning.

When he checked his phone, he found several worried messages from Valerie. They'd arranged to meet for lunch over on 42nd Street and she'd been waiting for him for an hour.

Andrew called to apologize, citing an impromptu work meeting. If his secretary had said he was out, that was only because no one at that paper ever paid attention to anyone else. His second lie of the day.

That evening, Andrew turned up at Valerie's with a bouquet of flowers. Since he'd asked her to marry him, he regularly had mauve roses, her favorites, delivered to her. But he found the apartment empty and a hastily scribbled note on the coffee table in the living room.

Called out to an emergency. Back late. Don't wait up. Love you.

He left the building and walked to Mary's Fish Camp for dinner. He didn't stop looking at his watch during the meal, and asked for the check before he'd even finished his main course. As soon as he was out the door, he jumped in a taxi.

Back in SoHo, he paced up and down the sidewalk in front of Novecento, longing to go in for a drink. The doorman, who doubled as a bouncer, took out a cigarette and asked Andrew for a light. Andrew had quit smoking years ago.

"Want to go in? It's real quiet tonight."

Andrew decided the invitation was another sign.

The doorman had been right. One quick glance was all it took for Andrew to realize the beautiful stranger from last night hadn't returned. Feeling ridiculous, he downed the Fernet and Coke he'd ordered and asked the bartender for the bill.

"Just one drink tonight?" the man asked.

"You remember me?"

"Sure. You knocked back five Fernet and Cokes in a row last night. I wouldn't forget that in a hurry."

Andrew hesitated, then asked for another drink. He watched the bartender pouring it and asked him a surprising question for a soon-to-be-married man.

"The woman who was sitting next to me—do you remember her? Is she a regular?"

The bartender looked pensive.

"I see a lot of pretty women in this bar," he said. "No, can't say I do. Is it important?"

"Yes," said Andrew. "Actually, no. Look, I have to go. What do I owe you?"

The bartender turned away to ring up the total.

Andrew slipped three twenty-dollar bills over the counter. "If she stops by again, and asks you about the Fernet and Coke man, here's my card. Please give it to her."

"You're with the *Times*?"

"Like it says on the card."

"Hey, if you want to do a write-up about this place someday, feel free."

"I'll do my best to remember," Andrew said. "You too, please."

The bartender winked at him as he stashed the card away in his till.

Andrew checked the time as he walked out of Novecento. If Valerie's emergency had run late, maybe he'd be home before her. Otherwise he'd tell her he'd been working overtime. One more lie hardly mattered.

* * *

From that evening on, Andrew could feel his composure progressively cracking with each passing day. He even got into a heated dispute with his colleague Freddy Olson when he caught him prying through his desk. Olson was envious of Andrew and an overall creep. But Andrew usually never lost his cool. He told himself he was stressed out because he had so much to do during the last two weeks of June. He still had to finish writing the article he'd researched on his two trips to Argentina; he was hoping it would be as widely read as his report from China. It was due to go to press the following Monday. Olivia Stern was a very punctilious editor, and he knew she'd be even pickier than usual when it came to an investigative story to be splashed over several pages in Tuesday's paper. She would spend all of Saturday reading through the story and making changes, which she would e-mail him that same evening. What a strange weekend it would be,

Andrew mused; on Saturday he'd be making his marriage vows before God, and on Sunday he'd be apologizing to Valerie for putting off their honeymoon because of his damn job and this story that was so important to his boss.

Meanwhile, Andrew couldn't get the stranger at Novecento out of his head. His desire to see the woman again was turning into an obsession, and he couldn't understand why.

He was feeling more lost than ever when he went to pick up his suit on Friday. The tailor heard him sigh as he stood looking at himself in the mirror.

"You don't like the cut?" he asked unhappily.

"No, Mr. Zanelli. You've done a perfect job."

The tailor surveyed Andrew and hitched up the right shoulder of the suit jacket.

"But you're upset about something, aren't you?" he asked, sticking a needle into the bottom of the jacket sleeve.

"It's complicated."

"Hmm. One of your arms is definitely longer than the other," he remarked. "I hadn't noticed that at the fitting. Give me a few minutes. We'll fix this right away."

"Don't bother. It's the kind of suit I'll only wear once in my life, isn't it?"

"I hope so. But it's also the kind of photograph you'll be looking at all your life, and when your grandchildren tell you that your jacket didn't fit properly, I wouldn't want you telling them you had a bad tailor. So let me get on with my job."

"It's just that I've got a very important story to finish by tonight, Mr. Zanelli."

"And I've got a very important suit to finish in the next fifteen minutes. You were saying something's complicated?"

"That's right," Andrew sighed.

"What kind of thing, if you don't mind me asking?"

"I guess you're bound by professional secrecy too, Mr. Zanelli."

"I will be if you say my name properly. It's Zanetti, not Zanelli. Take off that jacket and sit down. I'll fix it while we talk."

So while Mr. Zanetti adjusted the sleeve of Andrew's suit jacket, Andrew told him how he had been reunited with his high school sweetheart as she was coming out of a bar a year ago and how, days before his wedding, he'd come across a woman in another bar who he couldn't stop thinking about ever since he had set eyes on her.

"Maybe you should stop going out," the tailor said. "That would make your life easier. I have to say it's an unusual story," he added, hunting through a drawer for a spool of thread.

"My best friend Simon says exactly the opposite."

"He's got a strange way of looking at things, this Simon. Can I ask you something?"

"Anything you like, if it'll help me see things more clearly."

"If you could replay the whole thing, Mr. Stilman—if you could choose between not getting back together with the woman you're about to marry and not meeting the woman who's obsessing you, which would you prefer?"

"One of these women is my soul mate. As for the other one . . . I don't even know her name."

"So you see, it's not that complicated."

"Well, when you put it that way . . . "

"I'm a lot older than you, Mr. Stilman, so I'm going to take the liberty of talking to you like a father. But I should confess I've never had children, so I have no experience in the matter."

"Tell me anyway."

"Well, since you're asking. Life isn't like one of those modern gadgets where you just press 'rewind' to listen to your favorite song again. There's no going back. And some actions can have irreparable consequences—like falling for some total stranger, however mesmerizing she may be, right before your wedding. If you continue, I fear you'll regret it, not to mention the damage you'll be causing the people you love. And if you're going to say you have no control over your heart, just remember you have a head too, and remember to use it. There's no harm in being attracted to a woman, so long as it doesn't go any further than that."

"Have you ever felt like you'd met your soul mate, Mr. Zanetti?"

"A soul mate? What a delightful idea. When I was in my twenties I thought I'd met her each time I went out dancing on a Saturday night. I used to be a very good dancer, and I fell in love with every partner I had. I've often wondered how people know they've met their soul mate before they've built a relationship with that person."

"Are you married, Mr. Zanetti?"

"I've been married four times, so I should know what I'm talking about!"

As he said goodbye to Andrew, Mr. Zanetti assured him that since both sleeves of his jacket were now the right length, nothing could get in the way of the happiness awaiting him. Andrew walked out of the tailor's firmly resolved to wear his wedding suit with pride the next day.

5.

Valerie's mother came up to Andrew just before the cer-emony began, brushed his shoulder gently and whis-pered into his ear: "Ben, you old devil! Just goes to show you can always get what you want if you are persistent enough. I remember you mooning over my daughter when you were sixteen. I didn't think you had a snowball's chance in hell with her. And now here we all are in church!"

Andrew began to understand why his wife-to-be had been so keen to get away from her folks when the first chance came along.

Valerie had never looked lovelier. She was wearing a sim-ple, elegant white dress. She had her hair up under a small white pillbox hat like the ones the Pan Am stewardesses used to wear, except theirs had been blue. Her father led her up to the altar where Andrew was waiting for her. She smiled at him, her eyes brimming with love.

The priest's sermon was perfect and made Andrew very emotional.

They said their vows, exchanged rings and gave each other a long kiss. Valerie's parents, Colette and Simon burst into applause as they walked out of the church. Lifting his eyes to the sky, Andrew couldn't help thinking his own parents were looking down on them.

The little procession walked down the path through the garden of the Church of St. Luke in the Fields, where climbing roses bent under the weight of countless flowers and the tulip-filled flowerbeds were a riot of color. It was a beautiful day. Valerie was radiant, and Andrew was happy.

Until, as they came out on Hudson Street, he glimpsed a woman's face at the window of a black SUV stopped at a red light. A woman he wouldn't recognize if he bumped into her again, his best man had assured him; a woman with whom he'd exchanged a few trite words in a SoHo bar.

Andrew felt a lump in his throat, and a raging thirst for a Fernet and Coke despite the early hour.

"Everything okay?" Valerie asked, concerned. "You've turned pale all of a sudden."

"I'm just feeling emotional," Andrew replied.

He couldn't tear his eyes away from the SUV at the lights. His gaze followed it as it was swallowed up in the flow of traffic. Andrew felt his heart constrict. He could have sworn the stranger from Novecento had smiled at him.

"Ow, you're hurting me," Valerie complained. "You're crushing my hand."

"Sorry," he said, loosening his grasp.

"I wish the celebrations were over," she sighed. "I just want to be at home alone with you."

"You're full of surprises, Valerie Ramsay."

"Why is that, Andrew Stilman?"

"I can't think of any other woman who'd want to get her wedding day over with as soon as possible. When I asked you to marry me, I figured you'd want a huge ceremony. I pictured the two of us surrounded by at least two hundred guests whom we'd have to greet individually. I thought I'd have to meet all of your uncles and aunts and cousins and listen to them tell old family stories and feel totally left out. I was so afraid of today. But it's just the six of us on this sidewalk."

"No worries there. I've always dreamed of an intimate

wedding. I wanted to be your wife, not play Cinderella in a ball gown."

"Those options weren't mutually exclusive."

"Are you having regrets?"

"No. None at all," Andrew said, looking off down Hudson Street.

His fourth lie.

They had dinner at Mr. Chow's, a Chinese restaurant Valerie liked for its refined, avant-garde cuisine. It was a boisterous meal. Colette and Simon were getting along famously with Valerie's parents. Andrew said little, and his wife couldn't help noticing that he seemed miles away. She declined her father's suggestion that they take the party elsewhere. When he complained he was being deprived of a dance with his daughter, she told him she was sorry, but she couldn't wait to be alone with her husband.

Valerie's dad put his arms around Andrew and hugged him.

"You better make her happy, my boy," he whispered. "Or you'll have to answer to me," he added jokingly.

It was nearly midnight when the taxi dropped the newlyweds off at Valerie's apartment. She ran up the stairs ahead of him and stood waiting on the landing.

"What is it? What's up?" he asked, rummaging in his jacket pocket for his keys.

"You're going to pick me up and carry me over this threshold. Without banging my head on the door," she replied with a wicked smile.

"See? There are a few traditions you're still attached to," he said as he obeyed.

She took off her dress in the middle of the living room, unhooked her bra and slipped off her panties. She strolled naked across the room to where Andrew was standing, took off his tie, undid the buttons of his shirt and put her hands on his chest. She stood pressed up against him as her fingers slid down to unbuckle his belt and pull down his zipper.

Andrew took her hands in his. He caressed her cheek tenderly, then picked her up and carried her over to the sofa. He knelt in front of her, dropped his head in her lap and began to sob.

"What is happening, Andrew?"

Andrew looked up at her. "I'm sorry," he said.

"You've been acting happy all day, but it's clear you're not. On our wedding day! Are you having money problems? Is it work? Tell me."

Andrew took a deep breath. "You made me promise I wouldn't ever lie to you or cheat on you, remember? You made me swear I'd tell you straight out if something went wrong between us one day."

Valerie's eyes filled with tears as she stared silently at Andrew.

"You're my best friend, my lover, the woman I feel closest to . . . "

"We were married today, Andrew," Valerie said in a choked voice.

"I beg you. From the bottom of my heart. Forgive me."

"Is there someone else?"

"Yes. No. A shadow . . . but I've never felt this way before."

"You waited for us to get married before admitting to me and to yourself that you're in love with someone else?"

"I love you, I know I love you, but not like this other love. I was too cowardly to acknowledge it or to talk to you about it. I couldn't muster the courage to cancel our wedding. Your parents were coming all the way from Florida. Your best friend was coming from New Orleans. Then there's this article I've worked so hard on these past few months. It's turned into an obsession. I couldn't think of anything else. And I lost my way. I tried to bury my doubts. I wanted to do the right thing."

"Shut up," Valerie murmured.

She lowered her eyes. Andrew's gaze was drawn to her hands, which she was twisting together so hard her fingers had turned white.

"Please don't say another word. Get out. Go home. Go wherever you want to. Just go. Leave this apartment."

She got up. Andrew made as if to move towards her, but she backed off. She backed away as far as the bedroom and shut the door gently behind her.

* * *

Outside, a drizzle fell from a gloomy sky. Andrew pulled up the collar of his bridegroom's suit and trekked across town to get back to his apartment in the West Village.

Time and again he had to fight the urge to call Simon. But Andrew, who had always thought he wasn't afraid of anything, suddenly found he was scared to hear what his best friend would say.

Time and again he wished he could confide in his dad. He wished he could show up at his parents' place and tell them everything; hear his mom tell him it would all work out in the end, and that it was better to admit the marriage had been a mistake, however cruel that was, than to live a lie. Valerie would probably hate him for a few years, but she'd end up forgetting him. She was an amazing woman; she wouldn't stay single for long. If she wasn't the woman of his dreams, he probably wasn't the man of her dreams either. He was still young, and even if it felt like he'd never get over what he was going through right now, one day it would just be a bad memory. Andrew wished he could feel his mother's hand on his cheek and his father's arm on his shoulder and hear them talking to him. But his parents were no longer alive.

It was his wedding night, and he'd never felt lonelier.

* * *

When the shit hits the fan, it goes everywhere. That was Freddy Olson's favorite saying. Andrew kept muttering it to himself as he sat working on his article that Sunday. He'd got an e-mail from Olivia first thing. She'd said some very flattering things about his investigative skills, assured him it was one of the best pieces she'd read in a long time, and congratulated herself on entrusting him with it. But she had also sent it back full of comments and underlined passages. She wanted to know how authentic his sources were, and whether he'd checked every last detail. He'd made some pretty serious accusations and the legal department would undoubtedly want to make sure they were all well-founded.

As if he would have taken all those risks just to make up stories. He'd blown half his salary following up on the leads the barmaid at his seedy hotel had given him, and tracked down some reliable but rather cagey sources. He'd nearly got beaten up in the outer suburbs of Buenos Aires, but luckily he'd managed to give the slip to the thugs who'd been on his tail for two days. He'd almost ended up in prison, not to mention put his personal life on hold for the sake of this investigation. He wasn't a rookie! He grumbled all day as he sorted through his notes.

At least Olivia had ended her message with more praise, and told him she wanted to have lunch with him the next day. That was a first. Andrew would normally have been convinced the invitation meant he could expect another promotion, or maybe even an award, but he was in such a funk he was sure it wouldn't be anything good.

That evening he heard hammering on his door. Andrew thought it was probably Valerie's father come to smash his face in. He opened up, almost relieved: maybe a good thrashing would make him feel less guilty.

Simon pushed him roughly aside and strode into the apartment.

"Tell me you didn't do it!" he shouted, heading for the window.

"Did she call you?"

"No, I called. I wanted to stop by and give you guys your wedding present, but I was scared I'd walk in on you having sex or something. Man, was I wrong."

"What did she tell you?"

"What do you think? She's heartbroken. She doesn't get it. All she knows is that you've messed her around, and that you don't love her. Why did you marry her? Couldn't you have called off the wedding? You've acted like a total bastard."

"Look, you and everyone else said I shouldn't say or do anything, just go through with it. Everyone told me I was just imagining how I felt!"

"Who's 'everyone'? Who else did you confide in? Fallen for a new best friend, have you? Are you going to leave me too?"

"Don't be an asshole, Simon. I talked to my tailor."

"Oh, terrific. Couldn't you just try being married for a few months, at least give the two of you a chance? So what happened last night that was so serious you had to go and screw it all up?"

"If you really want to know, I couldn't make love to her. And Valerie's too smart to believe it was only because I'd had too much to drink."

"Do you feel like it's impossible for you to go see her and tell her you're sorry, that you made a mistake, and that this is all just some temporary madness?"

"I don't know what I feel anymore. I just know I've never been this unhappy."

Simon got up and went into the kitchen. He came back with a couple of beers and handed one to Andrew.

"I'm sorry for you, old buddy. Do you want to spend the week at my place?"

"Why?"

"Because I'm much better company than you are."

Simon put a hand on his friend's shoulder.

"Remember that story about the guy who was being tried for the murder of his parents and pleaded with the judge to let him off because otherwise he'd be sentencing an orphan?"

Andrew looked at Simon and the two of them laughed the way only good friends can when a situation is dire.

* * *

On Monday Andrew had lunch with his editor, just the two of them. She had chosen a restaurant some distance from the office.

Olivia had never shown this much interest in his work before. She had never interrogated him about his sources or the people he'd met or the way he'd carried out his investigation. Through lunch, she barely touched her food, hanging on to his words as he described his time in Argentina like a little girl listening to an adult reading her a heartbreaking story. Andrew thought she seemed on the brink of tears a couple of times.

When they'd finished lunch, she took Andrew's hand in hers, thanked him for the exceptional job he'd done and told him he should write a book about it one day. As they were getting up to leave, she informed him she was delaying the publication of his story by a week to get him a front-page lead and two full pages within the paper. A headline and two inside pages in *The New York Times*—it wasn't the Pulitzer, but it would certainly win him recognition. And when Olivia asked if he had enough material to flesh out the story, her tone making it clear she didn't doubt it in the slightest, Andrew assured her he would get to work straight away.

That's what he'd do all week, he promised himself. He'd get to the office early, grab a sandwich at lunchtime and work late into the night, except maybe to have dinner with Simon.

Andrew stuck to his schedule—until Wednesday, when, as he left the office, he was overcome by a sense of déjà vu. At the corner of 40th, he thought he glimpsed the face of the stranger from Novecento at the rear window of an SUV parked in front of the building. He started running towards her. In his haste, the folder he was carrying slipped out of his hand, spewing the pages of his article all over the sidewalk. By the time he had gathered them up, the car had disappeared.

From then on Andrew started going to Novecento every evening after work in the hope of finding the woman who was haunting him. He waited in vain, returning home each night disappointed and exhausted.

On Saturday he found an envelope in his mailbox, addressed in familiar handwriting. He placed it on his desk and promised himself he wouldn't open it until he had put the final touches on the article Olivia had been waiting for since the previous evening.

After he had sent it to her, he called Simon and told him he couldn't make dinner because he was still working.

Then he went to sit on the window ledge in the living room, breathed in great gulps of the night air, and finally opened Valerie's letter.

Andrew,

This Sunday without you was the first time since I was a teenager I spent wallowing in the pain of separation. I ran away at seventeen; you at nearly forty. How can I get used to not knowing how you're doing? How can I emerge from the depths of your silence?

I'm scared of my memories—they take me back to the way you used to look at me when we were young, to the sound of your voice brightening my day when we met again as adults, to the reassuring beat of your heart when I put my hand on your chest and listened to you sleeping at night.

Losing you, I've lost a love, a lover, a friend and a brother. It'll take me a long time to mourn them all.

I wished you dead for making me suffer so. But I want to be happy, and I know that I wouldn't be if you were not alive. So may your life be happy.

I'll sign off this short note by writing, for the first and the last time, "Your wife." Or rather, the woman who was your wife, for one sad day.

6.

He slept through most of Sunday. He had gone out the previous evening with the firm intention of getting monumentally drunk—he'd spent quite a few years honing that particular skill. Shutting himself away at home because he didn't have the guts to go out would have been even more unbearable.

He had pushed open the door of Novecento later than usual, drunk more Fernet and Cokes than usual and tottered out of the bar in a worse state than usual. And to top it all, he'd sat at the bar by himself the whole time, and only talked to the bartender. Wandering around the deserted streets in a drunken haze, Andrew had found himself breaking into a fit of hysterical laughter, which turned quickly into overwhelming sadness. He had sat sobbing for nearly an hour on the edge of a sidewalk with his feet in the gutter.

When he woke up with a hangover that reminded him he was long past the age of binge drinking, he found himself missing Valerie. He missed her intensely—as badly as he missed that apparition of a single night who had, for whatever reason, put him under her spell. But Valerie was his wife, and the other woman was an illusion. And Andrew couldn't stop thinking about Valerie's letter.

He had made a terrible mistake—one of the worst he had ever made. He thought about his article; if it brought him some fame and recognition then he wanted to share his sense of satisfaction with Valerie. He had to make things right with her again; he needed a second chance.

*

On Monday morning he went out for his run, going down Charles Street as he did every morning and jogging towards the river.

He waited for the lights to turn red and crossed the West Side Highway. When he reached the central traffic island the little illuminated figure was flashing, but Andrew stepped into the road anyway the way he did every morning, responding to the blaring horns by lifting his fist, his middle finger pointing to the sky. Then he turned into the Hudson River Park path and picked up his pace.

He'd knock on Valerie's door that very evening to explain and ask her to forgive him. He no longer had the slightest doubt about his feelings for her. He felt like hitting his head against a wall; he asked himself what madness had possessed him to make him act like he had.

A week had gone by since their separation—a seven-day nightmare he'd inflicted on the love of his life because he was a selfish bastard. But it would never happen again; he'd promise her that. Starting now, he'd do everything he could to make her happy. He would beg her to put it all behind her. And if she wanted him to jump through hoops before she'd forgive him, he'd do it.

When he got to Pier 40 there was only one thought running through his mind: how he could win back his wife's heart.

Andrew felt a sudden, vicious bite on his lower back and then a terrible tearing sensation inside, all the way up to his stomach. If the pain had been higher up, in his chest, he'd have thought he was having a heart attack. His breathing felt restricted. His legs gave way under him, and he had just enough strength left to stretch out his arms and protect his face as he fell.

Lying facedown on the asphalt, he tried to turn over and

call for help. He couldn't understand why there was no sound coming out of his mouth. Then a terrible coughing fit brought up a thick liquid.

Andrew realized the pool of reddish liquid trickling along the Hudson River Park path in front of him was his blood. It was draining out of him as if he were an animal in a slaughter-house. His vision blurred and darkened.

He thought he'd probably been shot, though he couldn't remember hearing a gun go off. Maybe he'd been stabbed. But who would want to kill him, Andrew thought, as he struggled to stay conscious.

He was now finding it practically impossible to breathe. His strength was ebbing out of him. He resigned himself to his fate.

He thought he would see his life flash before his eyes, a bright light at the end of a tunnel, a divine voice guiding him to some other world. None of it happened. His last few moments of consciousness were just a long and painful plunge into nothingness.

At 7:15 on a Monday morning in July, Andrew Stilman real-ized he was dying.

7.

Freezing cold air rushed into his lungs, and an equally icy liquid was flowing through his veins. A blinding light was making it impossible for him to open his eyes. He was terrified of what he'd see if he did open them. Where was he waking up: in purgatory or hell? Heaven was probably too good for him, considering the way he'd treated Valerie.

He could no longer feel his heart beating. And he was cold, terribly cold.

Death was supposed to last for eternity, and he could hardly stay in the dark the whole time. He plucked up his courage and managed to reopen his eyes.

To his amazement, he found himself leaning up against the traffic light on the corner of Charles Street and the West Side Highway.

Hell didn't look anything like the way it had been described in catechism class at the Catholic school he'd gone to in Poughkeepsie, unless this crossing was the entrance to it. But considering the number of times Andrew had run past it, surely he'd have figured it out before this.

He was trembling like a leaf in the wind, and his back was covered in sweat. He glanced at his watch without thinking. It was exactly 7 A.M.—fifteen minutes before he'd been killed.

That made no sense at all. He glanced around. Everything looked just the same as it did every morning. Cars were streaming north on the opposite side of the traffic island. The cars heading south towards the Financial District were bumper to bumper, while joggers advanced along the Hudson River Park path at a brisk pace.

Andrew tried to collect his thoughts. The only good thing about dying, as far as he knew, was that it freed you from physical suffering. But he was feeling acute pain in his lower back, and seeing stars. Surely that meant his soul was still firmly anchored to his body?

He was short of breath, but he was obviously still breathing; how else could he be coughing? A wave of nausea overcame him, and he leaned forward to throw up his breakfast in the gutter.

There was no way he could continue; he swore he wouldn't drink another drop of alcohol as long as he lived, not even a Fernet and Coke. Life had made him pay far too steep a price for him to get caught out again.

He gathered what strength he could and turned around. He'd get back home, have a nice long shower and a rest, and everything would be fine.

The pain in his back began to diminish as he walked, and Andrew persuaded himself he must have simply fainted for a few seconds—a brief loss of consciousness that had disoriented him totally.

And yet he could have sworn he had already reached Pier 40, several blocks past Charles Street, when he'd fainted. He would definitely go see his doctor to check it wasn't anything serious.

He thought again of Valerie and decided to call the newspaper when he had rested up a little to say he would be late. Then he would jump in a taxi and head for his wife's surgery ward at the NYPD stables. He needed to tell her he was sorry and ask her to forgive him.

Andrew pushed open the door of his building, climbed to the third floor, slipped his key in the lock and went in. The keys dropped out of his hand when he saw Valerie in the living room. She asked if he'd seen the shirt she had picked up from the dry cleaner's the previous evening. She'd been looking for it ever since he'd gone out for his run and still hadn't managed to find it.

She stopped searching to look at him, and asked why he was staring at her in that dazed way.

Andrew didn't know what to say.

"Well, don't just stand there. Help me look. I'm going to be late, and today really isn't the day for it—we've got a health inspector coming in."

Andrew didn't move. His mouth was dry. His lips felt like they'd been glued together.

"I've made you some coffee. And get yourself something to eat—you're pale as a ghost. You always overdo it when you go running," Valerie said, taking up her hunt again. "But help me find that shirt first. You've got to make some room for my things in your closet. I'm sick of lugging my stuff from my place to yours: look what happens!"

Andrew took a step towards Valerie and caught hold of her arm to capture her attention.

"I don't know what you're up to, but finding you here is the most wonderful surprise of my whole life. You're not going to believe this, but I was getting ready to come see you at the surgery. I absolutely have to talk to you."

"Good timing. I have to talk to you too. We still haven't decided about going to Connecticut for the weekend. When is it you're going back to Argentina? You told me yesterday, but I hate the idea so much I've already forgotten."

"Why would I be going back to Argentina?"

Valerie turned and stared at Andrew.

"Why would I be going back to Argentina?" Andrew repeated.

"Well, maybe because your newspaper's commissioned you to do, quote unquote, a story that's going to send your career through the roof. That's what you told me this weekend. You were ridiculously overexcited about it. And because your editor called you on Friday to suggest you go back to Argentina, even though you've only just been there. But she was insistent—she says it's an incredibly important piece."

Andrew could remember that conversation with Olivia perfectly. Except that it had taken place when he had returned from his first trip to Buenos Aires in early May, and it was now July.

"She called me on Friday?" he stammered.

"Go have something to eat. You're flipping out."

Andrew didn't answer. He ran to his bedroom, grabbed the remote control from the bedside table and switched on the television. He tuned in to the morning news on NY1.

He realized, dumbfounded, that he knew every single story the anchor was presenting. The spectacular fire that had burned down a warehouse in Queens, killing twenty-two people. The toll increase for drivers coming into the city, taking effect that day. But that day had been two months ago.

Andrew glanced at the headlines scrolling across the bottom of the screen and the date display: May 7. His legs gave way and he fell on the bed.

The weatherman announced the arrival of the season's first tropical storm. It was expected to begin losing strength before it hit the Florida coast. Andrew knew the weatherman was wrong. The storm would double in size by the end of the day. He also knew how many it would leave dead in its wake.

His tailor had once told him life wasn't like one of those modern gadgets where you just press "rewind" to listen to your favorite song again. He'd said there was no going back. Apparently Mr. Zanetti had got it all wrong. Andrew's life had just gone back to sixty-two days earlier.

He went to the kitchen, holding his breath as he opened the refrigerator. He found what he'd feared he would: a plastic bag containing the shirt his wife—except she wasn't his wife yet— had put away there by mistake with the yogurt she'd picked up at the grocery store on her way home.

He took it to her. Valerie wanted to know how come the shirt was so cold. When Andrew told her why, Valerie promised she wouldn't accuse *him* of being absentminded ever again.

"So why were you coming to see me at the surgery this morning?" she asked, picking up her handbag.

"No reason. I was missing you, that's all."

She gave him a quick kiss and left hurriedly after asking him to wish her good luck and warning him she'd probably be home late.

Andrew knew there would be no health inspection, because the health inspector was in a car crash on the Queensboro Bridge right this minute. Valerie would call him at the newspaper at around half past six that evening to suggest they go to the movies. Andrew wouldn't get out of the office in time and so they'd miss the beginning of the movie. He'd take out her out to dinner to make it up to her.

Andrew had an impressive memory. He had always congratulated himself on it. It had never occurred to him that this gift of his might one day plunge him into a state of utter panic.

Alone again in the apartment trying to come to grips with the unthinkable, Andrew realized that what he had decided was a fainting fit was nothing of the sort. He had been killed, and now he had sixty-two days to find out who had killed him, and why.

8

W hen he got to the office, Andrew decided not to make any changes to his routine. He needed to take a step back from the situation and consider it before deciding anything. Besides, he'd read a few science fiction books about going back in time when he was a boy, and he remembered that changing the course of events could have unfortunate consequences.

He spent the day organizing his second trip to Argentina— a trip he'd already organized in his previous life. He figured he could allow himself to change his hotel in Buenos Aires; he kept a very bad memory of the one he'd stayed in last time.

He had a brief argument with Freddy Olson, who had the cubicle next to his. Olson kept shooting him down at editorial meetings and trying to steal his story ideas, the jealous bastard.

Andrew clearly recalled the reason for their spat. Never mind how he had reacted last time; he took the initiative to put an end to his meddling and sent Olson packing. This way he avoided getting their editor involved, who would make him go through the humiliation of apologizing to that moron in front of all his colleagues.

It wasn't as if he could follow in his exact footsteps, after all, he reasoned as he returned to his desk. He would probably squash a few insects that had survived his morning runs in Hudson River Park over the past two months . . . *the next two months*, he corrected himself silently.

He quite liked the idea of shaking up the natural order of

things. He hadn't asked Valerie to marry him yet—he would only do it in three days' time, after she had brought up the subject of his trip to Buenos Aires again. He hadn't broken her heart, and so there was nothing for which he needed to ask forgiveness. All in all, if it wasn't for the probability that he'd end up in a pool of his own blood in around sixty days' time, this return to the past was all for the better.

When Valerie phoned at half past six, he made the mistake of promising her he'd join her at the movie theater right away, even before she could ask.

"How'd you I know I was about to suggest going to the movies?" she asked in surprise.

"I don't know," he stammered, fingers clenching his pencil. "But it's a good idea, isn't it? Um, unless you want to eat out?"

Valerie thought for a second, and opted for dinner.

"I'll get us a table at Omen."

"Wow. It's like you've got ESP this evening. That's exactly the place I was thinking of."

Andrew's pencil snapped in the palm of his hand.

"Oh, you know, I just get lucky sometimes," he said. "Let's meet in an hour." Then he asked her how the health inspector's visit had gone, though he already knew the answer.

"It didn't happen," Valerie said. "The inspector was in a car crash on the way over. I'll tell you about it over dinner."

Andrew hung up.

"You're going to have to play it smart over the next two months if you don't want anyone getting suspicious," he told himself out loud.

"Suspicious about what?" Freddy Olson's head popped up above the cubicle wall.

"Olson, didn't your mother ever teach you it's bad manners to eavesdrop on other people's conversations?"

"I don't see any conversation here, Stilman; you're just talking to yourself. And since you're such an observant guy, haven't you noticed we happen to work in an open space? You need to tone down that voice of yours. Think I enjoy having to listen to you?"

"I bet you do."

"So? What was all that about, Mr. Soon-to-be-promoted?"

"What's that supposed to mean?"

"Oh, come on, Stilman. We all know you're Stern's protégé. I guess you can't help being a brownnoser."

"I know you're so short on journalistic talent you can't quite believe you've made it into the profession. I'm not casting stones, Olson. If I was as useless as you I'd have my doubts too."

"Very funny. But that wasn't what I meant, Stilman. Don't act stupider than you are."

"So what *did* you mean, Olson?"

"Think about it. Stilman, Stern . . . both Jewish?"

Andrew stared at Olson. He remembered that in his previous life—the idea was so absurd he was still having trouble getting his head around it—this argument with Olson had happened much earlier in the day; Olivia had still been in her office. But she wasn't there this time around. Like most of his other colleagues, she had left at least half an hour ago, around 6 P.M. Andrew's actions seemed to be altering the order of things, and he decided he might as well take advantage of it. He gave Olson a resounding slap. Olson reeled back and stared at him, mouth agape.

"Shit, I could make a formal complaint, Stilman," he threatened, rubbing his cheek. "There are security cameras all over this floor."

"Go right ahead. I'd be happy to explain why you got slapped. I'm sure that particular video would go viral pretty fast."

"You won't get off that easy!"

"Try me. Anyway, I'm off—I've got to be somewhere else, and you've made me waste enough time as it is."

Andrew grabbed his jacket and walked over to the elevator, giving Olson—who was still standing there holding a hand to his cheek—the finger as he went. He found himself swearing as the elevator descended to the ground floor, but told himself he'd better calm down before he met Valerie. He'd have a hard time explaining to her what had just happened.

* * *

Seated at the counter of the Japanese restaurant in SoHo, Andrew listened to Valerie's chatter distractedly. Then again, he had the excuse of already knowing the content of her entire conversation. While she told him about her day, he was thinking hard about how he could make the most of the troubling situation he was in.

He bitterly regretted that he had always been so indifferent to the financial news. If he had shown even the slightest interest in it, he could have made a killing on the stock market right now. If only he had memorized a few stock prices for the next few weeks—or rather the past few weeks, as far as he was concerned—he could have invested his savings and made himself a tidy sum. But he had always found Wall Street and its excesses a total bore.

"You're not listening to a word I'm saying," said Valerie accusingly. "What are you thinking about?"

"You've just told me that Licorice, one of your favorite horses, has a bad case of tendinitis, and that you're worried it's the end of her career with the mounted police. You also said that Officer Thingy who rides her would never get over it if they declared his horse unfit for service."

Valerie looked at Andrew, speechless.

"What?" he asked. "Isn't that exactly what you've just been telling me?"

"No, it's exactly what I was just about to tell you. What's

with you today? Did you swallow a crystal ball at breakfast or something?"

Andrew forced himself to smile.

"You might be more absentminded than you think, you know," he said. "I'm just repeating what you told me. How could I have known all that stuff?"

"That's exactly what I'm asking you!"

"Maybe you were thinking so loud I heard you even before you said it. Just goes to show how closely we're connected," he said, putting on his most disarming smile.

"You phoned the surgery and got Sam, and he told you everything," she said.

"I don't know any Sam, and I didn't call your office."

"Sam's my assistant."

"See, I don't have a crystal ball. I was sure he was called John," he said. "Can we change the subject?"

"How was *your* day?"

The question gave Andrew pause for thought. He had died when he was out running this morning; he had come to life again shortly afterwards around a mile away from where he'd been killed and then discovered, to his amazement, that it was two months before the attack. Apart from that, his day had been pretty much the same as when he'd lived it the first time around.

"Long," he replied tersely. "I've had a really long day. So long I almost feel like I lived it twice."

* * *

Next morning, Andrew found himself alone in the elevator with his editor Olivia. She was standing behind him, but he could make out from her reflection in the doors that she was looking at him strangely—the way people look at you when they're about to give you bad news. He hesitated, and then smiled.

"Actually," he said, as if he was picking up a conversation where they'd left off, "before Olson comes tattling to you, I might as well confess I slapped him on my way out yesterday."

"You what?" Olivia exclaimed.

"That's right. To be completely honest, I thought you already knew."

"Why did you do it?"

"The newspaper won't be involved, don't worry. And if that moron files a complaint, I'll take full responsibility."

Olivia stopped the elevator, then pressed the button for the lobby.

"Where are we going?" Andrew asked.

"To get some coffee."

"I'll buy you coffee, but I'm not saying anything more," Andrew said as the doors opened.

They settled down at a table in the cafeteria. Andrew went to order two mochaccinos and bought himself a ham croissant while he was at it.

"This is so unlike you," Olivia said.

"It was just a slap. Nothing dramatic. And he deserved it."

Olivia looked at him and started smiling.

"Did I say something funny?" Andrew asked.

"I should be lecturing you and telling you such behavior is unacceptable and could get you suspended or even cost you your job, but I'm totally incapable of it."

"What's stopping you?"

"I wish *I'd* given Olson that slap."

Andrew refrained from comment, and Olivia changed the subject.

"I've read your notes. Good stuff. But it's not good enough. If I'm going to publish your story, I'll need concrete facts, irrefutable evidence. I suspect you've deliberately watered down your text."

"Why would I have done that?"

"Because you're on to something big, and you don't want to disclose it all to me just yet."

"That's a funny thing to assume."

"I've got to know you, Andrew. Let's make this work for both of us. I agree to your request: you can go back to Argentina. But if you want the paper to cover your expenses, you'll have to satisfy my curiosity. Have you picked up this man's trail?"

Andrew looked at his boss for a moment. If there was one thing he had learned on this job, it was that you couldn't trust anyone. But he knew that if he didn't give her any information, Olivia wouldn't let him go back to Buenos Aires. And she'd guessed right: it was only early May and he hadn't wrapped up the investigation, not by a long shot.

"I think I'm on the right track," he admitted grudgingly, setting his coffee mug down on the table.

"And, as your notes seem to imply, he was mixed up in this traffic?"

"Hard to say for sure. Several people were mixed up in that business, and folks down there are tight-lipped. It's still a painful subject for most Argentinians. By the way, since we're swapping confidences: why are you so hung up on this investigation?"

Olivia stared at him.

"You've already tracked him down, haven't you? You've got hold of Ortiz."

"Maybe. But you're right—I need some more information before we can go to press with it. That's why I need to go back there. You haven't answered my question, by the way."

Olivia got up, motioning for him to stay on and finish his croissant. "This is your number one priority, Andrew. I want you on this story full-time. I'm giving you exactly one month, and not a day more."

Andrew watched his boss walking out of the cafeteria. Two thoughts occurred to him. He couldn't care less about her threats; he knew perfectly well that he'd be leaving for Buenos Aires at the end of the month, and that he'd finish his investigation. But Olivia had caught him unawares during their conversation. He'd had to think twice before saying anything because he wasn't sure what she was supposed to know and what she didn't know yet. He had no recollection of giving her his notes, either in this life or his other life that had ended in Hudson River Park. On the other hand, he was pretty sure they hadn't had this conversation before.

As he headed back to the office, Andrew told himself maybe he shouldn't have slapped Freddy Olson. He'd have to be careful not to change the course of things from now on.

* * *

Andrew used his lunch break to go for a stroll along Madison Avenue and stopped in front of a jeweler's window. He wasn't particularly flush moneywise, but his marriage proposal had a lot more riding on it than the first time. He had felt sheepish about not having the customary ring box on him when he'd gone down on one knee to propose to Valerie at Maurizio's.

He went into the shop and peered at the display cases. It wasn't that easy to fool around with the past, to upend the order of events. He recognized the ring Valerie had chosen when they'd gone to buy one, glinting up at him from among ten other rings. And yet Andrew was absolutely certain they hadn't come to this particular jeweler's.

He knew exactly how much the ring had cost. So when the jeweler tried to convince him it was twice that price, Andrew said confidently: "This diamond weighs just under 0.95 carats, and though it has quite a sparkle, the cut is old-fashioned and there are several flaws, so I'd expect to pay half of what you're asking for it."

Andrew was only repeating what the previous jeweler had explained when he had bought this ring in Valerie's company. He could remember being touched by his fiancée's reaction. He had expected her to pick a better-quality stone, but Valerie had slipped the ring on her finger and told the jeweler it was good enough for her.

"So I see two possible explanations," Andrew said. "Either you made a mistake when you checked the price tag—and I can't say I blame you, it's written quite small—or you're trying to con me. I'd hate to have to write a piece about dishonest jewelers. Did I mention I'm with *The New York Times*?"

The jeweler took another look at the price tag and frowned. Looking very embarrassed, he admitted he had indeed made a mistake, and that the ring was worth exactly the amount Andrew had offered.

They sealed the deal in a most civil manner, and Andrew walked back out on Madison Avenue with a delightful little box nestling in his jacket pocket.

His second purchase of the day was a small combination lock for his desk drawer at the office.

The third was a faux leather notebook with an elastic band. It wasn't notes about his article he wanted to jot down in there. He was going to find out who'd killed him, and stop them. He had less than fifty-nine days left to do it.

Andrew went into a Starbucks and grabbed a bite to eat. He settled down in a leather armchair and began to think about all the people who might want him dead. It made him very uncomfortable. Where had he gone so wrong that he now had to make up a list like this?

He jotted down Freddy Olson's name. You could never tell what a colleague was really capable of, or how far jealousy might take them. But he dismissed the thought immediately. Olson didn't have the balls for it. And anyway, they'd never actually come to blows in his previous life.

There were those threatening letters he had received shortly after the publication of his article about the child trafficking ring in China. His piece must have thrown into turmoil the lives of any number of American families who had adopted kids from China. Children are sacred; parents anywhere in the world can tell you that. They'd be prepared to go to any lengths to protect their children—maybe even murder.

Andrew wondered how he would react if he adopted a child and a journalist had turned him into an unwitting accomplice of a trafficking ring by revealing that his child might have been stolen from his birth parents.

I'd probably hate the guy who'd opened that Pandora's Box for the rest of my life, he muttered to himself.

But what would you do if you realized that your child was going to discover the truth sooner or later, now that it had been made public? Would you break his heart, and yours, by taking him back to his legitimate family? Or live out a lie and wait for him to grow up and accuse you of turning a blind eye to the worst kind of human trafficking?

When Andrew had written the piece, he had barely thought about the possible implications of his investigation. How many American mothers and fathers had he thrown into a heart-breaking dilemma? But only the facts had counted back then; his job was to get the truth out there. *Everyone's looking out for numero uno*, as his old man used to say.

He crossed out Olson's name and wrote a reminder to himself to reread the three anonymous death threats he'd received.

His thoughts turned to his investigation in Argentina. The military dictatorship in power from 1976 to 1983 had had no qualms about sending contract killers outside its borders to eliminate opponents to the regime and anyone who might denounce the atrocities it had committed. Times had changed, but the methods devised by twisted minds tend to stay the same.

His investigation must have bothered quite a few people, too. It was possible—even probable—that his killer was a former member of the armed forces, in charge of ESMA[1] or another of the secret camps where "the disappeared" were taken to be tortured and killed.

He fished out his other notebook and from it started copying down the names of all the people he had interviewed on his first trip to Argentina. For obvious reasons, the notes he'd taken on his second trip weren't in it. He would have to be very careful not to let his guard slip when he returned to Buenos Aires.

What about Valerie's ex? She never mentioned him anymore, but they had been together for two years—that's a considerable amount of time. It wouldn't be the first time a spurned lover had turned violent.

Thinking about all the people who might want him dead had ruined Andrew's appetite. He pushed his plate away and left.

He toyed with the little ring box in his pocket as he walked back to the office, refusing to entertain one possibility that had just occurred to him. No, Valerie wasn't capable of doing something like that.

Are you sure? his innervoice asked. The question made his blood run cold.

* * *

On the Thursday of the first week of his resurrection—the expression filled him with terror each time he thought it—

---

[1] The Naval Mechanics School, which housed one of the largest secret detention centers in Argentina during the dictatorship.

Andrew got down to finalizing the last details of his trip. He was in more of a hurry than ever to return to Buenos Aires. He gave up on the idea of changing hotels; he'd met some of his key informants thanks to his stay at the last one. Marisa, the cute girl who worked at the hotel bar, had told him about a café where former members of the ERP, the People's Revolutionary Army, and the Montoneros, an urban guerrilla group, hung out. These men had survived their stay in a detention center, and there weren't too many of them. She had also put him in touch with one of the Mothers of the Plaza de Mayo—women whose children had been kidnapped by army commandos and never been seen again. Braving the dictatorship, they had paced up and down the sidewalks of the Plaza de Mayo every single day for years, carrying signs with photographs of their disappeared loved ones on them.

* * *

Simon called him around 11 A.M. to remind him they were having lunch. Andrew didn't remember them making plans; maybe their conversation would come back to him over lunch.

* * *

As soon as Simon told him the woman he'd on met his ski trip last winter had called him the previous evening, Andrew remembered that this had been a totally uninteresting lunch. Simon had fallen yet again for some girl with a great body and no sense of humor. Andrew wanted to get back to work. He broke in and told Simon bluntly that this was going nowhere.

"You said this girl lives in Seattle and she's coming to spend a few days in New York, right?"

"Yup. And I'm the lucky guy who gets to show her around the city," Simon replied happily.

"Next week we'll be sitting at this same table and you'll be in a shitty mood, telling me you've been had. That girl's looking for some poor schmuck like you who'll take her out, pay the bills and offer her someplace to sleep. When you get back to your apartment every night she'll tell you she's exhausted, say 'not tonight, darling,' and fall asleep instantly. All you'll get by way of thanks is a peck on your cheek the day she's leaving."

Simon gaped at him.

"What do you mean, 'not tonight, darling'?"

"Want me to spell it out for you?"

"How do you know all that?"

"I just do."

"You're just jealous. You're pathetic."

"You got back from your ski trip five months ago. Have you heard from her before this?"

"No, but Seattle isn't exactly next door, you know."

"Trust me, Simon: she flipped through her address book and stopped at S for Sucker."

Andrew picked up the tab. The conversation had taken him back to the year-end holidays and that incident on Christmas Day. He had nearly been knocked over by a car backing out of the Charles Street police station. Journalistic investigations were right up his alley, but he didn't have the particular skills needed for a criminal investigation. The services of a police detective—even a retired one—could come in very handy right now. He flipped through his address book to find the telephone number Inspector Pilguez had given him.

9

After he'd left Simon, Andrew called Inspector Pilguez. He got his voicemail. Unsure whether to leave a message, he hung up.

As he walked into the newspaper's offices he found himself shivering, and felt a shooting pain in the small of his back. It was so strong that he had to lean on the stair's bannister for support. Andrew had never suffered from back pain, and this anomaly immediately reminded him of the grim deadline that was approaching. If this was the first sign of imminent death, he thought, he'd better stock up on prescription painkillers as soon as possible.

Olivia found him breathless and doubled up in pain at the bottom of the staircase when she came in from lunch.

"Are you all right, Andrew?"

"I've been better, to be honest."

"You're looking terribly pale. Do you want me to call 911?"

"No, it's just my back playing up. I'll be fine."

"You should take the afternoon off and get some rest."

Andrew thanked Olivia. He told her he'd go splash some water on his face and everything would be okay.

Looking at himself in the restroom mirror, Andrew got the impression death was lurking behind him. He murmured to himself: "You've had a stroke of luck, buddy, but you better start racking your brains if you want it to last. You don't think everybody gets a second chance, do you? You've written enough obituaries to have some idea what it means when your time's up. You can't overlook anything anymore, not a single detail. The days are slipping by, and they'll go by faster and faster."

"Talking to yourself again, Stilman?" asked Olson, coming out of a stall. He zipped up his pants and walked over to where Andrew was standing next to a washbasin.

"I'm not in the mood," Andrew said, sticking his face under the faucet.

"You've been acting really weird lately. I don't know what you're up to now, but it's got to be something fishy."

"Olson, why don't you mind your own business and leave me the hell alone."

"I didn't report you," Olson declared proudly, as if he'd done something laudable.

"Good for you, Freddy. You're finally becoming a man."

Olson went over to the towel dispenser and yanked with all his might.

"These things never work," he said, banging the lid.

"You should write an article about it, I'm sure it'd be a winner. Your finest story this season. 'The Hand Towel Conspiracy,' by Freddy Olson."

Olson shot Andrew a dark look.

"Hey, I was joking. Don't take everything so literally."

"I don't like you, Stilman. I'm not the only one on this paper who can't stand your arrogance, but at least I don't pretend. A lot of us are waiting for you to slip up. You'll topple off your pedestal sooner or later."

Andrew looked at his colleague.

"So who else is part of this merry anti-Stilman band?"

"You should be wondering who likes you, actually. You'll find it's not a long list."

Olson looked at him scornfully and walked out of the men's room.

Andrew followed him, grimacing with pain, and caught up with him in front of the elevator.

"Olson! I shouldn't have hit you. It's just that I'm feeling on edge right now. I want to apologize."

"Really?"

"Hey, we're colleagues. Let's cool it, okay?"

Olson stared at Andrew.

"Okay, Stilman. I accept your apology."

Olson stuck his hand out and Andrew made a superhuman effort to shake it. Olson had really clammy palms.

Andrew felt a lingering sense of fatigue all afternoon that made it impossible for him to write. He used the time to re-read the introduction to his article about the terrible things that had gone on in Argentina during the dictatorship.

Andrew Stilman, The New York Times

On May 24, 1976, a fresh coup d'état brought a tyrant to power once again in Argentina. After banning all political parties and unions and muzzling the country's press, General Jorge Rafael Videla and the members of the military junta began carrying out a campaign of repression on a scale that Argentina had never previously experienced.

Their self-proclaimed objective was to prevent any form of revolt and eliminate anyone suspected of opposing the regime. A manhunt for suspected dissidents was launched throughout the country. The regime's opponents, their friends and acquaintances, and anyone holding views contrary to conservative Catholic values were considered to be terrorists, regardless of their age or gender.

The ruling junta opened secret detention centers and set up special sections made up of police units and members of the three branches of the armed forces. Death squads were rampant. Under the authority of regional chiefs, their mission was to kidnap, torture, and kill anyone suspected of sympathizing with the opposition. Over the next ten years, the ruling junta would enslave and make "disappear" more than thirty thousand people—men and women of all ages, but most of them very young. Several hundred newborn babies were stolen from their "dissident" mothers and given to supporters of the regime. The identity of these children was systematically erased, and a new one created from scratch. The regime claimed it was upholding Christian values by removing innocent souls from parents with perverted ideals, and offering the children salvation by entrusting them to families worthy of raising them.

The "disappeared," los desaparecidos, as they were known, were buried in mass graves. Many of them were drugged in detention centers before being loaded into planes flying under the radar, from which they were thrown alive into the Río de la Plata and the ocean.

There would be no traces of the massacre to incriminate those in power.

For the umpteenth time, Andrew pored over his list containing the names of those who had committed these atrocities in every corner of Argentina, rural and urban. The hours ticked by as he read the names of the torturers and leafed through transcripts of first-person accounts, confessions, and minutes of trial proceedings that had come to nothing. Once democracy had been restored, an amnesty law was passed granting these monsters near-total immunity.

It was painstaking work, and as Andrew went on with it he kept looking for traces of a man named Ortiz. Going by the information his editor had given him, Ortiz's case was typical of the many ordinary soldiers who had become tacit accomplices to some of the worst atrocities.

Why him in particular? Olivia had told him it was because Ortiz's story was shrouded in mystery. In Argentina, as elsewhere, the same question kept cropping up time and again: what kind of fanaticism could have inspired the ruling junta to turn normal men into torturers? How could a good husband and father return home and kiss his wife and children after spending his day torturing and killing other women and children?

Andrew knew he'd come this close to cornering Ortiz. Was it possible that one of the man's former accomplices or comrades-in-arms had pursued him all the way to Hudson River Park?

Something about that theory wasn't quite right. Andrew had been killed two days before his article appeared, so it couldn't have been revenge. Even so, when he returned to Buenos Aires he'd have to be much more careful than he had been in his previous life.

The more Andrew thought about it, the clearer it became to him that he needed help. He tried Inspector Pilguez again.

The retired cop immediately assumed the phone call meant bad news: Andrew had decided to take legal action against him after all because of the accident.

"My back *is* hurting, but it's not your fault," Andrew reassured him. "This call's got nothing to do with your energetic way of exiting parking lots."

"Oh." Pilguez sounded relieved. "In that case, to what do I owe the pleasure?"

"I need to see you. It's an emergency."

"I'd ask you to come over for coffee, but I live in San Francisco now. Might be a bit far for you."

"I understand," Andrew sighed.

Pilguez hesitated, and then asked: "What kind of emergency?"

"A life-and-death one."

"If it's a criminal case, I'm retired. But I can suggest Inspector Lucas of the 6th Precinct."

"I know you're retired, but you're the one I want to talk to. Call it instinct."

"I see."

"I doubt it. The situation I find myself in is bizarre, to say the least."

"Try me," the inspector urged. "I've heard a few in my day."

"It's too complicated to discuss over the phone. You wouldn't believe me. Sorry for calling this late. Have a nice evening."

"It's still mid-afternoon in San Francisco."

"In that case, have a good afternoon, Inspector."

Andrew hung up. He dropped his head into his hands and tried to collect his thoughts.

He was meeting Valerie in an hour's time, and he had to get himself in a better mood if he didn't want to screw up this very important evening. He'd used up his share of selfishness in his previous life.

* * *

He proposed to her as if for the first time. She admired the ring Andrew had slipped on her finger and tearfully assured him she would have picked exactly that one.

When they'd finished dinner, Andrew called Simon and immediately held out the phone to Valerie so she could tell him the news. Then they called Colette.

They'd just gotten to Valerie's East Village building when Andrew felt his cell phone vibrate in his pocket. He answered, wondering who could be calling this late.

It was Pilguez. "I've been thinking about our conversation," he said. "My wife would be only too happy if I left her in peace for a few days. She says a little distraction would do me good. I'll be getting on a plane tomorrow morning. I'm going to visit some friends in New York while I'm there. Let's meet for dinner around nine at the same place as last time. Don't be late. You've piqued my curiosity, Mr. Stilman."

"See you tomorrow. 9 P.M. at Frankie's," Andrew replied, feeling relieved.

"Who was that?" Valerie asked.

"Nobody."

"Oh, so you're having dinner with nobody tomorrow evening?"

* * *

Inspector Pilguez was waiting for him at a table in the back of the softly-lit restaurant. Andrew glanced at his watch as he sat down.

"Got in early," Pilguez said, reaching across to shake Andrew's hand.

The waiter handed them the menus and the inspector frowned.

"Damn this craze for dim lighting in restaurants. When is it going to pass? I can't read a word of this menu." He took a pair of reading glasses out of his pocket.

Andrew scanned the menu and put it down.

"They do a good steak here," Pilguez went on, abandoning his attempt to read the menu.

"Okay, let's get the steak," Andrew said. "Did you enjoy your trip?"

"What kind of question is that? When was the last time you heard of anyone enjoying a flight? But let's get on to the reason we're here. What can I do for you?"

"Help me to stop the person who . . . " Andrew hesitated. " . . . who tried to kill me," he finished.

Pilguez put his bottle of beer down.

"Have you reported this to the police?"

"No."

"That is generally what one does."

"It's a little more complicated. Let's just say it hasn't happened yet."

"I don't get it. Has someone already tried to kill you, or is someone going to try to kill you?"

"If I give you an honest answer to that question, I'm afraid you'll think I'm nuts."

"Try me."

"Well, both of those, Inspector."

"I see. Someone tried to kill you and you think they're going to try again soon, is that it?"

"Sort of."

Pilguez beckoned the waiter to come and take their order. As soon as the man had left, he looked hard at Andrew.

"I've just spent six hours squeezed into a sardine can at thirty thousand feet because you called to ask for my help. You seem like a nice guy, and I feel I owe you for nearly running you over."

"You barely bumped into me, and I came out of it without a scratch."

"That's just it. In this city full of crazies who'd jump at the slightest excuse to slap a lawsuit on you, there was every chance you'd try and get my insurance company to fork out a hefty compensation. You didn't, so I'm guessing you're an honest man. I could tell from your voice you're really worried. My instincts rarely let me down in forty years on the force and believe me, you can't imagine all the weird things I've seen. If I told you about some of them you'd think I was crazier than you. So either you tell me exactly what this is all about, or I'll just finish my steak and head off to bed. Have I made myself clear?"

"Couldn't be clearer," Andrew said, lowering his eyes.

"I'm listening," Pilguez said. "I hate eating cold food," he added as he started tucking into his meal.

"I was killed on July 9."

Pilguez began counting on his fingers.

"That was ten months ago. You can tell me about the circumstances later, but first of all, what makes you think your life's in danger once again?"

"You didn't hear what I said. I was killed this summer."

"It's only May 11, and you look very much alive to me."

"I warned you."

"You're not very good with words, considering you're a journalist. If I've understood what you're implying, you're convinced you're going to be killed on July 9. Why that date?"

"It's even more complicated than that."

Andrew told him the whole story—what had happened to him in Hudson River Park on the morning of July 9, and the incredible existence he'd been leading for the past few days. When he'd finished talking, the inspector drained his beer in one gulp and ordered another.

"Either I have a gift for attracting nut jobs, or else there's a curse on me."

"Why do you say that?"

"You wouldn't understand."

"We've got this far; you might as well tell me."

"Some other time."

Okay, to recap: you say you were killed, and that as soon as you died, you went back in time two months. Have you had a scan to make sure your brain's working fine?" Pilguez asked, his tone mocking.

"No."

"Then maybe we should start with that. Could be there's a little blood clot someplace in your brain that's making you believe the moon's made of green cheese. I've got a really good neurosurgeon friend in San Francisco. An amazing woman, and she's seen some pretty bizarre stuff too. I could give her a call. I'm sure she'd have a colleague she could recommend in New York."

"What if I told you I could predict what's going to happen from now through July?"

"And you're clairvoyant, too!"

"No, it's just that I have an excellent memory, and I remember everything that happened to me in the last two months of my life."

"Oh, good. That rules out early-onset Alzheimer's. Do you seriously believe what you're saying, Stilman?"

Andrew remained silent. Pilguez gave him a friendly tap on the hand.

"Of course you do! And it had to happen to me. What did I ever do to the good Lord?"

"I didn't think there was much of a chance you'd believe me," Andrew said. "I wouldn't either, if I were you."

"You a sports fan?" Pilguez asked abruptly, glancing at the television mounted above the bar.

"Sure. Isn't everyone?"

"Don't turn around. The Yankees are playing the Seattle Mariners, and the game's nearly over. Can you give me the final score?"

"I don't remember exactly, but what I do know is that, contrary to all expectations, the Mariners are having a great start to the season. They must be wiping the floor with the Yankees."

"Yeah, yeah," Pilguez sighed. "That's what any Mariners fan would say."

"Me, a New Yorker, a Mariners fan? You must be joking. The Yankees will get the upper hand back in the last few minutes and pull off a win."

"Doesn't look like they're heading for one," Pilguez sighed.

"Buy *The New York Times* tomorrow morning. On the

front page, you'll read about a US Navy carrier firing on an Iranian ship that was blocking the Strait of Hormuz."

"Oh, come on! You're with the *Times*, Stilman—you want to try and wow me by making me believe you've guessed the front page story of the newspaper you work for?"

"The Pentagon will issue a press release about the incident at around 11:30 tonight. The paper's put to bed at midnight, and we're nowhere near midnight right now. But since you don't believe me, how about this. A tornado will hit the small town of Gardner in Florida just before noon tomorrow. The entire downtown area will be practically wiped off the map."

"And the reason you remember this is that you're addicted to the Weather Channel?"

"I remember it because my future in-laws live in Arcadia, a small town around thirty miles from Gardner. I can clearly recall that my wife-to-be was worried sick, and I remember the exact date because it happened just two days after I proposed."

"Heartfelt congratulations. Anything else you can predict, Mr. Soothsayer?"

"A colleague of yours in the mounted unit will be run over by an ambulance tomorrow afternoon. He'll get off with a fractured collarbone, but unfortunately his horse will have to be put to sleep. My future wife's a vet; she looks after the unit's horses. What with the tornado and losing a horse, Valerie got back home so stressed out that I was worried about her. But I've wasted enough of your time, and I don't want to keep playing this little game: I'm not exactly enjoying it. Let me pay for dinner, okay? And please tell me what I owe you for your plane ticket."

"I'll let you get the check. As for my travel expenses, I'm a big boy, but thanks anyway."

Andrew paid the bill and got up.

"One little thought has just occurred to me, Stilman.

Assuming you *can* predict what's going to happen in the next few months, why don't you try to forestall what you can?"

"Because I can't change the course of things. The few times I've tried to these past couple of days, all I've managed to do is delay events by a few hours."

"In that case, what makes you think you can prevent your murder from happening?"

"Hope. Or despair, depending on my state of mind."

Andrew said goodbye to the inspector and left.

Pilguez remained at the table, lost in thought. He watched the end of the game. In the last few minutes, the Yankees hit a game-winning home run.

10.

A ndrew didn't wait to get to the office to read *The New York Times* the next morning. He bought the paper from the newsstand at the corner of his street, and noted that the front page featured the article Freddy Olson had written in haste following the Pentagon's announcement half an hour before the paper went to print. A U.S. Navy cruiser had fired a warning shot across the bows of an Iranian frigate that had sailed a little too close to the Sixth Fleet at the mouth of the Strait of Hormuz. The shot had done no damage to the Iranian ship, which had turned back, but tension between the two countries was escalating by the day.

Andrew hoped Inspector Pilguez had read the article too. In the early afternoon, after a glance at the news tickers scrolling the latest stories on the television screens in the editorial offices, he called Valerie to inform her, before she heard it from someone else, that an F5 tornado had destroyed a town not far from her parents' home. He tacked on a little white lie: she had no reason to worry about them, because as soon as he'd heard the news he'd inquired about the situation in Arcadia, and nothing had happened there.

In preparation for what he couldn't tell her yet, he called a florist, ordered a bunch of peonies and wrote a romantic message on a card to slip in among the flowers. He'd make sure he took good care of her that evening.

He spent the afternoon doing research, but the inspector's remark the previous evening had set him thinking. Why not try to alter the course of events? When he'd tried to avoid the argument with Olson, all he'd done was postpone it by a few hours, and it had ended up being a lot nastier than their original quarrel. When he'd gone to buy a ring before making his marriage proposal, strangely enough he'd chosen the exact same ring, even though he'd gone to another jeweler.

Still, why not try and turn his past experience to his advantage? On his forthcoming trip to Buenos Aires, maybe he'd be able to trap the man whose confession he hadn't been able to obtain. If he could get Major Ortiz to talk, his editor would offer him the front page as soon as she'd read his story, and that meant he could whisk his wife away on honeymoon the day after their wedding.

What if I could replay my life? Andrew scribbled on the flyleaf of his notebook. Hasn't everyone dreamed of having that opportunity? Correcting their mistakes; succeeding where they'd failed. Life was offering him a second chance.

So you won't be hanging out at Novecento anymore, right? a little inner voice whispered.

Andrew chased the thought away. He started tidying up his desk, wanting to get home before Valerie. His office line rang. It was the switchboard operator transferring a call. A police inspector wanted to talk to him.

"You're very gifted," Pilguez declared without saying hello. "You got nearly all of it right."

"Nearly?"

"My colleague fractured his thighbone, not his collarbone—more bothersome. I won't lie to you. When I read the paper this morning I figured you were just a really good con artist. I saw those horrifying images on TV after the tornado's passage, but I still wasn't ready to change my mind. I talked to my friend at the 6th Precinct less than an hour ago. He made a few inquiries on my behalf, and confirmed there'd been an accident this afternoon involving an ambulance and one of our colleagues in the mounted police. You couldn't have guessed all of that."

"No, I couldn't."

"We have to meet again, Mr. Stilman."

"How about tomorrow?"

"A lot sooner. Hop in the elevator. I'm right here in the lobby waiting for you."

* * *

Andrew took Pilguez to the Marriott bar. The inspector ordered a Scotch, and Andrew unthinkingly asked for a Fernet and Coke.

"Who could want you dead?" Pilguez asked. "Why does that question make you smile?"

"I've started making a list. I didn't think it would be such a long one."

"We can go in alphabetical order, if that makes it easier for you," Pilguez said, taking out a small notebook.

"I first thought of Freddy Olson, a colleague. We can't stand each other—though I made up with him yesterday, as a precaution."

"Resentment can linger for a long time. What's he got against you?"

"Professional envy. I've swiped quite a few stories from under his nose these past few months."

"If we all bumped off a colleague each time he stepped on our toes, Wall Street would be littered with corpses. Then again, nothing's impossible. What else?"

"I was sent three death threats."

"You're a funny guy, Stilman. You said that as if you were talking about flyers."

"Journalists get threats once in a while."

Andrew summed up the findings of the investigation he'd gone to China for.

"Have you kept the letters?"

"I gave them to security."

"Get them back. I want to read them tomorrow."

"They're anonymous."

"Nothing's totally anonymous these days. We could find fingerprints."

"Mine, certainly, and the security agents.'"

"Our forensics people are good at separating the wheat from the chaff. Have you kept the envelopes?"

"I think so. Why?"

"The postmark could give us a lead. Letters of this kind are usually written in anger, and anger makes you careless. Whoever wrote it could have simply dropped their letter in a mailbox near where they live. It'll take a long time, but we'll have to look for all the parents who adopted children from that orphanage, and find their addresses."

"That idea wouldn't have occurred to me."

"You're not a police officer. So—an office colleague, and three threatening letters. You said it was a long list. Who else is on it?"

"I'm currently working on an equally sensitive investigation into the atrocities committed by various soldiers during the Argentine dictatorship."

"Are you investigating anyone in particular?"

"The protagonist of my article is a former air force major who's suspected of having participated in death flights. The courts have cleared him of all charges, but I'm using his story as the leitmotif of my piece."

"Have you met this guy?"

"Yes, but I wasn't able to get him to talk. I'm hoping to get a confession out of him on my forthcoming trip."

"If I believe these absurd claims of yours, you already made this trip in the past, right?"

"Yes, that's right."

"I thought you couldn't change the course of events?"

"That's what I'd been telling myself, up until yesterday. But the fact that you're here and that we're having this conversation, which never happened in my previous life, makes me think I could be wrong."

Pilguez clinked the ice cubes in his glass.

"Let's get one thing straight, Stilman. You've shown a certain flair for telling the future, but I'm not quite ready to swallow this story of yours hook, line and sinker. Why don't we agree on a version that'll be less of a problem for me."

"Like what?"

"You think someone's going to kill you, and as you're obviously gifted with admirable powers of intuition, I'm willing to help you out. Let's call it assistance to a person presumed to be in danger."

"If that makes things easier for you, sure. Coming back to our discussion, I don't think this former air force major could have followed me here."

"He could have sent his men after you. Why did you choose him in particular to be the protagonist of your article?"

"He's the key figure in the background information my editor gave me. 'If you want readers to be moved by the story of a people, it has to involve flesh and blood characters they can relate to. Otherwise, even the most in-depth story about the worst possible atrocities is only a succession of events and dates.' That's exactly what she told me. She had every reason to believe that describing this man's career would be a good way to show how governments and populist fervor can turn ordinary people into monsters. It's quite an interesting subject considering what's going on in the world these days, don't you think?"

"Is your editor above all suspicion?"

"Olivia? Absolutely. She's got no reason to have a grudge against me. We get along very well."

"How well exactly?"

"What are you insinuating?"

"You're getting married soon, aren't you? Jealousy isn't necessarily the preserve of your male colleagues, you know."

"There's nothing ambiguous about our relationship."

"What about her? Is it possible she could have seen things differently?"

Andrew thought about the inspector's question.

"No. I honestly don't think so."

"Well, let's rule out this Olivia . . . "

"Stern. Olivia Stern."

"With or without an 'e'?"

"Without."

Pilguez jotted down the name in his notebook anyway. "What about your fiancée?"

"What about her?"

"Look, Mr. Journalist, forty years as a cop taught me that once you've ruled out attacks by crazies, there are only two reasons people commit murder—money and love. I have three questions for you. Do you have any debts? Did you witness a murder?"

"No to both. What's the third question?"

"Did you cheat on your wife?"

* * *

The inspector ordered another Scotch, and Andrew told him about an incident that might be connected to his own murder.

Andrew had been so caught up in his work that he hadn't

had a chance to drive his old Datsun for months. He kept it in the lower basement level of a parking garage near the Marriott. It was probably covered in a thick shroud of dust by now. The battery must have gone flat; the tires too.

He had a mechanic coming by at lunchtime to tow the car to Simon's auto shop. He knew Simon would rake him over the coals for neglecting it so badly, as he did each time Andrew brought the car in to be repaired. He'd remind Andrew of all the time and energy his mechanics had put into restoring the Datsun, which he'd gone to such lengths to find to make him happy, then say that a slob like Andrew didn't deserve to own a vintage car like this one. He'd keep the car in the garage for double the amount of time required to get it running again, like a schoolmaster confiscating a toy to punish a student, but he'd give Andrew back the Datsun running as good as new.

Andrew left the office and crossed 8th Avenue. He greeted the attendant at the parking garage entrance, but the man was immersed in his newspaper and took no notice of him. As he went down the ramp, Andrew heard what sounded like the echo of his own footsteps behind him.

A single neon light cast a feeble glow over the lower basement level. Andrew walked along the central aisle to parking space 37. It was the smallest car in there, sandwiched between two pillars. Opening the door and squeezing himself in took a degree of acrobatics, but he'd gotten a discount rate on this spot where few other drivers would have been willing to park.

He ran a hand over the hood and realized the Datsun was even filthier than he'd expected. He gave the front tires a quick kick and was reassured: there seemed to be enough air in them for the car to be towed away safely. He hunted in his pocket for the keys; the tow truck would be here any minute. He skirted the pillar and, as he bent to slip the key in the door lock, felt a presence behind him. Before Andrew could spin round, a baseball bat struck his hip, making him double over. Instinctively, he turned to face his attacker. A second blow, to his stomach, knocked the breath out of him and he fell.

Curled up on the ground, Andrew struggled to make out the figure now pressing the baseball bat into his chest to force him flat on his back.

If it was the car he wanted, he could take it; he wouldn't be able to start it, anyway. Andrew waved the keys, but the man kicked his hand and sent them flying.

"Take my cash and let me go," Andrew pleaded, pulling his wallet out of his coat pocket.

With a terrifyingly precise swing of the bat, the wallet was knocked right to the far end of the garage.

"Bastard!" the attacker shouted.

Andrew thought the man was deranged. Either that, or he'd mistaken Andrew for someone else, in which case the faster he told him so the better.

He managed to prop himself up against the door of his car.

A swipe of the baseball bat smashed the window to smithereens. Another blow whistled past, skimming over Andrew's head, and knocked off the side view mirror.

"Stop!" Andrew cried out. "What the hell have I done to you?"

"Now you ask that question, do you? What about me? What did I ever do to you?"

So he *was* deranged, Andrew concluded, petrified.

"The time's come to make you pay," the man said, lifting his bat.

"I beg you," Andrew whimpered. "I have no idea what you're talking about. I don't know you. I assure you you're making a mistake."

"I know exactly who I'm dealing with. A bastard who's only interested in his miserable career. A sonofabitch with no consideration for others. A scumbag," the man screamed, sounding even more threatening.

Andrew discreetly slipped his hand into his jacket pocket and found his cell phone. He groped with his fingertips for the buttons to dial 911 before realizing that there was no way his phone would get a signal here this far below ground.

"I'm going to smash your hands. I'm going to make sure you don't hurt anyone ever again."

Andrew could feel his heart pounding. This nutcase was going to kill him. He had to try something, but the adrenaline rushing through his veins was sending his heartbeat crazy. His whole body was trembling; he wasn't even sure he could stand.

"Not so cocky now, are you?"

"Put yourself in my place," Andrew replied.

"Funny you have the gall to say that! That's just it—I wish *you* had put yourself in *my* place. If you had, we wouldn't be here right now," the man sighed, pressing the baseball bat against Andrew's forehead.

Andrew watched as the bat was lifted above his head and smashed down on the roof of the Datsun, which caved in under the impact.

"How much did you get paid for it? Two thousand dollars? Five thousand? Ten thousand?"

"What are you talking about?"

"Oh, sure. Play innocent! Don't tell me: it's not about the money; you work for the prestige of it. After all, you've got the greatest job in the world, haven't you?" the man continued, sounding disgusted.

They heard the sound of an engine and the squeal of a clutch, and saw two beams of light suddenly pierce the darkness.

The attacker wavered. Sheer desperation gave Andrew the strength to get to his feet, throw himself at the man and clutch at his throat. The man freed himself easily, threw Andrew an uppercut punch and fled toward the ramp, brushing past the tow truck that was now lighting Andrew up in the glare of its headlights.

The mechanic got down from his vehicle and hurried over to Andrew.

"What happened?"

"I've been beaten up," Andrew said, rubbing his face.

"Looks like I got here just in time!"

"Ten minutes earlier would've been even better, but thanks—it could've gotten much worse."

"I wish I could say as much for your car. He's really bashed it up. Still, better the car than you."

"Yes, though I can think of someone who might take a different view," Andrew sighed, looking at his Datsun.

"Well, at least I'm not wasting my time. Have you got the keys?" the man asked.

"They're on the ground somewhere," Andrew said, feeling around for them.

"Sure you don't want me to drive you to the emergency room?"

"No, thanks. Nothing damaged, except for my self-esteem."

By the light of the tow truck's headlights, Andrew spotted his car keys near a pillar and his wallet lying not far from a Cadillac. He gave the mechanic the keys and told him he wouldn't accompany him to Simon's auto shop after all. He scribbled the address on the towing receipt and handed it to the man.

"What do I tell the man at the auto shop?"

"Tell him I'm fine, and that I'll call him this evening."

"Hop in. I'll drive you out of here, just in case that loony's still hanging around. You should go see the cops."

"I'd be incapable of describing my attacker. The only thing I can tell them is that he was at least a head shorter than me, and I don't really feel like boasting about that."

Andrew got out of the tow truck on 40th Street and walked back to the office. The pain in his hip was fading, but his jaw felt like it had been set in concrete. He had no idea who his assailant was, but he doubted the man had laid into him by mistake.

* * *

"When did this attack happen?" Pilguez asked.

"During the Christmas holidays, between Christmas and New Year's Day, when I was on my own in New York."

"Sounds like he's handy with a bat. I wouldn't be surprised if the writer of one of those anonymous letters you got used more than a pen to let you know he wasn't happy. And you can't tell me what he looked like?"

"It was very dark in that garage," Andrew said, lowering his eyes.

Pilguez put a hand on Andrew's shoulder.

"Have I told you how many years I worked for the police before I retired? Nearly forty. A hell of a long time, right?"

"I guess so."

"How many suspects do you think I interrogated in the course of that forty-year career?"

"Is it important for me to know?"

"Even I don't remember how many, to be completely honest. What I *can* tell you is this: I may be retired, but I can still see when someone's hiding something. When somebody's bull-shitting you, there's always some little detail that's a dead give-away."

"What kind of detail?"

"Body language never lies. A frown, a guilty blush, pursed lips, avoiding eye contact—like you're doing right now. Checking your shoes are well polished, are you?"

Andrew looked up.

"It wasn't my wallet I picked up in the parking garage, it was my attacker's. He must have dropped it when he fled."

"And why were you hiding that from me?"

"I'm ashamed I got beat up by a guy who's shorter than me. And I found out from the content of his wallet he's a professor."

"What difference does that make?"

"He's not your average thug. That man didn't attack me for the heck of it—an article of mine must have caused him trouble."

"Have you still got his ID card?"

"It's in my desk drawer at the office."

"Then let's take a little walk to your office; it's only a block away."

11

Pilguez came by to pick up Andrew at 6:30 A.M. the next morning. If they wanted to catch Frank Capetta, a professor of theology at New York University, the best thing to do was wait for him outside his building before he left for work.

The taxi dropped them off at 101st Street and Amsterdam Avenue, in front of a row of rent-controlled apartment buildings owned by the city. Number 826 was a twenty-story building overlooking a basketball court and a small fenced-in park where the neighborhood kids played. Pilguez and Andrew settled down on a bench facing the entrance to wait.

He wore a trench coat and clutched a briefcase under his arm, hunched over as if he was carrying the weight of the world on his shoulders. Andrew immediately recognized the man whose driver's license he'd stared at time and again, wondering what he could have done to send him into such a fury.

Pilguez shot Andrew a look. Andrew nodded to confirm that this was their man.

They got up, quickened their pace and caught up with Capetta before he could reach the bus stop. The professor blanched when Andrew stepped in front of him.

"How about a coffee before you go to work?" Pilguez asked, his tone brooking no argument.

"I'll be late for class," Capetta snapped, "and I've no desire to have coffee with this man. Let me past, or I'll call for help. The police station's just down the block."

"What'll you tell the cops?" Pilguez asked. "That you beat up this gentleman with a baseball bat and smashed his vintage car for a little holiday fun last Christmas?"

"*And* he's a coward to boot!" Capetta spat, giving Andrew a scornful look. "Brought your heavy along to take revenge, have you?"

"Thanks for the compliment," said Pilguez. "At least you're not denying you did it. I'm not a bodyguard, just a friend. Considering the way you acted the last time the two of you met, you can't blame him for wanting some backup."

"I'm not here to get even with you, Mr. Capetta," Andrew broke in.

"How did you find me?"

Andrew held out the wallet, and Capetta took it. "Why'd you wait so long?" he asked.

"Why don't we get that coffee?" Pilguez asked, tapping his foot on the sidewalk.

They went into the Café Roma nearby and got a table at the back of the room.

"What do you want?" Capetta asked.

"A double shot of espresso," Pilguez replied.

"To understand why you attacked me," Andrew said.

Pilguez took his pen and notebook out of his pocket and slid them over the table to Capetta.

"While I go place my order, I'd be obliged if you could write down the following: One veal roast, four pounds of potatoes, oregano, two red onions, one pint of half-and-half, one packet of mustard seed, two packets of grated Swiss cheese, one bunch of asparagus. Oh, and a cheesecake."

"Why would I write down all that?" Capetta asked.

"Because I'm asking nicely," Pilguez said, getting up.

"What if I don't want to?"

"You don't want your administrator at NYU to find out what a member of his teaching body got up to over the Christmas holidays, do you? Okay, start writing! I'll be back in a second. Want something? Cup of tea?"

Andrew and Capetta exchanged an astonished glance. Capetta bent to his task. As he was writing down the words Pilguez had dictated, Andrew asked him the question he'd been dying to know the answer to.

"So what did I do to you, Mr. Capetta?"

"Are you pretending you don't know, or are you stupid?"

"A bit of both, I guess."

"What did that bulldog of yours say—a jar of mustard or mustard seeds? I can't remember."

"The seeds, I think."

"You destroyed my whole life," Capetta sighed, going back to writing his list. "Is that enough for you? Or do you want the details?"

He looked up at Andrew.

"You want the details, of course!" he said. "I had two children, Mr. Stilman—a seven-year-old boy and a three-year-old girl. Sam and Lea. My wife developed medical complications after Sam was born, and the doctors told us we couldn't have another child. We'd always wanted Sam to have a little brother or sister. Paolina, my wife, is from Uruguay. She is also a teacher; children are her life. She teaches history, and her students are much younger than mine. When we finally admitted to ourselves that there was no hope of a second child, we decided to adopt. I don't need to tell you it's a long and tedious process. Some families wait years before they attain their dream. Then we heard how, in China, they don't know what to do with the thousands of babies abandoned each year. Their population control laws allow only one child per family. The Chinese authorities are very strict about it, but many couples don't have the money to buy contraceptives. When they have a second child they can't afford to pay the fine, so sometimes they have no choice but to abandon the child at an orphanage.

"Many of these kids spend their whole lives inside the walls of an orphanage and receive only a very basic education—a pretty hopeless existence. I'm deeply religious and I was convinced the Lord had put us through this to open our eyes to the suffering of others, so we could become the parents of a child given up by its birth family. By going the China route—absolutely legally, I assure you—we stood a good chance of adopting in a reasonable amount of time. And that's what happened. We went through all of the background checks and were approved for adoption. After paying the orphanage a five-thousand-dollar processing fee—and I can tell you that was quite a chunk of our savings—we experienced the second-happiest moment of our lives, after Sam's birth. We went to China to get Lea on May 2, 2009. She'd just turned two, according to her documents. You should have seen how thrilled Sam was when we came back with his little sister. He was crazy about her. For several months we were the happiest family in the world. Of course it wasn't easy getting Lea used to us in the beginning. She cried a lot and she was scared of everything, but we were so loving and affectionate and gentle with her that after a few months she gave us a wonderful gift: she started calling us Mom and Dad." Capetta broke off. "Sit down," he told Pilguez. "I can feel you standing behind me, and it's very unpleasant."

"I didn't want to interrupt you."

"Well, you have," Capetta said.

"Go on, Mr. Capetta," Andrew pressed him.

"One evening last fall, I took the train home as usual. I sat down and opened up my newspaper the way I always do. That evening—I don't need to remind you what date it was, do I, Mr. Stilman?—my eye was drawn to an article about a Chinese orphanage in Hunan province. You wrote very movingly about the mothers who'd lost their reason for living because the most precious thing of all—their child—had been stolen from them. *They wait for death the way you'd watch for a friend to arrive*: those were your exact words. I don't cry easily, but I cried when I read your article, Mr. Stilman. I was crying as I folded up the paper, and I went on crying later that evening after I'd kissed my daughter goodnight.

"I immediately assumed she was one of those stolen children. It all added up—the dates, the place, the sum of money we'd paid the orphanage. I knew it with every fiber of my being, but for several weeks I refused to face up to it. True faith dictates compassion. We owe it to God to cherish the compassionate nature He entrusted to us when He gave us the gift of life. One second of desertion or cowardice or cruelty is all it takes for us to lose our dignity forever. Some believers fear the darkness of hell. As a professor of theology, that always makes me smile. Hell is a lot closer than we think: it opens its doors to us whenever we lose sight of our humanity.

"These thoughts haunted me day and night. How could I be an accomplice, even a passive one, to such an abomination? How could I keep hearing Lea call us Mom and Dad when I knew that in another house, in another place, her real parents were crying out her name and mourning her absence? We had wanted to give all our love to an unwanted little girl, not take in a stolen child.

"I was tormented by guilt, and finally told my wife everything. Paolina didn't want to hear it. Lea was her daughter as much as mine. Lea was our child. Here with us, she would have a better life, an education, a future. Over there, her parents couldn't provide for her or make sure she was healthy. Paolina and I had a terrible fight. I criticized her logic. To hear her talk, you'd have thought it was perfectly okay to kidnap the children of all the poor people in the world! I told her the things she was saying were shameful; that she didn't have the right to talk that way. I really hurt her, and that was the end of our discussion about Lea.

"While Paolina strived to carry on as if everything was normal, I set about searching, day after day. I have a few Chinese colleagues who respected what I was trying to do, and offered to help. I sent e-mails and made contacts, and bit by bit, information began to trickle in. I soon had to face the truth. Lea had been forcibly taken away from her parents when she was fifteen months old. You know the facts as well as I do: in August 2009, a squad of corrupt policemen burst into a number of small villages in Hunan province and kidnapped babies and toddlers. Lea must have been playing in front of her house when they arrived. The police grabbed her from under her mother's nose, and beat the woman black and blue when she started fighting for her child.

"I owe a great deal to a dear colleague, William Huang, who heads the Department of East Asian Studies. He travels to China often, and maintains many valuable contacts there. I gave him a photo of Lea. It only took him one trip to find out the terrible truth. The detectives dispatched by Beijing to arrest the bastards responsible for the trafficking had found Lea's birth parents. They live in a tiny village about a hundred miles from the orphanage.

"In early December last year, Paolina took Sam to Uruguay for a week to visit her parents. We'd agreed that Lea and I would stay here. She was so trusting. She trusted me . . . But the truth was staring at us both, and I had made up my mind. The day after my wife and son left, I got on a plane with Lea. Because of my daughter's origins and my intentions, I'd had no difficulty obtaining our visas. There was an official guide waiting for us at Beijing airport. He took the plane with us to Changsha, and then accompanied us to her village.

"You can't imagine how I felt during that twenty-five-hour trip, Mr. Stilman. I kept wanting to turn back each time Lea smiled at me, filled with wonder at the sight of the cartoons playing on the little screen on the seat in front of her, or called me 'Dad' and asked me where we were going. So when the plane started its descent, I told her the truth—well, most of it. I told her we were going to visit the country where she'd been born, and in her childish gaze I saw a mixture of amazement and joy.

"And then we reached her village. It was a far cry from New York: dirt roads and dry stone houses, most of them without electricity. Lea was surprised by everything she saw; she held on to my hand and kept letting out little cries of joy. The world's a wonderful place to discover when you're three years old, isn't it?

"We knocked on the door of a small farmhouse, and a man opened the door. When he caught sight of Lea he was speechless. Our eyes met, and he realized why we were there. His eyes filled with tears; so did mine. Lea was staring at him, probably wondering who the man was and why the sight of her should make him cry. He turned and shouted out his wife's name. When I saw her, the last shred of hope that I was still nurturing instantly vanished. The resemblance between them was striking—Lea was the spitting image of her birth mother.

"Have you ever contemplated the beauty of nature when it is reborn in spring, Mr. Stilman? It can make you doubt that winter ever existed. The face of that woman was the most heartbreaking thing I'd ever seen. She knelt down in front of Lea, her entire body shaking, and held out a hand to her. I watched as the most indestructible bond in life was forged anew. Showing no fear and not the slightest hesitation, Lea took a step towards the woman. She placed a hand on her mother's face and caressed her cheek, as she took in the features of the woman who had given birth to her, and then she put her arms around her neck.

"That frail-looking woman swept my little girl off the

ground and hugged her close. She was crying and covering Lea with kisses. Her husband went up to them and held them both tight in his arms.

"I stayed with them for seven days, and for those seven days Lea had two fathers. During that all too short week, I gradually made her understand that she had returned home; that her life was here. I promised her we would come back and see her, and that one day she'd cross the ocean again to pay us a visit. I was lying, but I knew there was no other way. I had no strength left in me.

"The guide, who'd also been our interpreter, understood what I was going through; we talked a lot. The sixth evening, as I lay weeping in the darkness, Lea's father came over to my bed and asked me to follow him. We went outside. It was cold. He placed a blanket over my shoulders, then we sat on the steps in front of the house and he offered me a cigarette. I don't smoke, but I accepted that evening. I was hoping the acrid taste of the tobacco would dull the pain that held me in its grip. The next morning, the guide and I agreed to leave in the early afternoon, when Lea would be taking her nap. There was no way I could have said goodbye to her.

"After lunch I laid her down for the last time and spoke to her lovingly. I told her that I was going on a journey, that she'd be very happy here, and that one day we'd see each other again. She fell asleep in my arms. I kissed her forehead and breathed in her smell one last time, storing it up to remember it until the end of my life. And then I left."

Capetta took a handkerchief out of his pocket, mopped his eyes, folded it back up and took a deep breath before continuing his story.

"When we'd left New York, I had written Paolina a long letter in which I explained what I was about to do—what I had to do on my own, because we hadn't found the strength to take Lea back together. I wrote that in time we would get through this terrible ordeal. I told her I was sorry, and begged her to think of what the future would hold in store for us if I didn't do this. Would we be able to watch our child grow up, constantly fearing the moment when she would learn the truth? Every adopted child wants to find its origins at some point. The ones who can't agonize over it all their lives. There's nothing anyone can do; it's just the way people are made. What would we have told her when she found out? That we had always known where her parents were? That we had been unwilling accomplices to her kidnapping? That our only excuse was that we loved her? We would have deserved it if she rejected us, but it would have been too late for her to start over with her birth family.

"In my letter, I told my wife that we hadn't adopted a child only to orphan her all over again when she grew up.

"My wife loved our daughter more than anything. You don't love someone just because you have the same genes. They'd never been apart, except when Paolina left for Uruguay with Sam.

"You must think I'm a monster, separating them like that, Mr. Stilman. But the thing was, when Lea first came to us, she kept repeating a word that we took for baby's babble. She would cry out *niang* all day long. *Niang, niang, niang*, she'd keep saying, looking at the door. Later on, when I asked my colleague if it meant something, he told me sorrowfully that in Chinese, *niang* means mother. Lea had been calling to her mother for weeks, and we hadn't understood.

"She was our daughter for less than two years. When she's seven or eight, maybe even sooner, she'll have erased us from her memory. As for me, I'll still be able to see her face if I live to be a hundred. Until the very last moment of my life, I'll be able to hear her childish laughter and shouts and smell the scent of her round little cheeks. You never forget your child, even if that child was never truly yours.

"When I got back from China, the apartment had been cleared out. Paolina had taken everything except our bed, the kitchen table and a chair. There wasn't a single toy left in Sam's room. And on the kitchen table, in the spot where I'd left the letter in which I'd begged her to forgive me one day, she had written just one word in red ink: *Never*.

"I don't know where they are. I don't know if she's left the U.S., if she's taken my son to Uruguay, or if she's simply in another city."

The three men remained silent for a moment.

"Why didn't you go to the police?" Pilguez asked.

"What would I have said to them? That I'd kidnapped my daughter and that my wife had paid me back for it by running away with our son? So they could hunt her down? So they could arrest her? So that social services could place Sam with a foster family until a judge sorted out our story and decided on his fate? No, I didn't do it. We've had our share of suffering. You see, Mr. Stilman, desperation can sometimes transform itself into anger. I've damaged your car, but you've destroyed my family and my life."

"I'm truly sorry, Mr. Capetta."

"Now you are, because you sympathize with my pain, but tomorrow morning you'll tell yourself it wasn't your fault, that you were only doing your job, and that you're proud of doing it. You reported the truth. Fair enough. But there's one question I want to ask you, Mr. Stilman."

"Anything."

"You wrote in your article that five hundred American families, maybe even a thousand, had been mixed up—in all innocence—in this child trafficking business. Before that article went to press, did you think for one single moment about the tragedy you were going to inflict upon them?"

Andrew lowered his eyes.

"That's what I thought," Capetta sighed. Then he handed Pilguez the list of words the policeman had ordered him to write.

"Here's your stupid list."

Pilguez took the sheet of paper. He took the copies of the three letters Andrew had recovered from the newspaper's security division out of his pocket and placed them on the table.

"I don't get it," he said. "It's not the same handwriting."

"What are you talking about?" Capetta asked.

"Mr. Stilman received some death threats. I thought perhaps you'd written one of them."

"Is that why you came?"

"Among other things, yes."

"I went to that parking garage to get revenge, but I wasn't capable of it."

Capetta took the letters and glanced at the first one.

"I could never kill anyone," he said, putting the sheet of paper back on the table.

He paled as he picked up the second letter.

"Have you still got the envelope this letter came in?" he asked, his voice trembling.

"Yes, why?"

"Can I see it?"

"First answer the question," Pilguez broke in.

"I recognize this handwriting," Capetta murmured. "It's my wife's. Do you remember if there was a foreign stamp on it? I suppose you'd have noticed a stamp from Uruguay?"

"I'll check first thing tomorrow," Andrew replied.

"Thank you, Mr. Stilman. It's important for me to know."

Pilguez and Andrew got up and said goodbye to the theology professor. As the three of them exited, Capetta called out to Andrew.

"Mr. Stilman, I told you back there I'd be incapable of killing anyone."

"Have you changed your mind?" Pilguez asked.

"No, but after what's happened, I can't say the same for Paolina. I wouldn't take her threats lightly if I were you."

* * *

Pilguez and Andrew took the subway back downtown. At that time of day, it was the fastest way to get to Andrew's office.

"I have to admit you've got a talent for winning people over," said Pilguez.

"Why didn't you tell him you're a cop?"

"If he knew he was talking a cop he'd have invoked his right to remain silent and insisted on having his lawyer present. Believe me, it was better for him to think I'm your bodyguard, even if it's not very flattering."

"But you're retired, aren't you?"

"Yes, that's right. What can I say? I can't get used to it."

"I wouldn't have thought up that idea of dictating a list to compare the handwriting."

"What, you think I make it up as I go along? I've been a cop for a long time."

"But the list of ingredients was totally stupid."

"I promised the friends I'm staying with I'd make them dinner tonight, and it so happens that that is my shopping list. I was worried I'd forget something. Not so stupid after all, huh, Mr. Journalist?" Pilguez grew serious. "Capetta's story was heartbreaking. Does it ever occur to you to think about the consequences of what you write about people?"

"Have you never made a mistake in the course of your long career, Inspector? Haven't you ever ruined the life of an innocent person just because you were sure your suspicions were correct, or because you wanted to wrap up an investigation at any price?"

"You bet I have. In my line of business, choosing whether or not to turn a blind eye is an everyday dilemma. Do you send a petty criminal behind bars, with all that that entails, or do you let it slide? Do you give your report an accusatory slant or not? Depends on the circumstances. Every crime is a special case. Every criminal has his own story. Some you'd like to shoot in the head; others, you want to give them a second chance. But I was just a cop, not a judge."

"Did you turn a blind eye often?"

"This is you, Mr. Stilman. Don't miss your stop."

The train slowed, then came to a standstill. Andrew shook the inspector's hand and stepped out onto the platform.

12

At twenty-four, Isabel was the mother of a two-year-old girl. Her husband Rafael Santos, only slightly older than her, was a journalist. The couple lived in a small apartment in the Barracas neighborhood of Buenos Aires. Isabel and Rafael had met in college. Like him, she was studying journalism. He always maintained that she had a snappier, more confident writing style than him, and a particular gift for writing profiles. But when their daughter was born, Isabel had chosen to put her career on standby until María Luz went to school. Journalism was the couple's shared passion, and Rafael never sent in an article for publication without getting his wife to read it first. Once their daughter had gone to sleep, Isabel would sit at the kitchen table, pencil in hand, and revise his drafts. Rafael, Isabel and María Luz led a happy existence, and the future held the promise of even better things to come.

The coup d'état that placed the country under the control of a military dictatorship destroyed all of their plans.

Rafael lost his job. The moderate newspaper that employed him, La Opinion, was shut down, even though it had taken a "prudent" editorial stance toward the new ruling power. The couple began to have serious money problems, but for Isabel the newspaper's closure was almost a relief. The only journalists still publishing articles had sworn allegiance to General Videla. As left-wing Peronists, there was no way Isabel and Rafael would agree to write so much as one line to appear in Cabildo or any of the other dailies still in print.

Rafael, who was good with his hands, changed jobs and started working for a neighborhood carpenter. Isabel and her best friend shared one job as supervisor at the science school, each working one day and caring for both of their children the next.

Rafael and Isabel struggled to make ends meet, but their combined salaries enabled them to scrape by and to provide for their daughter's needs.

When Rafael returned home from the carpentry shop, they would sit at the kitchen table after dinner. Isabel completed sewing jobs she'd started taking in to earn a little extra money, while Rafael wrote about the injustices being committed and repression under the regime, the corruption of the state, the complicity of the Church and the sad state of affairs that had taken hold of Argentina.

Each morning at 11, Rafael would step out of his workshop for a smoke. A cyclist would stop next to him and ask for a cigarette. Rafael would give him a light and discreetly slip him the article he had written the previous night. The messenger would carry the forbidden text to an abandoned factory housing an underground print shop. Rafael was a regular contributor to a dissident newspaper that was printed daily and distributed in the utmost secrecy.

Isabel and Rafael dreamed of one day leaving Argentina and going to live in a country where they would finally be free. Some evenings, when Isabel's spirits flagged, Rafael would take a little notebook with a red cover out of the chest of drawers. He would count their savings and tick off the number of days left before their departure. Once they were in bed, he would recite the names of cities to her in a low voice as if he were recounting a dream, and this was how they fell asleep, Rafael usually being the first to drop off.

After dinner one early summer evening, with little María Luz already fast asleep, Rafael put aside the article he was writing and Isabel her sewing work, and they went to bed earlier than usual. Isabel slipped naked under the sheets. Her skin was pale and smooth. Rafael's hands had become callused since he'd started his carpentry job, so he had taken to stroking her very gently, afraid she'd find their touch unpleasant.

"I like your worker's hands," Isabel murmured, laughing into his ear. "Tell them to hold me tighter."

Rafael was making love to his wife when they heard someone banging on the door of their small apartment.

"Don't move," said Rafael, grabbing his shirt from the bottom of the bed.

The banging got louder, and Rafael worried the racket would wake their daughter.

When he opened the door, four men in hoods threw him on the floor, raining blows on him to force him down on his belly.

One of the men kept him on the ground by pushing a knee into his back. Another grabbed Isabel by her hair as she came out of the bedroom in a panic. He pushed her up against the wall of the kitchen, rolled a dish towel around her neck and pulled it tight. When Isabel's screaming was stifled, the man loosened his grip just enough to let her breathe. The third man quickly searched the apartment and returned to the living room carrying María Luz and holding a knife to her throat.

The men wordlessly motioned Rafael and Isabel to get dressed. They were dragged outside and shoved into the back of a small truck. María Luz was put in front.

The vehicle raced across the city. The noise of the engine filled their ears, but Rafael and Isabel could still hear their daughter calling out to them through the partition between them and the cab. Isabel sobbed uncontrollably each time she heard her little girl scream "Mamá." Rafael held her hand and tried to soothe her, but how does one soothe a mother who can hear her child screaming?

The truck came to a stop thirty minutes later and the doors

were thrown open to reveal a courtyard. They were pulled out. Rafael got another blow to his head when he tried to turn back toward the truck where his daughter was being held. When Isabel tried to break free, one of the men dragged her back by her hair.

They were pushed roughly along to an open door in the building enclosing the paved courtyard. Isabel screamed her daughter's name, and was given a punch in the jaw that sent her hurtling down the staircase in front of her. Rafael was kicked in the back, and tumbled down the stairs after her.

They landed at the bottom of the steps on a patch of bare earth stinking of urine. Isabel was taken off to be locked up in a cell, and Rafael in another . . .

"What are you doing?" Andrew asked, coming into the living room.

Valerie put the sheaf of paper she'd been reading back down on the coffee table.

"Is it because they were journalists that you're so obsessed with this investigation?"

"Dammit, Valerie, that's confidential! I'm not going to put my notes under lock and key in my own apartment! Look, try and understand. This is my work, okay? I just need you to respect that," Andrew said in a calm voice, collecting up the papers.

"Isabel was allowed to read what her husband wrote, and even make suggestions."

"I'm sorry. Don't hold it against me. I hate for anyone to read my notes."

"'Anyone' just happens to be your future wife. 'Anyone' puts up with being alone when you're off on work for weeks on end. 'Anyone' understands about you being distracted even when you're around because you're so taken up with your job. 'Anyone' accepts all of that because she loves you. But don't ask me to live with you if I can't share a little of your passion."

"Did you like what you read?" Andrew asked.

"I'm terrified thinking of what will happen to that family, to María Luz, but I couldn't help envying Rafael and Isabel for being so close and working together at their kitchen table."

"It's only a draft," Andrew muttered.

"It's more than that."

"I can never publish their story if I don't go back to Argentina. It's not a made-up story, you know? Those people really existed. And one or two accounts just aren't enough."

"I know you have to go back there. This passion that drives you is one of the reasons I love you. I'm only asking you not to exclude me."

Andrew sat down next to Valerie, took her hand and kissed it.

"You're right. I'm an idiot. I'm paranoid about my work. I'm obsessed with secrecy, I'm afraid of deforming the truth, being partial, or influenced, or manipulated. That's why I only wanted you to find out about my crusade after this article is published. But I was wrong," he said. "From now on, I'll let you read what I'm writing as I go along."

"And?" Valerie asked.

"And what?"

"And will you show a little more interest in *my* job?"

"Hey, everything about you interests me. You want me to read your post-surgery reports?"

"No, Valerie replied, laughing. "I'd like for you to come to my office at least once so I can show you what a typical day is like for me."

"You want me to come see the mounted unit stables?"

"That, and my office, and the operating room, and the lab."

"I wish you looked after poodles. The only reason I've never come to visit you is that I'm terrified of horses."

Valerie smiled at Andrew.

"No need to be scared of them. What I've just been reading is a lot scarier than the most spirited horse in our stables."

"How spirited?" Andrew asked. He got up.

"Where are you going?" Valerie asked.

"Let's go get a breath of fresh air. I want to take a walk through the Village and I'll show you where we're going to have a romantic dinner."

As Andrew helped Valerie into her coat, she turned to him and asked:

"What happened to Rafael and Isabel and María Luz?"

"Later," Andrew replied, shutting the apartment door behind them. "I'll tell you the whole story later."

* * *

Andrew arrived at work around 8:30 A.M. He went through security and stopped in the cafeteria to have a coffee before going up to his office.

Sitting at his desk, he switched on his computer, entered his password, and began searching a few websites. After a while, he grabbed a notepad and a pen.

> *Dear Mr. Capetta,*
> *Your wife sent her letter from Chicago. The stamp has been postmarked by a post office near Warren Park.*
> *I am deeply sorry about everything that has happened to you.*
> *Yours sincerely,*
>
> *Andrew Stilman*

> *PS Please check for yourself, but I looked at some online photos of that park, and I think I could make out a playground.*

Andrew slipped his note into an envelope, copied out Mr. Capetta's address and took it over to the outgoing mail basket.

Back at his desk, he couldn't help but remember the last thing Capetta had said about his wife: *I wouldn't take her threats lightly if I were you.* And Chicago was only a two-hour flight from New York.

His telephone rang and the receptionist informed him that he had a visitor. In the elevator on his way down to the lobby, Andrew felt a shiver surge through his body, followed by a dull ache at the base of his spine.

* * *

"You don't look very good," Inspector Pilguez remarked.

"Just tired. I don't know what's wrong with me. I'm frozen stiff."

"That's odd—you're sweating."

Andrew wiped his hand across his forehead.

"Do you want to sit down for a moment?" Pilguez suggested.

"Let's go out. I need some fresh air," Andrew replied.

The pain suddenly became so intense that it stopped him in his tracks. Pilguez caught Andrew as his legs gave way and he fell.

When Andrew came to, he was lying on a bench in the lobby with Pilguez beside him.

"Good, you're getting your color back. You scared me. You just went out like a light. Do you faint often?"

"No. I mean, I never used to before."

"Probably stress," sighed Pilguez. "I know what I'm talking about. You start cracking up when you're scared. Your heart races, you hear ringing in your ears, you start feeling like you're wrapped up in cotton, sounds become distant and then—bam!—you're on your ass on the floor. You've just had a little anxiety attack."

"Maybe you're right."

"Have you discussed your story with anyone other than me?"

"Who do you think I'd have told? Who'd believe my story?"

"Don't you have any friends?"

"Of course I do."

"Friends you can count on in any situation?" Pilguez asked, a hint of sarcasm in his tone.

Andrew sighed.

"Okay, I'm a bit of a loner, but there's Simon, who's like a brother to me. Our friendship is worth more than lots of superficial acquaintances."

"No reason you can't have both. You should talk to Simon and tell him what happened to you. You've got eight weeks left to find your killer."

"Thanks for reminding me. I think about it morning, noon and night. Even if I do manage to forget it for a moment, the pain comes back to remind me I'm running out of time."

"The closer you get to the date, the more you're going to need someone to rely on."

"Is that your way of telling me you're giving up on me?"

"It's sound advice, Stilman. I've no intention of ditching you, but I have to go home at some point. My wife is waiting for me. I'll stay in New York until you leave for Argentina. After that, there's always the phone, and I've recently started using the internet. After all those years tapping out reports on typewriters, I'm pretty good at typing. But in the meantime I want you to go tell your friend everything. That's an order!"

"Why did you drop by to see me this morning? Anything new?"

"The list of people who have it in for you got longer yesterday, which doesn't help matters. I'm going to follow up on Mr. Capetta's ex-wife. Meanwhile you should take a closer look at your colleague Freddy Olson. I'd also like to find out more about your boss."

"I've already told you, you're on the wrong track with Olivia."

"If it were my life at stake I wouldn't exclude anyone, I assure you. Speaking of which, and I'm sorry to bring it up again, but there's another person on my list."

"Who's that?"

"Your wife. The woman you ditched on her wedding day."

"Valerie wouldn't hurt a fly."

"That's no surprise—she's a vet. But a man who'd hurt her that much? You wouldn't believe all the imaginative ways to get revenge people come up with when they've been humiliated. Plus she's around police officers all day long."

"So what?"

"If my wife decided to get rid of me, she'd be way more inventive than any cop show screenwriter."

"Are you just here because it'll make a good story or do you really believe me now?"

"I'm not playing games, Stilman. Follow me."

"Where are we going?"

"To the scene of a crime that hasn't taken place yet."

13

I s this a rental?" Andrew inquired when Pilguez led him over to a black Ford SUV parked outside the newspaper and gestured for him to climb in.

"Borrowed from a friend."

"It's got a police radio," Andrew let out a low whistle. "Who's the friend?"

"Put your seat belt on and stop touching things. If I'd been a doctor, I'd have borrowed an ambulance."

"I've never been in a cop car before."

Pilguez looked at Andrew and smiled.

"Oh, right. I get it," he said, leaning over to the glove compartment.

He took out the strobe light, put it on the dashboard and switched on the siren.

"How do you like that?"

"Great!" replied Andrew, clutching his seat as Pilguez sped off.

Ten minutes later the inspector parked the Ford at the corner of Charles Street and the West Side Highway.

Andrew led him along the footpath where he took his regular morning run. They stopped when they reached Pier 40.

"This is where it happened. Just being here sets off the pain."

"It's psychosomatic. Breathe deeply and you'll feel much better. When you think back to this premonition of yours, can you identify the murder weapon?" Pilguez asked, scouring the horizon.

"It wasn't a premonition!"

"Fine, it happened, and it'll happen again if we waste time arguing."

"I was attacked from behind. When I realized what was happening to me, I was already lying in a pool of my own blood."

"Where was the blood coming from?"

"My mouth and nose."

"Try to remember: did you feel anything in your stomach?"

"No, why?"

"A bullet shot at close range creates more damage at its exit point than its entry point. If you'd been shot, your intestines would have been thrown out onto the blacktop. Believe me, you'd have noticed."

"And if someone had aimed at me from much further away, using a sniper rifle, for instance?"

"That's exactly what I was just thinking. But look, none of the roofs on the other side of the highway is high enough to let you pick out one runner in a crowd at that distance. And you told me you died on July 10, right?"

"July 9. Why?"

"Look up. In a couple of weeks, you won't be able to see this path for the leaves on the trees. The injury was made horizontally, by someone who was following you."

"I didn't feel any pain in my stomach."

"It's got to be a knife that killed you, then. We just need to find out what kind. Take some deep breaths—you're looking very pale again."

"I'm not enjoying this conversation."

"Where can we find this Simon guy?"

"At work right now. He's got a vintage auto shop on Perry Street."

"I'm in luck. That's a short walk from here, and I love old cars."

* * *

Pilguez's jaw dropped as he walked into the garage. A Chrysler Newport, a De Soto, a beige Plymouth cabriolet, a 1956 Thunderbird and a 1954 Ford Crestline, among others, were lined up in perfect rows along the immaculate floor of the garage. The inspector made his way over to a Packard Mayfair.

"Amazing," he murmured. "My father had one of these. I haven't seen one for years."

"That's because very few were ever made," Simon explained, joining him. "I won't have it for long. It's such a rare model, I bet it'll have a new owner by Friday."

"Forget the sales pitch. We haven't come to buy a car," Andrew said, coming up behind them. "This gentleman's with me."

"Oh, it's you! You could have said you were on your way."

"What, now I need to send you a note before dropping by?"

"Of course not. It's just that . . . "

"He hates for me to overhear him doing his salesman routine," Andrew told Pilguez. "But you've got to admit he's great at it. 'Such a rare car, I bet it'll have found a new owner by Friday.' Don't believe a word! He's been stuck with it for the past two years. We did a weekend trip in it last summer, and guess what? It broke down."

"Okay, you've made your point. Did you want something? I don't know about you, but I have work to do."

"Some friendship you two have," Pilguez smirked.

"Can we go into your office?" Andrew asked.

"You look strange. Are you in trouble?"

Andrew didn't reply.

"What kind of trouble?" Simon pressed.

"It'd be better if we could talk in your office," Pilguez reiterated.

Simon signaled to Andrew to take the stairs up to the mezzanine.

"I don't want to be nosy," he asked Pilguez, bringing up the rear, "but who are you?"

"A friend of Andrew's. But don't be jealous—I'm not a rival."

Simon sat his visitors down opposite him in two club chairs, and listened to Andrew tell his story without interrupting. When Andrew finished an hour later, Simon took a long look at him and then picked up the phone.

"I'm calling a doctor friend I go skiing with every winter. He's a very good general physician. You've probably got diabetes. I've heard that if your blood sugar levels get too high, it can mess with your brain. Nothing to worry about. We'll find . . . "

"Don't waste your time," Pilguez said, putting his hand on the telephone. "I offered him the services of a neurologist friend, but your buddy here is absolutely certain of what he's saying."

"And you're backing up his story?" Simon asked, turning to Pilguez. "Some friend you are."

"Listen. I don't know if your friend's deranged or not, but I do know how to recognize someone who's telling the truth; as I once told your friend here, I worked some pretty weird cases during my time, and that's one thing I learned. During my four decades with the police, I came up against cases that were completely out of the ordinary. But that didn't make me resign."

"You're a cop?"

"I used to be."

Simon turned back to Andrew. "Just a quick checkup to

put our minds at rest," he begged. "I'm not asking for much, unlike you, Andrew."

"I don't remember asking anything of you."

"You're asking me to believe that someone's going to murder you in a few weeks, and that you're absolutely certain of this because you already died. Apart from that, no, you're not asking anything of me. So can I go ahead and make this doctor's appointment? Because from what you've said, we don't have much time."

"My initial reaction was much the same as yours," said Pilguez, "but your friend does have a special gift."

"And that is?" Simon inquired.

"Being able to announce news before it happens."

"That's it! Maybe *I* should be examined—it appears I'm the only one who finds this story far-fetched."

"Stop it, Simon. I shouldn't have bothered you with all this. But Pilguez insisted. Let's go," Andrew said, standing up.

"Let's go where?" Simon asked, blocking his way.

"You're staying here, seeing as you're up to your eyes in work. And we're going to carry on our investigations and find the person who wants to kill me, before it's too late."

"Just a minute! I don't like this one bit, not one bit," Simon muttered, pacing around his office. "Why would I stay here on my own while you two go . . . "

"Goddammit, Simon! This isn't a joke. My life's at stake here."

"Yeah, yeah," sighed Simon, grabbing his jacket off the back of his chair. "And may I know where you're going?" he said, turning to Pilguez.

"I've got to make a quick trip to Chicago," Pilguez said, walking out the door. "I'll be back as soon as I can. Don't worry, I'll find my way out."

Simon went to the window overlooking the workshop and watched the inspector leave the garage.

"Can you really predict what's going to happen over the coming weeks?"

"Only what I can remember," Andrew replied.

"Am I going to sell any cars?"

"The Pontiac, at the beginning of July."

"How do you remember that?"

"You invited me out for a meal to celebrate it. And to cheer me up."

Andrew paused, then looked at his friend and sighed.

"Only the Pontiac? Times really are hard. I was selling two a month last year. Any more good news to tell me?"

"You're going to live longer than me. That's good news, isn't it?"

"Andrew, if you're pulling my leg, tell me now and I'll give you an Oscar for best actor. I'm this close to believing you."

Andrew didn't answer.

"Anyway, it doesn't matter. All that counts is that *you* believe what you're saying. I've never seen you look so lost. So where do we start?"

"Do you think Valerie would be capable of killing me?"

"If you really did leave her on your wedding night, I can understand her holding it against you. Or maybe it's her father wanting to take revenge."

"I hadn't put him on my list—that's one more name!"

"I've got a simple idea to keep you out of harm's way: when you get married next time round, try to stay out of trouble for a few months before. That'll eliminate two suspects straight off."

"It's all your fault."

"What do you mean, my fault?"

"If you hadn't dragged me to Novecento, I'd never have . . . "

"You've got some nerve. In that story you were just telling me, you were the one who begged me to go back there."

"I can't believe she'd be capable of murder, even in the throes of anger."

"You say you were killed with a knife—she could've stabbed you with a surgical instrument. They're easy to get hold of in her job, plus didn't you say it was done with real precision? You'd need quite a bit of dexterity to do that."

"Stop it, Simon!"

"No way. You're the one who came to me to discuss it! And you can tell your retired inspector that. I'm the one who's going to find your killer, not him! What's he doing in Chicago anyway?"

"I'll explain on the way."

Simon opened his drawer and took out a ring of keys. He showed Andrew down to the workshop and gestured to the Packard.

"I've got to take her to show a customer over on 66th Street. Shall I drop you off on the way? Although I'm wondering why I'm going to meet this guy, seeing as you've told me I won't sell anything before July."

"Because you don't totally believe me yet, that's why."

Andrew spent the car journey answering Simon's rapid-fire questions about their meeting with Capetta. They parted company in front of the *New York Times* Building.

When Andrew got to his desk, he found an e-mail from Olivia Stern asking him to come and see her ASAP. He could hear Freddy Olson whispering into the phone behind the partition. When Freddy spoke in hushed tones, it meant he was onto a scoop he wanted to keep for himself. Andrew slid his chair over to the wall and pressed his ear to it.

"When did this murder take place?" Olson asked the person he was speaking to. "And it's the third attack of its kind? I see, I see," he continued. "Then again, a knife in the back isn't exactly original in New York. You might be jumping the gun, deducing it's the work of a serial killer. I'll take a look into it. Thank you. I'll get back to you if anything new comes up. Thanks again."

Olson put down the phone and stood up. *Probably going to*

the restroom, Andrew thought. He'd long suspected that Freddy didn't just go there to relieve a weak bladder. His colleague was in a constant state of agitation, and Andrew supposed he often disappeared to do a line of coke.

As soon as Freddy had disappeared, Andrew hurried over to his desk and began rifling through his papers.

A man had been stabbed the previous day in Central Park, near the Turtle Pond. His attacker had knifed him three times before running off, leaving him for dead. The victim had survived his injuries and ended up in the ER at Lenox Hill Hospital. The incident had been covered in the *New York Post;* the tabloid adored that kind of sensational news. Olson had scribbled two dates and two addresses at the foot of the page: January 13: 141st Street; and March 15: 111th Street.

"What are you doing?"

Andrew jumped.

"I'm working, as you can see. Unlike some people, by the looks of things."

"And you're working at my desk?"

"So *that's* why I couldn't find my things!" Andrew exclaimed. "I've got the wrong cubicle," he went on, standing up.

"Do you take me for an idiot?"

"Fairly often. Excuse me, the boss has asked to see me. Maybe wipe your nose—there's something white above your lip. Were you eating something with powdered sugar?"

Freddy wiped his nostrils.

"What are you implying, Stilman?"

"I'm not implying anything. Are you covering run-over dogs now?"

"What are you talking about?"

"Those dates and addresses you've noted down—mutts that have been squashed by buses? My partner's a vet, you know, if you need a hand with your investigations."

"A reader made a connection between three knifings in New York. He's convinced it's a serial killer."

"And you agree?"

"Three stabbings in five months in Manhattan, with its two million inhabitants, is a rather insignificant statistic, but Olivia's asked me to investigate."

"How reassuring. Anyway, it's not that I'm bored by your company, but I'm expected elsewhere."

Andrew turned on his heel and walked over to Olivia Stern's office door. She gestured for him to enter.

"How are your inquiries coming along?" she asked, continuing to tap away on her keyboard.

"My contacts on the ground have sent me new information," Andrew lied. "I've got several meetings lined up, and an interesting lead that could take me further afield than Buenos Aires."

"What lead is that?"

Andrew racked his brain. Since his journey back in time had begun, he'd devoted barely any time to his investigations because he was too preoccupied with his own fate. To satisfy his editor's curiosity, he drew from his memory details of a trip he wasn't supposed to have gone on yet.

"Apparently Ortiz has moved to a small village at the foot of the mountains, not far from Cordoba."

"Apparently?"

"The situation will become clearer once I'm there. I'm off in less than two weeks."

"I've already told you I want concrete evidence: documents, a recent photo et cetera. A few witness accounts just aren't enough. Unless your sources are one hundred percent trustworthy."

"I really feel like you take me for an amateur when you talk to me like that."

"You're too sensitive, Andrew. And paranoid, too."

"I've got reason to be, believe me," he replied, standing up.

"I've taken on huge expenses for this piece, so don't let me down. Neither of us can afford to make a mistake."

"I've got strangely used to hearing that warning recently. By the way, did you ask Olson to investigate a serial killer case?"

"No. Why?"

"No reason," Andrew replied as he walked out of her office.

Andrew returned to his desk, pulled up a map of Manhattan on his screen and located the addresses from Olson's notebook. The first two murders had been committed on the edge of parks: one on 141st Street on January 13 and another on 111th Street on March 15. The most recent occurred close to 79th Street. If it was the same killer, it looked like he was committing his crimes as he worked down the island. It occurred immediately to Andrew that the attack he'd been a victim of had fit in perfectly with this southward trajectory. He did a search on the most recently stabbed man, snatched his jacket and hurried out of the office.

When he got to the lobby, something caught his eye as he looked through the plate glass window toward the street. He took out his phone and dialed a number.

"Why are you hiding behind a plant outside the entrance to the newspaper?"

"How did you know?" Simon asked.

"Because I can see you, imbecile."

"Did you recognize me?"

"Obviously. Why the raincoat and hat?"

"A disguise."

"You must be kidding! What are you doing?"

"Nothing. I'm keeping an eye on your colleague Olson's comings and goings. Each time he leaves the building, I tail him."

"You've gone crazy!"

"What else do you want me to do? Now that I know I'm not going to sell a car for two months, I'm not going to waste my time at the garage while someone's plotting to kill you. And shh! You're blowing my cover."

"You don't need me for that. I'm coming out to join you. Get out from behind that greenery!"

Andrew joined Simon on the sidewalk, took him by the arm and steered him well away from the building.

"You look like Philip Marlowe, in other words, ridiculous."

"This raincoat cost me a fortune. It's Burberry."

"It's hot as hell, Simon."

"Are you just here to give me a lecture about playing private detective?"

Andrew hailed a taxi, told Simon to get in, and asked the driver to take them to Park Avenue and 77th Street. Ten minutes later the taxi pulled up in front of the entrance to Lenox Hill Hospital's emergency department. Simon went in first and made his way over to the reception desk.

"Hi," he said to the nurse. "We've come to see my friend, Doctor . . . "

Andrew grabbed him by the arm again and yanked him to one side.

"What've I done now? Aren't you here for an appointment with a psychiatrist?"

"Simon, either behave properly or leave right now, got it?"

"I thought you'd made a wise decision for once. If we aren't here for you, why are we in this hospital?"

"A guy got stabbed in the back. I want to question him. You're going to help me get into his room as inconspicuously as possible."

Simon's delight at taking part in something like this was written all over his face.

"What do you want me to do?"

"Go back and see that nurse at reception and claim to be

142 · MARC LEVY

the brother of someone called Jerry McKenzie. Say you've come to visit him."

"Consider it done."

"And take off the raincoat."

"Not until you've admitted that you're not pulling my leg," Simon replied as he walked away.

Five minutes later he came back to Andrew waiting in the lobby.

"Well?"

"Room 720, but visiting hours don't start until 1 P.M and we can't go in—there's a police officer at his door."

"We're screwed," Andrew said irately.

"Unless we have a visitor's badge," Simon added, popping a sticker onto his coat. "Like this one."

"How did you get that?"

"I showed her my ID, said that poor Jerry was my brother, that we had the same mother, but not the same father, hence the name difference, that I'd just arrived from Seattle, and that I was his only family."

"And she believed you?"

"I appear to inspire confidence. And with this raincoat, Seattle was completely convincing; it rains there year-round. I also asked for her phone number so I could take her out to dinner, as I'm all alone in the city."

"Did she give it to you?"

"No, but she felt flattered so she gave me a second badge . . . for my driver," Simon continued, sticking one onto Andrew's jacket. "Shall we go, James?"

In the elevator on the way up to the seventh floor, Simon put his hand on Andrew's shoulder.

"Go on, say it. It won't hurt, you know."

"Say what?"

"'Thank you, Simon.'"

* * *

Andrew and Simon were frisked thoroughly before the police officer would let them in.

Andrew walked over to the dozing patient, who opened his eyes.

"You're not doctors. What do you want?"

"I'm a journalist. I'm not looking for trouble."

"Go try that on some politician," the man said, sitting up in bed. "I don't have anything to tell you."

"I'm not here for a story," Andrew said, drawing closer.

"Get out of here or I'll shout for help!"

"I was stabbed too. And two other people have met the same fate in similar circumstances. I'm wondering if it's the same assailant. I just want to know if you remember anything. His face? The weapon he used on you?"

"Are you stupid or what? I was stabbed in the back."

"And you didn't see anything coming?"

"I heard footsteps behind me. I was with several other people leaving the park. I felt a presence close in on me. I was lucky—half an inch higher and the bastard would have hit an artery. I would have bled out before I got here. The doctors told me that if the hospital weren't so close, I wouldn't have made it."

"I wasn't as lucky," Andrew sighed.

"You look like you're in good shape."

Andrew's face reddened. Simon rolled his eyes.

"Did you lose consciousness immediately?"

"Almost," McKenzie replied. "I thought I saw my attacker walk past me then run off, but my vision was blurred. I couldn't give you a description of him. I was on my way to see a customer and he robbed me of ten thousand dollars' worth of merchandise. It's the third time I've been attacked in five years. This time I'm going to apply for a gun license—authorized beyond the 215 square feet of my jewelry store. But you're a journalist—did he take anything from you?"

While Andrew and Simon were at Lenox Hill Hospital, Freddy Olson cracked the combination of his padlock and rifled through his colleague's drawer looking for the password that would give him access to Andrew's computer.

* * *

"What are we doing now?" Simon asked out on the sidewalk in front of the hospital.
"I'm going to see Valerie."
"Can I come with you?"
Andrew said nothing.
"I understand. I'll call you later."
"Simon, promise not to go back to the paper."
"I'll do what I want."
Simon ran across the road and jumped into a taxi.

* * *

Andrew announced himself at the reception desk. The sergeant on duty made a call and sent him off in the right direction.

Valerie's workplace didn't look anything like Andrew had imagined. He found himself in a square courtyard. A long, surprisingly modern building stretched along the far end. The ground floor was occupied by stables. A central door opened onto a long corridor that led to the veterinary offices.

Valerie was in the operating theatre. One of her colleagues sent Andrew to wait in the staff lounge. A police officer jumped up when he entered.

"Any news?" he asked. "Did the operation go well?"

Andrew was taken by surprise once again. This imposing,

burly man, whom Andrew normally wouldn't want to cross, was a nervous wreck.

"No news yet," Andrew replied, taking a seat. "But don't worry, Valerie is the best vet in New York. Your dog couldn't be in better hands."

"He's more than a dog, you know," the man sighed. "He's my partner and my best friend."

"What breed is he?" Andrew inquired.

"A retriever."

"He must look a bit like my best friend, then."

"Do you have a retriever too?"

"No, mine's more of a mutt, but very intelligent."

Valerie came into the room and was amazed to find Andrew there. She told the police officer he could go and see his dog in the recovery room, and that the operation had been successful. He'd be fit for service again in a few weeks, after a period of rehabilitation. The officer rushed out of the room.

"This is a nice surprise."

"What was wrong with his dog?" Andrew asked.

"A bullet to the abdomen."

"Will he get a medal?"

"Don't poke fun. That dog got between an assailant and his victim. I don't know many men who'd have done that."

"I wasn't poking fun," Andrew said pensively. "Will you show me around?"

Valerie's office was bright and uncluttered with white-washed walls and two large windows overlooking the court-yard. Her desk was a glass tabletop set on two antique trestle legs, with just a computer screen and two pots of pens on it. Behind it was a Windsor chair she must have unearthed in a vintage store. Files were piled up on a console table. Andrew looked at the photos standing on a small metal cabinet.

"That's Colette and me in college."

"Is she a vet as well?"

"No, a veterinary anesthesiologist."

"Here are your parents," Andrew said, peering at another photo. "Your father hasn't changed! Well, hardly after all these years."

"Neither physically nor mentally, unfortunately. As narrow-minded as ever, and still convinced he knows better than everyone else."

"He wasn't very fond of me when we were teenagers."

"He hated all my boyfriends."

"You had that many?"

"A few."

Valerie pointed at another frame.

"Look at this one," she said, smiling.

"Wow! Is that me?"

"From back when people called you Ben."

"Where did you find that photo?"

"I've always had it. It was among the few belongings I took with me when I left Poughkeepsie."

"You kept a photo of me?"

"You were an important part of my life back then."

"I'm very touched. I'd never have imagined you wanting to take me with you, even in a photo."

"If I had asked you to come with me, you wouldn't have, would you?"

"I have no idea."

"You dreamed of being a journalist. You started the school newspaper all by yourself. You used to jot down everything that happened in your little notebook. I remember you wanting to interview my father about his job, and him sending you packing."

"I'd forgotten that."

"I'm going to let you in on a little secret," Valerie said, walking over to him. "You were much more in love with me than I was with you. But now, when I watch you sleeping at night, I feel like it's the other way round. Sometimes I say to myself it won't work, I'm not the woman you hoped for, the wedding won't happen and you'll leave me. You can't imagine how unhappy those thoughts make me."

Andrew hugged Valerie.

"Well, you're wrong. You're the woman I always dreamed of—far more than my dream of becoming a journalist. If you think I've waited for you all that time only to leave you . . . "

"Did you keep a photo of me, Andrew?"

"No. I was too angry that you'd run away from Pough-keepsie without leaving an address. But I never forgot your face. You don't realize how much I love you."

Valerie showed Andrew to the operating theatre. The bloody compresses on the linoleum floor made him feel queasy. He walked up to a trolley and scrutinized the array of differ-ent-sized surgical instruments laid out on it.

"They're incredibly sharp, these things, aren't they?"

"Sharp as scalpels," Valerie replied.

Andrew leaned over, picked up the longest of them in his fingertips and gauged its weight as he held it by the handle.

"Careful you don't hurt yourself," Valerie said, taking it delicately out of his hand.

Andrew noticed how deftly she handled the object. She rolled it between her index and middle finger and placed it back down on the trolley.

"Come with me. Those instruments haven't been disinfec-ted yet."

Valerie led Andrew over to the basin fixed to the tiled wall. She turned on the tap with her elbow, pressed the soap dis-penser foot pedal and washed Andrew's hands between hers.

"Surgery's very sensual," Andrew whispered.

"It all depends on who your assistant is," Valerie replied.

She wrapped her arms around Andrew and kissed him.

* * *

Sitting in the canteen surrounded by police officers suddenly reminded Andrew he was waiting to hear from Inspector Pilguez.

"Is something worrying you?" Valerie asked.

"No, it's the company. I'm not used to eating among so many uniforms."

"You get used to it. Anyway, if your conscience is clear, you're safer here than anywhere else in New York."

"As long as we don't go and see your horses."

"I was planning to show you around the stables once you'd finished your coffee."

"No way—I've got to get back to work."

"Chicken!"

"Next time, if you don't mind."

Valerie looked Andrew in the eye.

"Why did you come today, Andrew?"

"To have coffee with you and to see where you work. You asked me to come and I wanted to."

"You came all the way across town just to make me happy?"

"And for you to kiss me over a surgical instrument trolley. It's the romantic in me."

Valerie walked Andrew outside to hail a taxi. Before shutting the door, he turned to her.

"What did you father do again?"

"He was an industrial designer in a factory."

"And what did the factory manufacture?"

"Sewing equipment: hem markers, tailors' scissors, and all sorts of needles, including knitting needles. You used to make fun of him and say he did a woman's job. Why do you ask?"

"No reason."

He kissed Valerie, promised not to be home late and closed the taxi door.

14

T wo men took Rafael out of his cell. One of them dragged him by the hair while the other repeatedly struck his calves with a club to make sure he couldn't stand up. The pain in his head was so intense he thought his scalp was going to be ripped off. He kept trying to straighten up as they moved forward, but his knees caved in each time from the strength of the blows. His torturers' little game ceased for a moment when they reached an iron door.

It opened onto a large windowless room. Long red streaks stained the walls. The beaten-earth floor reeked with the unbearable, acrid stench of dried blood and excrement. Two bare bulbs hung from the ceiling.

The light was blinding, unless it was just the contrast with the darkness of the cell where he'd spent two days without being brought food or drink.

They made him strip naked, then forced him into an iron chair cemented into the ground. Two straps were nailed to the armrests and another two to the legs. The leather cut into Rafael's flesh as they strapped him in.

An army captain wearing a pristinely ironed uniform entered the room. He sat down on the corner of a table, stroked his hand across the wood to remove the dust, and put down his cap. Then he stood up in silence, walked over to Rafael and punched him in the jaw. Rafael tasted blood in his mouth. He didn't mind; his tongue was stuck to the roof of his mouth because it was so parched.

"*Antonio* . . . (a punch shattered his nose), *Alfonso* . . . (a second his chin), *Roberto* . . . (a third split his eyebrow open) *Sánchez. Will you remember my name or do you want me to say it again?*"

Rafael had passed out. A bucketful of stinking water was thrown in his face.

"*Repeat my name, scum!*" *the captain ordered.*

"*Antonio Alfonso Roberto sonofabitch,*" *murmured Rafael.*

The captain raised his arm, but stopped himself from striking. Instead he smiled and signaled to his two henchmen to get this uncooperative dissident ready.

They fixed copper plates to his chest and thighs so the current would circulate properly, then wrapped bare electric wires around his ankles, wrists and testicles.

The first electric shock propelled his body forwards. He understood why the chair had been fixed to the ground. It felt as if thousands of thorns were rushing through his veins just under his skin.

"*Antonio Alfonso Roberto Sánchez,*" *the captain said again coolly.*

Each time Rafael lost consciousness, another bucket of putrid water brought him back to that room and his tortures.

"*Ant . . . Alfonso . . . Rob . . . ánchez,*" *he mumbled after the sixth electric shock.*

"*Claims to be an intellectual and doesn't even know how to pronounce a name correctly,*" *the captain sneered.*

He lifted Rafael's chin with the end of his rod, then slashed it across his cheek.

Rafael's only thoughts were of Isabel and María Luz, and of not dishonoring his family by begging for mercy.

"*Where's your goddam printing works?*" *the captain asked.*

At the mention of the place, Rafael escaped momentarily from the reality of his swollen face and battered body by imagining himself within the room's blue, peeling walls, inhaling the smell of paper and ink and the methylated spirits his friends used to make the duplicating machine work. These olfactory recollections restored an inkling of lucidity.

Another electric shock bolted through him. He began convulsing and his sphincter muscles opened. Blood-tinged urine trickled down his legs. His eyes, tongue and genitals had been burned to ash. He lost consciousness.

The doctor accompanying the captain listened to Rafael's heart, examined his pupils and said that was enough for today if they wanted to keep their prisoner alive. Captain Antonio Alfonso Roberto Sánchez definitely did. If he'd wanted to kill him, he could have simply put a bullet in his head. He wanted to take pleasure in Rafael's suffering, not his death, to make him pay for his treason.

As the men dragged him back to his cell, Rafael regained consciousness. He suffered the worst torture yet when he heard Captain Sánchez call out from the end of the corridor: "Bring me his wife."

Isabel and Rafael spent two months at ESMA. They had their eyelids stuck open with surgical tape to prevent them from sleeping. If they drifted into unconsciousness, they were kicked and beaten awake.

During their time at ESMA, Isabel and Rafael, who didn't once cross each other's paths in the corridor leading to the torture room, became more and more dissociated from a world in which humanity existed. Through the long days and nights that passed without them knowing the difference, they sank deeper and deeper into a dark abyss that even the most fervent of believers could not imagine.

Yet, when Captain Sánchez had them brought to the room where he tortured them, he spoke of the treachery they had committed against their homeland and against God. As he uttered the word "God," Sánchez would hit them even harder.

The captain had Isabel's eyes gouged out. But one light

refused to go out in her: María Luz's face. Sometimes she wished her daughter's features would disappear so she could give in to death. Only death would set her free. Only death would restore her humanity.

One evening, when Captain Sánchez was bored, he had Rafael's genitals severed. One of his men cut them off with a pair of scissors. The doctor stitched up the wound. They had no intention of letting all the blood drain from his body.

At the beginning of their second month of captivity, they had the tape ripped off their eyes, and their eyelids came off in the process. Each time the captain summoned back his victims, they lost a little more of their human appearance. Isabel was unrecognizable. Her face and breasts were covered with burns from cigarettes the captain put out on her skin (he smoked two packs a day). Her intestines, also charred from the electric torture, couldn't digest the gruel she was force-fed with a spoon. Her nostrils had long ago stopped smelling the odor of her own excrement, in which she lay. Reduced to this animal state, Isabel held on to the image of María Luz's face in the shadows, uttering her name over and over again.

One morning, the captain tired of his task. Neither Rafael nor Isabel would reveal the address of their printing works. He didn't care; he never had. A captain of his rank had more important things to do than track down some old copy machine. Looking at his victims with disgust, he was delighted to have achieved at least part of his mission: breaking the spirits of two immoral individuals who had disowned their homeland and refused to submit to the only regime capable of restoring to Argentina the greatness it deserved. Captain Sánchez was a devoted patriot. God would reward his devotion.

At dusk, the doctor went into Isabel's cell. In a final moment of irony, he disinfected the crook of her arm with a cotton swab soaked in alcohol before administering an injection of Pentothal. The drug sent her into a deep sleep, but did not kill her. That was the idea. Rafael was given the same treatment in his cell at the other end of the corridor.

Once night fell, they were transported in the back of a van to a clandestine airfield in the sprawling Buenos Aires suburbs. A twin-engine Air Force plane was waiting for them in a hangar. Isabel and Rafael were laid out in the cabin alongside twenty or so other lifeless prisoners guarded by four soldiers. With the cargo loaded, the aircraft took off without lights. Its pilot had been given instructions to fly towards the river, then head in a southeasterly direction at very low altitude. He was instructed not to go anywhere near the coast of Uruguay. When he reached the ocean he should turn around and fly back to his point of departure. A routine mission.

Major Ortiz followed these instructions to the letter. The aircraft climbed into the Argentinean sky, flew across the Río de la Plata and reached its destination an hour later.

Once there, the soldiers opened the rear door and in a matter of minutes threw the ten men and ten women, all unconscious but alive, into the sea below. The roar of the engines shielded their ears from the thud of the bodies as they hit the waves and sank. Schools of sharks had made a habit of lurking in these gloomy waters, waiting for the meal that fell from the sky at the same time every evening.

Isabel and Rafael spent the final moments of their lives side by side but unaware of each other's presence. By the time the plane arrived back at the airfield, they had joined the ranks of the thirty thousand people who were made to disappear forever by the Argentinean dictatorship.

Unable to utter a word, Valerie put down the sheets of paper and went over to the window. She felt a pressing need for fresh air.

Andrew came up behind her and wrapped his arms around her waist.

"You insisted on reading it. I warned you not to."

"What happened to María Luz?" Valerie asked.

"They didn't kill children. They gave them to the families and friends of the ruling military junta and created new identities for them under the names of their adoptive parents. María Luz was two when Rafael and Isabel were kidnapped, but hundreds of women were pregnant when they were arrested."

"You mean those bastards tortured pregnant women too?"

"Yes, but they made sure they kept them alive until they gave birth, then they stole their newborns. The military boasted that they were saving innocent souls from perversion by handing them over to families who could raise them in keeping with the dictatorship's values. They claimed that what they were doing was Christian and charitable, and that they had the wholehearted support of Church officials, who knew what was going on.

"For the final months of their pregnancy, the mothers-to-be were shut up in makeshift maternity units in the detention centers. As soon as the babies were born, they were taken away. You know now what lay in store for those women," Andrew said, pointing to his article. "Most of the stolen children, now adults, aren't aware their birth parents were tortured and then dropped into the ocean alive. María Luz among them, probably."

Valerie turned round. Andrew had never seen her so distressed and angry. The look in her eyes almost frightened him.

"Please tell me the perpetrators are in jail and that they'll stay there for the rest of their lives."

"I wish I could. The men who committed the atrocities were protected by an amnesty passed in the name of national reconciliation. By the time it was repealed, most of the criminals had slipped under the radar or gotten new identities."

"Swear to me you'll go back there and finish your investigation. You've got to find Ortiz and those other bastards!"

"That's been my intention since the start. Do you see why I'm devoting so much of my time to it? Do you forgive me for neglecting you?" Andrew asked.

"I'd like to rip their guts out."

"I know. Me too. But come on, calm down."

"If I found them . . . I'd feel less remorse about killing monsters who torture pregnant women than about destroying a pack of rabid dogs."

"And end up in prison for life? Very smart."

"Trust me—I'd know how to go about it without leaving a trace," Valerie continued, still seething.

Andrew looked at her closely, then hugged her a bit tighter.

"I hadn't realized my article would put you in such a state. Maybe I shouldn't have let you read it."

"I've never read anything so horrendous. I'd like to come with you to track down those brutes."

"I'm not sure that's a good idea."

"Why not?" asked Valerie, getting carried away.

"Because most of those monsters, as you call them, are still alive, and the passing of time hasn't necessarily made them any less dangerous."

"Says the man who's scared of horses . . . "

* * *

When he left home the following morning, Andrew was surprised to find Simon outside of his apartment building.

"Got time for a coffee?" Simon asked.

"And a very good morning to you too."

"Follow me," instructed his friend, who looked more anxious than Andrew had ever seen him.

They walked up Charles Street in silence.

"What's the matter?" Andrew asked worriedly as they went into Starbucks.

"Go get a couple of coffees. I'll save us this table," Simon replied, sitting down in an armchair next to the window.

"Yes, sir!"

Andrew waited in line, not taking his eyes off Simon, puzzled by his behavior.

"A mochaccino for me and a cappuccino for His Highness," he said, joining Simon at the table a few minutes later.

"I've got bad news," Simon announced.

"Go ahead."

"It's to do with Freddy Olson."

"You tailed him and realized the guy isn't going anywhere. I've known that for a long time."

"Very funny. I spent the whole of yesterday evening at my computer browsing your newspaper's website, looking up your stories."

"Simon, if you were that bored you should've called me."

"You'll stop playing the wise guy in a couple of minutes. It wasn't your wonderful prose I was interested in, it was the comments section. I wanted to see if there was some lunatic out there writing evil stuff about you."

"I bet there are quite a few."

"I'm not talking about people who think you're a bad journalist."

"Do readers post that kind of comment on the website?"

"Some do. But . . . "

"I didn't know that," Andrew interrupted.

"Can I finish?"

"Wasn't that your bad news?"

"There was a series of messages that were so hostile, they went way beyond criticism of your professional skills. They were incredibly abusive."

"Saying what?"

"Things nobody would like to read about themselves. Some

of the most aggressive ones were written by someone calling themself SpookyKid. They caught my eye because there were so many of them. I don't know what you've done to that guy, but he sure doesn't like you. I searched some more to see if the person behind that username also comments on any forums, or has a blog."

"And?"

"He's got it in for you real bad. Every time you publish an article, he lays into you. Even when you don't publish any-thing. If you read everything I found on the net posted by him, you'd be amazed. Like I was."

"Let me get this straight—a failed writer, whose bedroom is probably a shrine to Marilyn Manson, hates my work. Was that your bad news?"

"Why do you say Marilyn Manson?"

"I don't know—it just came to me. Carry on."

"Seriously, it just came to you like that?"

"Spooky Kids was the name of Manson's first group."

"How do you know that?"

"Because I'm a journalist. Get on with it!"

"I happen to know a computer whiz kid, if you get what I mean."

"No, I don't."

"A hacker. A good one. The kind of guy who can tell you who you were dating fifteen years ago and where you went on your first date."

"How come you know a hacker?"

"When I first opened the shop, I used to rent out my cars to rich kids on the weekends to make some extra money. One of them left something behind inside the central armrest when he returned a Corvette to me."

"A gun?"

"Weed. Enough for a herd of cows to graze on. I've never been into smoking dope. If I had taken his stuff to the police, his acne would have cleared up long before he would have been able to get back to his cherished computer. But I'm not a snitch, so I gave him back what was rightfully his. He said I was 'super honest' and vowed to be there for me if I ever needed his help. At eleven o'clock last night, I realized I needed a favor that was right up his alley. Don't ask me how he did it—I know nothing about computers—but he called me this morning saying he'd found Spooky Kid's IP address. It's like his computer's license plate, and it appears every time he goes online."

"Has your hard-drive raider identified this Spooky Kid who's spitting his venom at me?"

"Not his identity, but the location he publishes his comments from. And you'll be surprised to hear he posts his messages from the *New York Times* network."

"What did you say?" Andrew asked, stunned.

"You heard me. I've printed off a few examples. They're not actually death threats, but they're so hate-filled they nearly could be. Who at your newspaper could be writing such hateful things about you? Look, here's the latest one," Simon continued, handing Andrew a printout. "*If a bus ran over that bastard Andrew Stilman, its tires would be covered in shit and national press would be spared this disaster.*"

"I think we both know the answer," Andrew replied, shocked by the comment he'd just read. "I'll take care of Olson myself, thanks."

"You'll do nothing of the sort, pal. First off, I have no proof it's him. He's not the only other person working at the *Times*. Plus, if you stick your nose in, he'll only get suspicious. Let me do my thing, and don't budge until I give you the green light. Agreed?"

"Agreed," Andrew replied.

"At the office, keep acting like nothing's wrong. Who knows what a guy who hates you so much is capable of? The main thing is to make sure it's him. As far as I'm concerned, whether or not he's Freddy Olson, this Spooky Kid character is now at the top of the list of the people that want you dead, and he's certainly taking every opportunity to let everyone know."

Andrew got up and said goodbye to his friend.

"Shall I keep following him, or do you still think I'm being ridiculous?" Simon asked with a smile as Andrew walked away.

* * *

Andrew spent the rest of the day getting ready for Argentina, making one phone call after another to organize his trip. At dusk, still at work, he began to drift off at his desk. The figure of a little girl appeared to him in a dream. She was standing still, alone at the end of a long avenue of cypress trees leading up a hillside. Andrew put his feet up on the desk and sank back in his chair.

The little girl led him toward a village set high in the mountains. Each time he thought he was catching up with her, she quickened her pace and the gap between them widened. Her peals of laughter guided him in the absurd chase. The wind lifted as night fell. Andrew shivered. He was cold. So cold he started to tremble. He came to a derelict barn and went in. The little girl was waiting for him, sitting on the ledge of a window just under the roof, swinging her legs. Andrew walked over to the wall and looked up at her, but couldn't make out the child's features. He only saw her smile—a strange, almost adult smile. The young girl breathed words that the wind carried down to him.

"Seek me, find me, Andrew. Don't abandon me. I'm counting on you. We can't afford to make a mistake. I need you."

She fell forward into the void. Andrew ran to catch her, but she disappeared before she'd touched the ground.

Alone in the barn, Andrew knelt down, shaking. His back was aching. A sharp twinge made him pass out. When he regained consciousness, he found himself strapped into a metal chair. He could hardly breathe. His lungs burned. He was suffocating. An electric shock surged through his body. All of his muscles contracted and he felt himself being propelled by a great force. In the distance he heard a voice shout "again." An even more powerful shock flung him forward, his arteries thumping, his heart in flames. The smell of smoldering flesh entered his nostrils. The straps shackling his limbs cut into him. His head lolled to one side and he begged them to stop.

His racing heart began to calm. The air he'd been desperate for entered his lungs and he inhaled deeply, as if he'd been holding his breath for an age.

A hand touched his shoulder and shook him roughly.

"Stilman! Stilman!"

Andrew opened his eyes to see Olson's face pressed right up to his.

"Sleep at the office if you want, but don't dream so loudly! Some of us are working."

Andrew sat up with a jump.

"Shit! What are you doing here, Freddy?"

"I've been listening to you groaning for the past ten minutes. You're making it impossible to concentrate. I thought you were ill or something, so I came to see what was up. But if that's the greeting I get, I don't know why I bothered."

Beads of sweat stood out on Andrew's forehead, yet he felt frozen stiff.

"You ought to go home and get some rest. You must be coming down with something. Even I don't like seeing you in this state," Freddy sighed. "I'm leaving soon. Do you want me to drop you somewhere in a taxi?"

Andrew had had a few nightmares in his life, but none that had seemed so real. He looked at Freddy for a moment, then replied, "No thanks. I'll be okay. Must be something I ate at lunch."

"It's eight o'clock in the evening."

Andrew wondered how long he'd been disconnected from reality, lost in his dreams. As he tried to recall what time he'd seen displayed on his screen before he'd dropped off, he asked himself what was real in his life anymore.

Exhausted, he headed home. He called Valerie on the way to warn her he wouldn't wait up, but Sam informed him that she'd only just gone into surgery and probably wouldn't be finished until late.

15

His night consisted of a long succession of nightmares in which the little girl with blurred features appeared to him. Each time he woke from one, shivering and dripping in sweat, he was still trying to find her.

In the most terrifying one, she stopped, turned to him and gestured for him to be quiet. A black car came to a halt between them and four men got out, not paying any attention to either of them. They went into a small building. From the deserted street where Andrew stood, he could hear screams: a woman screeching and a child crying.

The little girl was standing on the sidewalk on the opposite side of the road, swinging her arms and singing a nursery rhyme as if she didn't have a care in the world. Andrew wanted to protect her and as he walked toward her, he met her gaze. Her eyes were smiling and menacing at once.

"María Luz?" he whispered.

"No," she replied in an adult's voice. "María Luz doesn't exist anymore."

Suddenly a child's voice gushed out of the same small body. "Please find me!" it said. "Without you I'll be lost forever. You're on the wrong track, Andrew. You're not looking where you should. You're wrong. They're all wrong. You'll pay dearly if you get lost. Come and help me. I need you, and you need me. We're connected now. Hurry, Andrew, hurry! You can't afford to make a mistake."

Crying out, Andrew awoke for the third time. Valerie wasn't

home. He turned on the bedside lamp and tried to calm down, but he was sobbing uncontrollably.

In his last nightmare, María Luz's face appeared to him fleetingly. He was convinced he'd already seen those dark eyes staring at him, somewhere in a past that wasn't his own.

Andrew got out of bed and went into the living room. He sat down at his computer, deciding he'd rather spend the rest of the night working. But his thoughts prevented him from concentrating and he couldn't write a single line. He looked at his watch, hesitated, then picked up the phone and called Simon.

"Am I disturbing you?"

"Of course not. It's two in the morning. I was just rereading *As I Lay Dying* while waiting for you to call me."

"You don't know how appropriate that is."

"Gotcha. I'm getting dressed right now. I'll be with you in fifteen."

Simon arrived sooner than expected. He'd put his Burberry trench coat on over his pajamas and slipped on a pair of sneakers.

"I know," he said, walking through Andrew's apartment door. "You're going to make another negative comment about my attire. I'll have you know I've just bumped into two neighbors walking their dogs in robes. The owners in robes, not the dogs, obviously."

"Sorry I disturbed you in the middle of the night."

"No you aren't, otherwise you wouldn't have called. Are you getting your ping-pong table out, or are you going to tell me why I'm here?"

"I'm frightened, Simon. I've never been so frightened in all my life. My dreams are terrifying. I wake up every morning with my stomach in knots, realizing I've got one less day to live."

"It's not like I want to downplay your situation, but there

are seven billion other human beings in the same predicament as you."

"Except that I've only got fifty-three days left!"

"Andrew, this preposterous story of yours is getting out of hand. I'm your friend and I don't want to take any risks, but you've got as much chance of being murdered on July 9 as I have of getting run over by a bus on my way out of here. Though with these red plaid pajamas, a bus driver would have to be blind not to see me in his headlights. Do you like them? I bought them in London, they're flannelette. Much too warm for the season, but they're my most flattering pair. Don't you have any PJs?"

"Yes, but I never wear them. They make you look old."

"Do I look old?" Simon asked, flinging open his arms. "Now put on your robe and let's go for a stroll. You got me out of bed so I could take your mind off things, right?"

As they walked past the Charles Street police station, Simon said hello to the police officer on duty and asked him if he'd seen a short-haired dachshund. The answer was no. Thanking him, Simon carried on, calling out "Freddy" enthusiastically.

"I'd rather not walk along the river," Andrew said as they got to the West Side Highway .

"Any news from your inspector?"

"None so far."

"If it's your colleague who wants you dead, we'll take care of him, no problem. If it isn't, and we don't have any other concrete leads by the start of July, I'll take you on a trip. We'll be a long way from New York by the 9th."

"I wish it were that simple. Supposing we did go, I can't just give up my work and go into hiding for the rest of my life."

"When are you off to Argentina?"

"In a few days. I have to admit I like the idea of getting away for a bit."

"I'm sure Valerie would be delighted to hear that. You'll

have to be careful over there all the same." They arrived outside Simon's building. "Here we are. You okay going home on
your own in that getup?"

"I'm not on my own. I'm walking Freddy," Andrew
answered, then walked away, pretending he was holding a dog
on a leash.

* * *

Andrew was woken from his short night by the telephone
ringing. He picked it up in a daze and recognized the inspector's voice. He was waiting for Andrew in the café on the corner of his street.

Andrew went into Starbucks and found Pilguez sitting in
the chair Simon had occupied the day before.

"Have you got bad news for me?" he asked, sitting down.

"I've found Mrs. Capetta," the inspector replied.

"How?"

"I don't think that really matters, and I can only spare an
hour right now if I don't want to miss my plane."

"You're leaving?"

"I can't stay in New York forever. Anyway, you're off soon
too. San Francisco is less exotic than Buenos Aires, but it's
where I live. My wife's waiting for me. She misses my ram-
blings."

"What did you find out in Chicago?"

"She's a very beautiful woman, Mrs. Capetta—ebony eyes
and a gaze that could knock a man off his feet. Mr. Capetta
can't have tried too hard to track her down, she hasn't even
changed her identity. She and her son live there alone, two
streets from the place where she posted that charming letter to
you."

"Did you speak to her?"

"No. I mean yes. But not about you."

"I don't get it."

"I played at being the sweet old grandpa out for some air on a park bench. I told her my grandson was the same age as her kid."

"You're a grandfather?"

"No. Natalia and I met too late to have children. But we do have an adorable little substitute nephew—the son of that neurosurgeon friend I told you about and her architect husband. We're very close. He's five, and my wife and I tend to spoil him. Right, stop making me tell you my life story, or I really will miss my flight."

"Why the roleplay if you didn't question her?"

"Because there are different ways of questioning someone. What did you want me to say to her? 'Mrs. Capetta, while your kid's playing in the sandpit, would you please be so kind as to tell me if you're planning to stab a journalist from *The New York Times* next month?' I spent a couple of afternoons in the park chatting with her about this and that, trying to win her over. Would she be capable of committing a murder? To be completely honest, I've got no idea. She's definitely a headstrong woman, and there's something cold in her gaze. I also thought she seemed extremely intelligent. But I find it hard to believe she'd risk being separated from her boy. Even when you convince yourself you're committing the perfect crime, you can never entirely dismiss the possibility of getting caught. What got me the most was how she lied when I asked her if she was married. Without missing a beat, she answered that her husband and daughter had died on a trip abroad. If I hadn't met Mr. Capetta, I'd have bought her story wholesale.

"When I get back to San Francisco, I'm going to continue investigating the people on my list—including your wife and your editor, even if that annoys you—with the help of my contacts in New York. I'll call you as soon as I have some news.

Maybe I can fly out again when you're back from Buenos Aires. But if I do, I'll bill you for the plane ticket."

Pilguez held out a piece of paper to Andrew and stood up.

"Here's Mrs. Capetta's address. It's up to you whether you decide to pass it on to her husband. Take care of yourself, Stilman. Your story's one of the craziest I've heard in my whole career, and I get the impression something bad is brewing."

* * *

Andrew went to the office and sat down at his computer. A red light on his telephone indicated that a voicemail message was waiting for him. Marisa, the bartender from his hotel in Buenos Aires, had information for him, and wanted him to call her back as soon as possible. Andrew vaguely remembered their conversation, but he'd started to get muddled with dates and events. It wasn't easy to keep track, living everything twice. He bent to get his notes out of his drawer and froze when he saw the lock. Someone had tried to get into his things. When he'd last closed the padlock he'd left it displaying the first three numbers of his date of birth, as he always did. They'd changed—someone had tried to break into his things. Andrew poked his head over the top of the partition wall. Olson wasn't at his desk. He flicked through his notebook looking for the page where he'd jotted down the details of his last phone conversation with Marisa and sighed when he found nothing. He dialed the number she'd given him.

Marisa informed him that a friend of her aunt's was sure she'd recognized an ex-air force pilot corresponding to the description of the man who went by the name of Ortiz under the junta. He'd become the owner of a profitable little tannery that supplied leathers to bag, shoe, saddle, and belt manufacturers all over the country. He was making a delivery to one of his clients in a Buenos Aires suburb when the family friend recognized him.

This woman was a Mother of the Plaza de Mayo too, and had a poster in her living room displaying photos of all the soldiers who had been tried for crimes committed during the Dirty War, then granted amnesty. She'd lived with those photos day and night since her son and her nephew had disappeared in June 1977. Both boys were seventeen at the time. This mother had never agreed to sign the documents confirming her son's death, and refused to do so until she saw his remains for herself. And yet, like the parents of the other thirty thousand disappeared, she knew she never would. For years and years, she'd gathered with other mothers on the Plaza de Mayo and protested the government by brandishing portraits of their lost children.

When she'd crossed paths with this man as he entered a saddler in Calle 12 de Octubre, her blood ran cold. She clutched her shopping bag to her as hard as she could to conceal her sudden surge of emotion. Then she sat down on a wall to wait for him to come out again. She followed him up the street. Who would have found an old lady carrying a shopping bag suspicious? As he was climbing into his car, she'd memorized the model and license plate. After a series of phone calls, the Mothers of the Plaza de Mayo network had managed to come up with the address of the man she was convinced was formerly called Ortiz and now went by the name of Ortega. He lived not far from his tannery, in Dumesnil, a small town on the outskirts of Córdoba. The vehicle she'd seen in Calle 12 de Octubre in Buenos Aires had been a rental car that he'd returned to the airport before taking his flight.

Andrew offered to send Marisa money so she could fly to Córdoba, buy a digital camera, and follow Ortega. He had to be absolutely certain that Ortega and Ortiz were the same man.

Something like that would require Marisa to take at least

three days off work, and her boss wouldn't allow it. Andrew begged her to find someone trustworthy to travel there in her place; he'd make it up to her, even if it meant paying out of his own pocket. Marisa made just one promise: to call him back if she found a solution.

* * *

Olson arrived at the paper at around noon. He walked straight past Andrew without saying hello and sat down in his cubicle.

Andrew's phone rang. It was Simon, asking him to come and join him as discreetly as possible at the corner of Eighth Avenue and 40th Street.

"Why the urgency?" Andrew asked when he met up with Simon.

"Let's not stay here. You never know," Simon replied, leading him to a barber shop.

"Is this why you made me leave the office? To take me to get a shave?"

"Say what you want, but I need a good haircut. I also need to talk to you someplace quiet."

They went into the barber's and sat down next to each other on red leatherette chairs in front of a big mirror.

The two Russian barbers, who looked so alike they must have been brothers, came over at once and got to work.

While Simon was getting shampooed, he told Andrew how he'd waited for Olson to leave home, then tailed him.

"How did you get his address? Even I don't know it."

"My evil computer genius! I know all your colleague's numbers—social security, cell, gym membership, credit cards, and all the loyalty programs he's registered with."

"You do realize that stealing that kind of data constitutes a violation of the most basic rights and is a criminal offense?"

"Shall we turn ourselves in right now, or do you want to know what I found out this morning?"

At just that moment the barber smeared shaving cream across Andrew's face and he couldn't answer Simon's question.

"First off, your colleague's a junkie. He exchanged a wad of dollars for a plastic sachet in Chinatown this morning before he'd even had breakfast. I took a couple of photos of the transaction, just in case."

"You're out of your mind, Simon!"

"Wait till you hear the rest: you might think differently. He went to NYPD headquarters around ten o'clock—some nerve he has, considering what he was carrying in his pocket. I've gotta give it to him, he's one cool customer—either that or he's completely crazy. I don't know why he went there, but he was in there for at least half an hour. Then he went to a hunting supply shop. I saw him talking to the salesman and being shown various hunting knives. Well, not exactly knives, maybe . . . I was keeping my distance, but some strange-looking tools. By the way, I wouldn't fidget like that if I were you. You'll end up getting your throat slit with that razor."

The barber confirmed that Simon was right.

"I can't tell you if he bought anything; I moved on before he could notice me. He came out shortly afterward, looking more delighted than ever. Of course he might have just gone to the bathroom to powder his nose. Next, your guy went to buy himself a croissant, which he ate walking up Eighth Avenue. After that he went into a jeweler's. He stayed there for a while, chatting to the owner, then came out and walked all the way back to the paper. I called you as soon as he got there. That's it. I don't want to be too optimistic, but it does look like the noose is tightening around Olson."

The barber asked Andrew if he'd like his sideburns trimmed.

Simon answered for him, requesting he take off at least half an inch on either side.

"Maybe I should ask you to come to Buenos Aires with me," Andrew said, smiling.

"Don't tempt me. I've got a soft spot for Argentine women, and I could go pack my case right now!"

"It's a bit soon for that," Andrew pointed out. "Meanwhile, it's probably high time I went to grill Olson."

"Give me a few more days. At the rate I'm going, I'll know more about him than his own mother before long."

"I don't have much time, Simon."

"Up to you. I'm merely your humble servant. But think about Buenos Aires: we could have a blast there together!"

"What about your garage?"

"My car dealership, you mean. I thought I wasn't selling anything before early July."

"You won't be selling anything in July either if you're never at work."

"I didn't realize I'd invited my mother to the barbershop with me. I'll let you pay," Simon added, admiring himself in the mirror. "I look good with short hair, don't I?"

"Shall we get some lunch?" Andrew asked.

"Let's go see that knife salesman first. You wanted to grill someone. You can flash that press card of yours at him and find out what Olson was doing there."

"Sometimes I wonder how old you actually are."

"Wanna bet the salesman will fall for it?"

"What are we betting?"

"That lunch you were talking about."

When they arrived, Andrew entered the store first. Simon followed and stationed himself a few yards behind his friend. While Andrew spoke, the salesman kept darting worried glances at Simon out of the corner of his eye.

"Late this morning," Andrew said, "a journalist with *The New York Times* visited this store. Can you tell me what he bought?"

"What's it got to do with you?" the salesman replied.

As Andrew rummaged through his pockets for his business card, Simon walked up to the counter, looking intimidating.

"It's got everything to do with us. That man is a felon using a false press card. I'm sure you'll understand that we need to stop him before he does something dangerous, with a weapon from your store, no less."

The salesman looked Simon up and down, hesitated briefly and sighed.

"He was interested in some very special equipment, the kind only serious hunters use. And there aren't too many of those in New York."

"What type of equipment?" Andrew asked.

"Hunting knives, awls, hooks, elevators—that kind of thing."

"Elevators?" Andrew inquired.

"I'll show you," the salesman answered, disappearing into the back of the store.

He returned carrying a wooden-handled tool with a long, flat needle.

"Designed as a surgical instrument. Then trappers started using them to skin their kill. You lift the pelt away without tearing off flesh. Your man wanted to know if owners need to register this type of product, like for firearms and combat knives. I told him the truth: you don't need a license for an elevator. You find things that are a lot more dangerous at any hardware store. He asked me if I'd sold any recently. I hadn't, but I promised I'd ask my employee. It's his day off today."

"And did this man buy any from you?"

"Six. One of each size. Now, if you're not buying anything, I have to get back to work. I've got to do the books."

Andrew thanked the salesman. Simon merely nodded his head.

"So which one of us lost the bet?" Simon asked as they walked down the street.

"That guy thought you were some kind of weirdo, and I can't say I blame him. He only answered our questions to get rid of us as quickly as possible."

"Cheater!"

"Okay, okay. Lunch is on me."

16.

The next day, Andrew arrived at the office to a new message from Marisa. He called her back at once.

"I think I have a solution," she told him. "My boyfriend can follow Ortega's trail. He's unemployed, and it would do him good to earn a bit of money."

"How much?" Andrew asked.

"Five hundred dollars for the week. Plus expenses, of course."

"That's quite a sum," Andrew sighed. "I'm not sure my bosses will accept."

"Five ten-hour days; that's ten dollars an hour—same as what cleaners get paid in New York. Just because we're not American doesn't mean we should be treated with less respect."

"I totally agree, Marisa. But newspapers aren't doing well, budgets are tight, and my employers think this investigation has already cost too much."

"Antonio could leave tomorrow. If he drives to Córdoba, that'll save the cost of the plane ticket. He'll sort out his own accommodation—he has family living nearby, at San Roque Lake. All you'll need to pay for is his wage, gas and food. It's up to you. But of course, if he finds a job he'll no longer be available."

Andrew mulled over Marisa's terms, smiled and decided to give her the go-ahead. He took down the details she gave him and promised to transfer the money that same day.

"We'll set off as soon as I receive the money. We'll call you every evening with an update."

"You're going with him?"

"If we're driving, it won't cost more for me to tag along," Marisa replied. "And two of us traveling together will attract less attention. We'll look like a couple on vacation. San Roque Lake is very beautiful."

"I thought you said your boss wouldn't let you take any days off."

"You may not know this, Mr. Stilman, but my smile can work wonders."

"I'm not giving you a weeklong vacation at the paper's expense."

"How dare you call it a vacation? We're going to be trailing a war criminal!"

"Maybe I should call on your services next time I ask for a raise, Marisa. I look forward to hearing your first update."

"Talk to you soon, Mr. Stilman," she said, then hung up.

Andrew rolled up his sleeves, girding himself to confront Olivia Stern about green-lighting these extra expenses, but on his way to her office he thought better of it. This arrangement with Marisa hadn't taken place in his previous life, and the outcome remained uncertain. He decided to advance the cost of the trip from his own pocket. If he obtained interesting information as a result, it'd be easier to ask for more money. If he didn't, he'd avoid being called out as an extravagant employee.

He left the paper and went to the nearest Western Union to wire seven hundred dollars: five hundred for Antonio's wage plus a two hundred advance for expenses. Then he called Valerie to say he'd be home early.

By mid-afternoon, Andrew could feel there was another fainting fit in the offing. He was sweating and shivering, tingles ran up and down his arms and legs, and a dull ache—stronger than last time—had reappeared at the base of his spine. A shrill whistling sound pierced his eardrums.

Andrew went to the bathroom to splash some water on his face. He found Freddy Olson bent over the sink, his nose in a line of powder.

Olson jumped.

"I was sure I'd locked it."

"Well, you didn't. But if it makes you feel better, I'm not at all surprised."

"Fuck, Stilman. If you breathe a word about this, I'm done for. I can't lose my job. Please, don't be a bastard."

Being a bastard was the last thing on Andrew's mind as he felt his legs give way beneath him.

"I don't feel so good," he groaned, leaning on the sink.

Olson helped him sit down on the floor.

"Are you ill?"

"I'm in great shape, as you can see. Lock the door? It'd look pretty bad if someone came in right now."

Olson hurried to bolt the door.

"What's up, Stilman? This isn't the first time you've fainted like this. Maybe you should go see a doctor."

"Your nose looks like you dunked it in a vat of flour. You're the one who needs to get treatment. You're a cokehead, Freddy. You'll end up frying your neurons with that shit. How long have you been doing it?"

"What the hell do you care about my health? Tell me straight, Stilman: are you trying to get me thrown out? I'm begging you, please. I know we've had our differences, you and me, but you know better than anyone else that I'm no threat to your career. What would you stand to gain if I got fired?"

Andrew's dizzy spell began to pass. He was getting the feeling back in his limbs and his vision was clearing. A gentle warmth flooded through him.

Something Pilguez had said suddenly popped into his mind: if you have your criminal but haven't understood his motives, your job is only half done. He concentrated as hard as he could. Had he already caught Olson with his nose in a line of coke in his previous life? Was Olson threatened by him? It was possible that someone else had let the cat out of the bag, and Olson—convinced the snitch was Andrew—had decided to get his revenge. Andrew contemplated how to uncover Olson's motives. What had prompted him to buy a collection of elevators from a hunting store? What were they for?

"Can you help me up?" Andrew asked.

Olson looked at him threateningly. He slipped his hand into his pocket. Andrew thought he could make out the tip of a screwdriver or an awl.

"First, swear you'll keep your mouth shut."

"Don't be a jerk, Olson. You said so yourself: what would I gain apart from a guilty conscience? What you do with your free time is no concern of mine."

Olson held out his hand to Andrew.

"Maybe you're not such a bad guy, Stilman."

"It's all right, Freddy. Spare me the ass-kissing. I won't say anything—you have my word."

Andrew splashed water on his face. The paper towel roll was jammed, as usual. He left the bathroom with Olson close on his heels, and they bumped straight into their editor, who was waiting in the corridor.

"Were you plotting something, or is there something you two want to tell me?" Olivia Stern inquired, looking first one then the other of them in the eye.

"What on earth are you talking about?" Andrew retorted.

"You've been shut up alone together in a small bathroom for a quarter of an hour. What do you want me to think?"

"Andrew had a dizzy spell. I went to see if everything was okay and found him lying on the floor. I stayed with him until he started feeling better. But everything's back to normal now, right, Stilman?"

"You fainted again?" Olivia asked in an anxious voice.

"Nothing serious, don't worry. Those damn back pains of mine are so strong sometimes, they literally have me flat on the floor."

"Go see a doctor, Andrew. This is the second time it's happened at the newspaper, and I presume it's happened elsewhere too. That's an order. I don't want to have to bring you home from Argentina because of a stupid case of lumbago. Got it?"

"Yes, boss," Andrew replied in a deliberately impertinent tone.

Back at his desk, Andrew turned to Olson and said, "You've got a nerve, making me the scapegoat."

"What did you want me to tell her? That we were smooching in the bathroom?" Freddy replied.

"Come take a walk with me before I punch you in the face. I need to talk to you, but not here."

"What the hell were you doing buying hunting knives?" Andrew asked as they entered the cafeteria.

"I had a roast to carve. What's it got to do with you? You're spying on me now?"

Andrew tried to think of a way to respond without making him suspicious.

"You sniff coke all day long and you buy specialist knives. If you've got debts, I'd rather know about it before your dealers show up at the paper."

"Chill out, Stilman. Me going to that shop has nothing to do with that. I went there for a story."

"You're going to have to elaborate."

Olson hesitated for a moment, then gave up and decided to confide in Andrew.

"Okay. I told you I was investigating three knifings. Well, I have my contacts too. I went to see a cop buddy of mine who'd got hold of the forensic scientist's reports. Turns out the three victims weren't stabbed with a knife, but a pointed object, sort of like a needle, that leaves behind a series of asymmetrical incisions."

"An ice pick?"

"No, because each time it was pulled out, the weapon caused much more damage than a simple needle, however long. The forensic scientist thought it might be some kind of hook. The problem is that with a hook, the victims would have had to be stabbed in the side for the internal wounds to reach the belly.

"When I was a kid, I used to go hunting with my dad. He worked the traditional way, like a trapper. I won't bore you with the details, but I remembered something my old man would use to dismember stags. I wondered whether that kind of tool could still be bought today, and went to check somewhere they sold hunting equipment. Has that satisfied your curiosity, Stilman?"

"Do you really believe a serial killer is loose on the streets of Manhattan?"

"I'm totally convinced of it."

"And the paper put you on this half-baked story?"

"Olivia wants us to be the first to publish the scoop."

"If we were second, it wouldn't really be a scoop, would it? Why all these lies, Olson? Olivia hasn't asked you to investigate any serial killer."

Freddy shot Andrew a dark look and sent his cup of coffee flying.

"Your arrogance really pisses me off, Stilman. Are you a cop or a journalist? I know you don't like me, but I won't let you ruin my career. I'll defend myself—by any means."

"Chill out, Olson. For someone who's trying to play it cool, hurling your cup across the cafeteria wasn't very smart. Everyone's looking at you."

"To hell with them. I'm just trying to protect myself."

"What are you talking about?"

"What planet are you living on, Stilman? Can't you see what's brewing at the paper? They're going to fire half the staff. Are you the only person who doesn't get it? Of course *you* don't feel threatened. When you're the editor's pet, you don't fear for your job. I, on the other hand, am not in her good graces, so I'm fighting as best I can."

"You've lost me, Freddy."

"Fine, play dumb. Your piece on the Chinese orphanage hit it big. Right after, you get an investigative report in Argentina. You're in solid with the bosses. As for me, I haven't published anything significant for months. I work the night shift, praying for something out of the ordinary to happen. Do you think I like sleeping under my desk and spending my weekends here to try and save my job? If I lose my job, I lose everything. It's all I've got.

"Do you ever have nightmares? Of course not—why would you? But I do. I often wake up in a sweat from a nightmare where I'm in a seedy office in some godforsaken provincial town, working for the local rag. In this nightmare I'm looking up at a yellowed copy of *The New York Times* hanging on the wall of my grimy office, dreaming of better days. And then the phone rings, and I'm told I have to rush to the grocery store because a dog's been run over. I have that goddam nightmare every night.

"So you're right, Stilman: Olivia didn't ask me to do that investigation. She hasn't put me on anything since you became her golden boy. This is all me. If there's any chance I could be the first to identify a serial killer—the slightest chance I'm onto a scoop—I'll visit all the hunting shops in the tri-state area so I don't miss it. Whether you like it or not."

Andrew stared at his colleague. Freddy's hands were shaking and his breathing was erratic.

"I'm sorry. If I can help you with your investigations, I'd really like to."

"Of course! Looking down his nose, Mr. Stilman offers sympathy. Fuck you!"

Olson got up and left the cafeteria without looking back.

* * *

The conversation with Olson occupied Andrew's mind for the rest of the day. Knowing his colleague's situation made him feel less alone. That evening, at dinner with Valerie, he described Freddy's misery.

"You should help him," Valerie said. "Work alongside him instead of turning your back."

"That's just how the cubicles crumble."

"Don't be dumb. You know exactly what I mean."

"My life's been disrupted enough by my own investigation. If I have to start following an imaginary killer, I won't be able to hold it together."

"I wasn't talking about that. I meant you should help him with his cocaine addiction."

"That nutcase went to buy some elevators so he could play at being a forensic scientist. He thinks that's the weapon his serial killer's using."

"I have to admit that's pretty extreme."

"Do you know anything about them?"

"They're used as surgical instruments. I can bring one home from the office tomorrow night, if you want," Valerie replied with a slight smile.

These words left Andrew pensive. He was still reflecting on them when he fell asleep that night.

* * *

Andrew woke up as dawn was breaking. He missed his

morning runs along the Hudson River. He had good reason for not going back there since his "resurrection" but as he thought about it, July 9 was still a long way off. Valerie was fast asleep. He got out of bed without a sound, slipped on his running gear and left the apartment. All was quiet in the West Village. Andrew jogged down Charles Street. He sped up at the bottom of the road and managed, for the first time in his life, to cross the West Side Highway's eight lanes before the second traffic light turned green. Thrilled with his achievement and with resuming his morning exercise, he turned onto the Hudson River Park footpath.

He broke off from his run for a moment to watch the lights of Hoboken go out as the sun rose. He loved that sight; it reminded him of his childhood. When he lived in Poughkeepsie, his father used to come to his room early on Saturday mornings and wake him. They would have breakfast together in the kitchen, and then his dad would sit him in front of the steering wheel and push the Datsun out into the lane so they didn't wake his mother. *God, I miss my parents*, he thought. Once they were in the street, Andrew would carry out the maneuver he'd learned: pull down into second, release the clutch, wait for the engine to start sputtering then give a quick press on the accelerator. When teaching him to drive, his father would make him cross the Hudson Bridge, then turn off into Oaks Road and park along the river. From their observation point, they'd sit waiting for the lights of Poughkeepsie to be switched off. Every time he watched it happen, Andrew's father would clap as if a fireworks display had come to an end.

As the lights of Jersey City went out too, Andrew left his memories behind and continued on his run.

Looking behind him as he rejoined the flow of joggers, he suddenly recognized a familiar figure in the distance behind him. He squinted and saw Freddy Olson running towards him with his right hand inside the pocket of the sweatshirt he had on. Andrew immediately sensed danger. He could have confronted Freddy, tried to reason with him, but he knew already that Freddy would mortally wound him before he would have the chance to dodge his attack. Andrew started running as fast as he could. Panic-stricken, he turned around again to estimate the distance separating him from Olson. He was gaining ground. Try as he might, Andrew wasn't fast enough to shake him off. Olson must be high as a kite. How could he fight off someone who did coke morning, noon and night? Andrew noticed a small group of joggers in front of him. If he caught up with them, he'd be safe; Freddy couldn't attack him then. They were only a hundred or so feet ahead—he had to catch up with them, no matter how out of breath he was. He prayed to God to give him the strength he needed. It wasn't July 9 yet, and he still had an assignment to carry out in Argentina, and so many things to say to Valerie. He didn't want to die today— not yet, not again. The joggers were only some forty feet ahead of him now, but he could sense Freddy closing in on him.

Try harder, he groaned to himself. *Faster, dammit, faster!*

He wanted to shout for help, but there wasn't enough air in his lungs.

Suddenly Andrew felt a terrible pain rip into the base of his spine. He screamed in pain. One of the joggers ahead of him heard his cry and turned around. Andrew's heart stopped beating when he saw Valerie's face smiling calmly at him, watching him die. He collapsed onto the tarmac and everything went dark.

* * *

When Andrew opened his eyes again, he was lying shivering on a cold, hard plastic bed. A voice was addressing him through a speaker: he was in the midst of a scan; it wouldn't take long and he should remain as still as possible.

How could he move when his wrists and ankles were bound? Andrew tried to control the beating of his heart; he could hear it echoing around the white room. Before he had time to look around to see where he was, the bed began sliding into a large cylinder. He felt as if he were being imprisoned inside a modern-day sarcophagus. He heard a muffled sound followed by a series of loud hammering noises. The voice coming out of the speaker was trying to sound soothing: it said everything would be fine, he had nothing to fear, it was a painless exam and would soon be over.

After several minutes the noises stopped, and the bed slid slowly out again, bringing Andrew back into the light of the room. A nurse came right away and transferred him onto a bed with wheels. He knew that face—he'd already seen it someplace. He was almost certain it was Sam, Valerie's assistant at the veterinary office. No doubt he was delirious from the drugs he'd been administered.

Andrew wanted to put the question to the nurse all the same. But the man just smiled and left him in the room to which he'd wheeled him.

What hospital am I in? he wondered. But it didn't really matter. He'd survived his attack and identified the perpetrator. Once he'd recovered from his injuries, he'd be able to live a normal life again. That bastard Freddy Olson would spend the next ten years behind bars. That had to be the minimum for attempted murder.

Andrew would always be angry for letting himself be duped by his story. Olson must have guessed that Andrew suspected something and decided to act earlier than planned. It occurred to Andrew that he'd have to postpone his trip to Argentina, but since he'd managed to save his skin this time, he now had proof that the course of things could be changed.

There was a knock at the door. Inspector Pilguez came in, accompanied by a ravishing woman in a white doctor's coat.

"I'm sorry, Stilman. I failed, and that guy pulled it off. I'd backed the wrong horse. I'm getting old and my instincts aren't what they used to be." Andrew wanted to reassure the detective, but hadn't recovered enough to speak.

"When I found out what had happened to you, I jumped on the first plane with my neurosurgeon friend I've told you so much about. May I introduce you to Dr. Kline."

"Lauren," said the doctor, holding out her hand.

Andrew recalled her name, Pilguez had mentioned it once over dinner. He was surprised he did, because every time he'd hesitated about getting himself examined, he'd tried in vain to remember it.

The doctor took his pulse, inspected his pupils and got what looked like a pen out of her coat pocket, except it had a tiny lightbulb instead of a nib.

"Follow this light with your eyes, Mr. Stilman," she said, moving her pen back and forth from left to right.

She replaced it in her pocket and took a few steps back.

"Olson," Andrew uttered with difficulty.

"I know," Pilguez sighed. "We questioned him at the office. He tried to deny the facts, but your friend Simon told us about the hunting knives and when we threw that at him, he ended up admitting to it. I wasn't completely off-base, unfortunately: your wife was his accomplice. I'm sorry—I'd have preferred to be wrong about that."

"Valerie . . . But why?" Andrew stammered.

"I told you there are only really two types of crime? In ninety percent of cases, the killer is a close relation. Your colleague let on to her that you were in love with someone else and were about to call off the wedding. She couldn't bear the humiliation. We arrested her at her office. Given the number of police officers around her, she didn't put up any resistance."

Andrew was overwhelmed with sorrow, a sadness that suddenly drained him of his will to live.

The doctor walked over to him.

"Your scan results are normal. There's no trace of a brain lesion or tumor, so that's good news."

"But I'm so cold, and my back hurts so much," Andrew mumbled.

"I know—your body temperature is low. We've consulted and all reached the same conclusion. You're dead, Mr. Stilman. Well and truly dead. That cold feeling shouldn't last long, just the time it takes for your conscience to die too."

"I'm sorry, Stilman, really sorry I failed," Pilguez said again. "I'm going to take my friend to lunch, then we'll come back and take you to the morgue. We won't leave you on your own at a time like this. I was delighted to know you, even if it was only briefly."

Dr. Kline said goodbye politely, and Pilguez patted Andrew on the shoulder in a friendly manner. They turned out the light and left the room.

Alone in the darkness, Andrew began to wail his heart out.

* * *

He was being shaken violently, as if he was being tossed about on a stormy sea. A ray of light hit his eyelids. He opened his eyes wide and saw Valerie's face above him.

"Andrew, my love, wake up. You're having a nightmare. Wake up, Andrew."

He inhaled deeply and sat up with a jolt, covered in sweat. He was in his own bed, in his bedroom in his West Village apartment. Valerie was nearly as scared as Andrew. She took him in her arms and hugged him tight.

"You have nightmares every night. You've got to see someone—this can't go on."

Andrew pulled himself together. Valerie handed him a glass of water.

"Here, drink this. It'll do you good, you're bathed in sweat."

He glanced at the alarm clock on the nightstand. It read 6 A.M. and the date was Saturday, May 26.

He had six weeks left to identify his murderer, if his terror-filled nights didn't destroy him first.

17

V alerie did her best to comfort Andrew. He was exhausted, and it worried her. Around noon, she suggested they go for a stroll in Williamsburg to browse the antique shops. Andrew was fascinated by a miniature steam engine dating back to the 1950s, but it cost a lot more than he could afford. Valerie encouraged him to go and have a look around the back of the store. As soon as he'd turned away, she bought the coveted object and slipped it into her bag.

Simon spent the whole of Saturday tailing Olson. He'd gone to wait in front of Olson's apartment building at first light. Seated at the wheel of an Oldsmobile Eighty-Eight that attracted attention from passersby each time he stopped at a traffic light, Simon wondered if he should have picked another car, but this was the most inconspicuous one in his collection.

Olson spent his lunch hour in a shady-looking massage parlor in Chinatown. He emerged around 2 P.M. with his hair slicked back against his head. The next stop was a Mexican restaurant. Simon parked in front of it and waited as Freddy wolfed down tacos, licking every last drop of sauce off his fingers.

Simon had bought himself a camera and a telephoto lens that any tabloid photographer would be proud to own; he'd decided these accessories were essential to the success of his stakeout.

Towards mid-afternoon Olson went for a walk in Central Park. Simon watched as he attempted to strike up a conversation with a woman reading on a bench. *If you can swing it wearing that Tabasco-splattered shirt of yours, bud, I'll go join a monastery*, he thought. He breathed a sigh of relief when he saw the woman shut her book and walk away.

While Simon spied on Freddy, the hacker he'd recruited was busy copying the content of Olson's computer. It had taken him less than four minutes to break into it. Once he'd decrypted all the duplicate files, he'd know whether Olson was the person behind the Spooky Kid username.

Simon's computer whiz wasn't the only one tapping away at a keyboard. On the other side of the country, a retired detective was exchanging e-mails with a former colleague he'd mentored at the 6th Precinct back in the day and who now headed the Chicago Police Department's Bureau of Detectives. Pilguez asked him for a small favor. The legality of his request was highly questionable without a judge's order, but he figured it was between him and his friend and for a good cause, so to hell with the paperwork.

The information he'd just been given worried him considerably, and he hesitated for quite some time before calling Andrew.

"You sound like you're in bad shape," he said.

"I had a rough night," Andrew replied.

"I'm an insomniac too, and it doesn't get any better with age. But I wasn't calling to tell you about my problems. I wanted to let you know that Mrs. Capetta bought herself a plane ticket to New York this morning. And what caught my eye is that she's arriving on June 14, but it's an open return ticket. You'll probably tell me that it's cheaper this way, but still. Those dates are just a little too close for comfort."

"How did you find that out?"

"If a policeman asked you to reveal your sources, would you?"

"No way," Andrew replied.

"Then be happy with what I'm willing to tell you. The rest is my business. I've made a few arrangements regarding Mrs. Capetta. There'll be someone on her tail from morning to night from the moment she sets foot in New York. Especially in the morning—you and I know why."

"Maybe she's decided to see her husband again."

"That would be the best news I've heard in weeks. But I've got this unfortunate character flaw: I never believe good news. What about you? Have you made any progress on your end?"

"I can't think clearly anymore," Andrew said. "Olson bothers me, and he's not the only one. I find myself suspecting everybody."

"You need a change of scenery. You should get out of New York for a while. You're on the front line of this investigation and you have to stay focused, but time is running out. Unfortunately I know you're not going to take my advice."

Pilguez said goodbye to Andrew and promised to call again as soon as he had any news.

"Who was that?" Valerie asked, finishing the ice cream she was eating on the patio of the café where they'd found a table.

"Nothing important. It was a work thing."

"That's the first time I've heard you say your work isn't important. You must be even more tired than I thought."

"Would you like to go to the beach for a night?"

"Of course I would."

"Come on. I know a charming little beachfront hotel in Westport. We can catch a train from Grand Central. The sea air will do us good."

"We'll have to stop off at home first to pick up a few things."

"Not necessary. We can buy a toothbrush there, can't we? That's all we need for an overnight trip."

"What's going on? It's like you're running away from something or someone."

"I just feel like getting out of the city. A little romantic jaunt with you, somewhere calm and quiet."

"And may I ask how come you know about this charming little beachfront hotel?"

"I wrote the owner's obituary."

Valerie looked at him tenderly. "Well, this is very chivalrous of you," she said.

"You're not jealous of my past, are you?"

"Of your past *and* your future. You have no idea how jealous I was of all those girls that hung around you back when we were in college," she replied.

"What girls?"

Valerie gave a knowing smile and hailed a taxi.

They reached Westport in the early evening. From their room they could see the headland and the constant swirl and clash of the currents.

After dinner they went for a walk along a deserted strip of beach near the inlet. Valerie spread a towel she'd borrowed from the hotel on the sand. Andrew laid his head on her knees, and together they watched the angry ocean.

"I want to grow old with you, Andrew, so I have time to really get to know you."

"You know me better than anyone else."

"Since leaving Poughkeepsie, all I've experienced is loneliness. Being with you is drawing me out of my solitude. I'm finally starting to feel happy."

They snuggled up together in the cool of the evening, silently watching the waves break on the shore. Andrew thought back to their teenage years, musing that some memories were like faded old photographs where the details only came into focus in certain kinds of light. He felt like the two of them were closer right now than they'd ever been.

In three days' time he would be in Buenos Aires, thousands

of miles away from her and from this peaceful interlude. He hoped he'd be able to relive this moment when the summer days began to wane.

* * *

A peaceful night's sleep and breakfast in the sunshine helped Andrew to recover his strength. His back pain had disappeared.

When they returned to New York on Sunday evening, he called Simon and asked him to meet him at Starbucks around nine the next morning.

* * *

Simon was late. Andrew read the paper while he waited.

"Don't say anything," Simon warned. "I've had the shittiest Saturday of my life."

"I haven't said anything."

"That's because I've forbidden you to."

"What was so terrible about your Saturday?"

"I spent the day in Freddy Olson's shoes. You have no idea what a revolting disguise it was."

"That bad?"

"Worse. Whores, tacos, and coke, and that was only the morning's activities. After lunch he treated himself to a visit to the morgue. Don't ask me what he was doing there. If I followed him in he would have spotted me and anyway, I'm not crazy about seeing the inside of one of their iceboxes. Then he bought some flowers and went to Lenox Hill Hospital."

"And after the hospital?"

"He went for a walk in Central Park. Then he went to your neighborhood and hung around your place. After walking past the door of your building four times, he went in and hunted for your mailbox. Then all of a sudden he turned around and left."

"Olson went to my place? That guy is out of his mind!"

"I'd say he's at the end of his rope. I tailed him all the way back to his place. That man's loneliness is bottomless, an abyss. He's totally lost."

"He's not the only one feeling lost. It's nearly June. Although I shouldn't be complaining. Who else can brag that they've lived through the same month of May twice?"

"Not me, at least," Simon replied. "And considering my stellar turnover this month, it's just as well. Come on, June—and here's to July," Simon said, raising his coffee cup in a mock toast.

"May was the month my life changed," Andrew sighed. "Up until then, I was happy. I hadn't screwed up every good thing that had ever happened to me."

"You have to forgive yourself, Andrew. Any number of people would dream of being able to start over, to go back to the moment just before they messed everything up. If you say that's what's happening to you, make the most of it instead of complaining about it."

"I'm going to be murdered, Simon. It's not a dream, it's a nightmare. Will you look after Valerie when I'm gone?"

"You'll look after her yourself! We're all going to die: life's a terminal illness that afflicts us all. I don't know when the fateful day will arrive for me, and it's not a deadline I'll be able to postpone. Which is no more reassuring, come to think of it. Want me to take you to the airport tomorrow?"

"No need."

"I'll miss you, you know."

"I'll miss you too."

"Right, you'd better get back to Valerie. I have an appointment."

"Who with?"

"You're going to be late, Andrew."

"Answer me."

"With the receptionist at Lenox Hill Hospital. I went back there yesterday evening to see if she was doing okay after Freddy's visit. It's the perfectionist in me—can't help it."

Andrew got up and said goodbye to Simon. He turned back just before leaving the café. "I want to ask you to do me a favor, Simon."

"I thought you already had. But go ahead, I'm listening."

"I need you to go to Chicago. There's this woman I'd like you to follow for a few days. Here's her address."

"Does this mean we're not going to be meeting up in Buenos Aires?"

"Did you really think we would?"

"I had my suitcase packed, just in case."

"I'll call you. I promise I'll ask you to come over if it's at all possible."

"Don't bother. I'll go to Chicago as soon as I can, and you take care of yourself over there. Is this Mrs. Capetta pretty?"

Andrew gave his friend a hug.

* * *

Andrew spent the morning at the office. Olson wasn't around. Andrew called the receptionist and asked her to let him know the minute Olson arrived. He told her he was supposed to be meeting him in the lobby.

As soon as he'd put down the phone, Andrew went to snoop around Olson's cubicle. He rummaged through his desk drawers, but all he found was a lot of notebooks filled with memos and totally uninteresting ideas for stories the newspaper would never publish. How could Olson be so useless? Andrew was about to give up when a Post-it that had stayed stuck to the wastebasket caught his eye. It had the password to his own computer scribbled on it. How had Olson gotten ahold of it? And what had he been doing on Andrew's computer?

Same thing as you, said a little voice in his head. *Looking for dirt.*

"It's not the same thing," Andrew murmured to himself. "Olson is a potential threat to me."

And I'm a threat to him—to his career, anyway.

A crazy thought occurred to him. He tapped out his own password on the keyboard of Olson's computer to see if he could gain access. It worked. Andrew concluded that Freddy was about as imaginative as a goldfish. Either that, or he was incredibly Machiavellian. Who would think of using the password of the very individual they were spying on?

There were several folders on Olson's hard disk, including one named "SK." Andrew opened it to find it contained the prolific writings of Spooky Kid. Olson was certifiably insane, he thought as he read through the torrent of abuse directed at him. But, unpleasant though it was to read a litany of this kind, he was glad a jealous colleague was behind it and not a reader. Andrew slipped a flash drive into the computer and started copying Olson's files to read them at leisure. He was scrolling through the file names on the screen when he heard his telephone ring on the other side of the cubicle wall, and the ping of the elevator doors opening on the landing. Andrew just had time to copy a file named "Punishments," and got up hastily as Freddy came walking down the corridor.

Slipping back into his own cubicle, Andrew realized he'd left his flash drive in Olson's computer, and prayed he wouldn't notice.

"Where were you?" he asked as Olson passed him.

"Why? Since when do I owe you any explanations?"

"Just curious," replied Andrew.

"When are you leaving for Buenos Aires, Stilman?"

"Tomorrow."

"If you could stay there, it'd give me a break."

Olson's cell phone rang. He went out of the office to take the call. Andrew seized the opportunity to retrieve his flash drive. Then he picked up his notebooks, glanced one last time at his desk and decided to go home. Valerie would be waiting for him; it was their last evening together before he went off to Buenos Aires, and he didn't want to be late.

* * *

He took her to dinner at Shanghai Café in Chinatown. The restaurant was a lot cozier than Joe's. Valerie was feeling down and made no attempt to hide it. Though Andrew was happy to be taking his investigation further, he couldn't help feeling guilty. They should have made the most of their evening out, but the knowledge that their separation was imminent made it impossible.

Valerie decided to sleep at her own place. She said she would rather not be there early next morning when Andrew zipped up the small suitcase she'd packed for him. He accompanied her back to her apartment in the East Village. They stood in each other's arms in front of the building for a long time.

"I hate you for leaving me here alone, but I'd hate you even more if you decided not to go."

"What can I do to make you love me, just a little?"

"On the eve of your departure? Not much. Come back soon. That's all I'm asking. I miss you already."

"It's only for ten days."

"And eleven nights. Look after yourself, and find that guy. I'll be proud to become your wife, Andrew Stilman. Now get out of here before I decide not to let you go."

18

A ndrew's flight landed at Ezeiza International Airport in the early evening. To his surprise, Marisa had come to meet him. He'd sent her several e-mails, but he hadn't heard from her at all since the last time they'd spoken on the phone. On his earlier trip, they'd met at the hotel the morning after his arrival.

Andrew was noticing that the more time went by, the more things seemed to be happening in a different order than they had the last time around.

He recognized Marisa's old VW Beetle. Its side runners were so rusty that, on his previous trip, each time the car had hit a bump he'd wondered if his seat would go through the floor.

"I thought you really had gone on vacation with the money I sent you," he told her. "You promised me you'd be in touch."

"It turned out to be more complicated than we thought. Antonio's in the hospital."

"What happened?" Andrew asked.

"We had a car accident on our way back."

"A serious one?"

"Serious enough that my boyfriend's got one arm in a cast, six fractured ribs and head trauma. It's a miracle we didn't both end up in the hospital."

"Was it his fault?"

"If you consider that he didn't brake at the red light, yes. But since the brakes had stopped working, I suppose he isn't responsible."

"Was his car as well maintained as yours?" asked Andrew, who was struggling to extricate the jammed seat belt.

"Antonio's fanatical about his car. I sometimes wonder if he loves it more than me. There's no way he'd have started out on a trip without checking everything first. Someone deliberately cut our brakes."

"Do you suspect anyone in particular?"

"We located Ortiz. We watched him and took photos of him. We asked about him—too many questions, probably, and his friends aren't exactly choirboys."

"That's not going to help me with my investigation. He'll be on his guard now."

"Antonio's in serious condition and all you can think of is your investigation? I'm extremely touched by your concern, Mr. Stilman."

"That was tactless of me. I'm sorry about your boyfriend. Don't worry, I'm sure he'll pull through. But I can't help being nervous about my work. I haven't come all the way here for vacation, you know. When did this accident happen?"

"Three days ago."

"Why didn't you let me know?"

"Because Antonio only regained consciousness yesterday evening, and you were the last thing on my mind."

"Have you still got the photos?"

"The camera case was badly damaged in the crash. We were using an old camera because we didn't want to attract too much attention with an expensive model. The film will probably turn out grainy. I'm not sure we'll be able to see much. I've given it to a photographer friend. We can pick it up tomorrow."

"You'll have to go on your own. I'm leaving for Córdoba tomorrow."

"There's no way you'll be doing anything that stupid, Mr. Stilman. With all due respect, if Antonio and I, who are locals, managed to get ourselves noticed, it'll take Ortiz's men less than half a day to spot you. Besides, there's no need for you to drive all the way there. Ortiz comes to Buenos Aires every week."

"When's his next visit?"

"Tuesday, if he sticks to his routine. That's what we were told when we questioned some of his neighbors, which is probably why we had the accident."

"I'm sorry, Marisa," Andrew said sincerely. "I had no idea I'd be making you run any risks. If I'd known . . . "

But Andrew didn't remember this accident. Nothing was happening like it had the last time. On his former trip, *he'd* been the one to photograph Ortiz, and he'd had his camera stolen in an alleyway in a Buenos Aires suburb after being attacked by three men.

"Do you really think a man who's put so much effort into changing his identity to avoid going to prison will just sit there and let himself be unmasked? What planet are you living on?" Marisa asked.

"You'd be surprised if I described it to you," Andrew replied.

Marisa pulled up in front of the Quintana Hotel in Recoleta, a middle-class neighborhood.

"Let's go see how your boyfriend's doing," Andrew suggested. "I'll drop my stuff off here later."

"I appreciate your concern, but Antonio needs his rest, and visiting hours are over. We'll go tomorrow. He's in intensive care at General de Agudos hospital. It's close to here. I'll come by and pick you up at nine o'clock tomorrow."

"You aren't working at the bar this evening?"

"No, it's my day off."

Andrew said goodbye to Marisa, got his suitcase out of the back seat, and walked towards the hotel.

A white van stopped outside the hotel entrance. The man

sitting in the front seat aimed his camera at Andrew and took a series of shots. The rear door opened, and another man got out and strolled into the lobby. The van started up again and fell in behind Marisa's car. Its driver had been tailing her ever since she and Antonio left Córdoba.

Andrew smiled when the receptionist handed him the key to room 712. It was the same room he'd been given in his previous life.

"Could you ask housekeeping to change the batteries in my TV remote control?" he asked.

"Our cleaning service checks them daily to make sure they're working," the employee intoned.

"Trust me, whoever did my room didn't do his job properly."

"How would you know that, sir? You haven't been up to your room yet."

"I have ESP!" Andrew said, opening his eyes wide.

Room 712 was exactly the way he remembered it. The window wouldn't open, the closet had a squeaky door hinge, the shower leaked and the mini-fridge made coughing noises like a cat with tuberculosis.

"Some cleaning service!" Andrew snorted, throwing his suitcase on the bed.

He hadn't had a bite to eat since New York—the food on the plane had looked so disgusting he didn't want to risk it— and he was starving. He remembered having eaten on his last trip in a *parrilla* right across from the Recoleta cemetery. He pulled his room door shut behind him, amused by the thought of eating the same steak for the second time.

When Andrew left the hotel, the man in the lobby got up from his armchair and followed him. He sat on a small bench in front of the restaurant.

While Andrew was enjoying his meal, a cleaning service

employee at the Quintana hotel was going through the belongings of the guest in room 712 in exchange for a sizeable
amount of cash. He carried out his mission meticulously,
opened the tiny room safe with his staff key and photographed
all the pages of Andrew's address book, passport and diary.
When he'd put everything back in its place, he checked to see
if the remote control was working, changed the batteries and
left. He found his generous benefactor waiting for him at the
service entrance of the hotel and returned his digital camera.

* * *

Feeling pleasantly full, Andrew slept like a log and didn't
have any nightmares. He woke up refreshed early in the morning. After having breakfast in the hotel dining room, he went
outside to wait for Marisa.

"We're not going to see Antonio," she announced as soon
as Andrew got into the Beetle.

"He hasn't gotten worse, has he?"

"No, he's actually feeling better this morning. It's my aunt.
She received a very unpleasant phone call in the middle of the
night."

"What do you mean?"

"A man who didn't bother to introduce himself told her she
should keep an eye on the people her niece is getting involved
with. He told her I could get into serious trouble otherwise."

"Ortiz's pals don't waste any time, do they?"

"What really worries me is that they already know you're in
town and that we know each other."

"Am I the only bad company you could be keeping?"

"Is that a serious question?"

"There must be quite a few guys, upstanding and otherwise,
hanging around you."

"No, because I love my boyfriend very much."

202 · MARC LEVY

"It was a compliment, nothing more," Andrew assured her. "Do you know which street the service entrance of the hospital is on?"

"It won't do us any good to try and play smart. Ortiz's men probably have an accomplice inside the building. I don't want to put Antonio in any more danger. He's taken enough risks as it is."

"What do we do next?"

"I'm taking you to see my aunt. She knows more than I do—more than most other people in this city, actually. She was one of the very first Mothers of the Plaza de Mayo. But keep in mind I'm not here to be your tour guide."

"I wouldn't really call this sightseeing, but I'll remember that. And that you're in an excellent mood."

* * *

Luisa lived in a small house in the Monte Chingolo neighborhood. A courtyard shaded by a huge purple jacaranda, its walls covered in passionflower, preceded her front door.

Marisa took him through to the living room.

"So you're the American journalist who's investigating our history," Luisa said, getting up from the armchair where she'd been sitting and doing the crossword. "I thought you'd be better looking."

Marisa grinned. Her aunt beckoned Andrew to a place at the table and she then went into the kitchen. She reappeared holding a plate of cookies.

"Why are you interested in Ortiz?" she asked, pouring Andrew a glass of lemonade.

"My editor finds his career interesting."

"Your boss has some funny interests."

"She does, like understanding what makes an ordinary man become a torturer," Andrew replied.

"She should have come here instead of you. I'd have given her the names of hundreds of soldiers who turned into monsters. Ortiz wasn't an ordinary fellow, but he wasn't the worst of them. He was a coast guard pilot—small fry. We've never found hard evidence that he participated in the torture. And don't think I'm trying to make excuses for him. He did some terrible things, and he deserves to rot in prison for his crimes, like a lot of other people. But, like many others, he's gotten away with it—until now, anyway. If you can help us prove that Ortiz has become the trader who calls himself Ortega, we can have him taken to court. Or at least we can try."

"What do you know about him?"

"About Ortega? Not much so far. As for Ortiz, all you need to do is go through the ESMA archives to find his pedigree."

"How has he managed to evade justice?"

"What justice are you talking about, Mr. Journalist? The one that granted amnesty to those jackals and gave them time to manufacture new identities for themselves? After the transition to democracy in 1983, we—the victims' families—thought the criminals would be convicted. We didn't expect that President Alfonsin would be so spineless and the army so powerful. The military regime had time to erase its tracks, clean its bloodstained uniforms and hide the torture equipment in anticipation of better times. And there's no guarantee those times won't return one day. Our democracy is fragile. If you think you'll be shielded from the worst of it because you're American, you're mistaken; as mistaken as we were. In 1987, Barreiro and Rico, two high-level army officers, provoked unrest and managed to declaw our legal system. Two shameful laws were passed—the 'due obedience' law, which established a hierarchy of responsibility based on military rank, and the even more disgraceful 'full stop' law, which set a deadline for bringing charges for all the crimes that hadn't yet been judged. So Ortiz and hundreds of his comrades were basically offered a pass that protected them from being prosecuted. And the ones who were in prison were freed. We had to wait fifteen years for those laws to be repealed. But as you can imagine, fifteen years gave those lowlifes plenty of time to cover up their tracks."

"How could the Argentine people let such a thing happen?"

"How can you ask me that question? Did you Americans take your President Bush, Vice President Cheney or Defense Secretary Rumsfeld to court for authorizing the use of torture in the interrogation of Iraqi prisoners in the name of national security? Or for setting up the detention center in Guantanamo? Have you closed down that center, which has violated the Geneva Conventions for more than a decade? You see how fragile democracy can be, so don't judge us. We did what we could in the face of an all-powerful army manipulating the machinery of the state to its maximum advantage. Most of us were merely trying to send our children to school, to fill their plates and put a roof over their heads. That alone took a great deal of effort and sacrifice on the part of impoverished Argentines."

"I wasn't judging you," Andrew assured her.

"You're not a judge, Mr. Journalist, but you can help us to ensure that justice is done. If you expose the man hiding behind the name of Ortega and he really is Ortiz, he'll get the treatment he deserves. That is why I'm prepared to help you."

Luisa got up from her chair and went over to the sideboard that held pride of place in her living room. She took a file out of a drawer and placed it on the table. She turned the pages one by one, licking her finger each time, until she got to the page she was looking for. She handed the page to Andrew.

"There's your Ortiz," she said. "That was in 1977. He would have been around forty—already too old to pilot anything other than coast guard planes. His career as an officer was fairly run-of-the-mill. According to the investigation report I found in the archives of the National Commission on the Disappeared, he piloted several of the death flights. Many young men and women, some of them barely out of adolescence, were thrown alive into the waters of the Río de la Plata from the plane he was flying."

Andrew couldn't help grimacing in disgust as he looked at the photograph of the officer in his haughty pose.

"He didn't report to Massera, the head of ESMA. That's probably why he managed to slip by unnoticed during those few years when he could have been arrested. Ortiz was under the orders of Héctor Febres, the Coast Guard chief. But Febres also headed ESMA's intelligence service. He was in charge of Sector 4, which included a number of torture rooms and the maternity unit—if you could call it that, considering it was a tiny hole measuring a few square feet where women prisoners were made to give birth like animals. Worse than animals, even, because their heads were covered with burlap sacks.

"Febres forced those brand-new mothers to write a letter to their families asking them to look after their babies while they were in prison. You know what happened next. Now listen carefully, Mr. Stilman, because if you really want me to help you, we'll have to make a pact, you and I."

Andrew refilled Luisa's glass with lemonade. She gulped it down and put the glass back on the table.

"It's very likely that Febres did Ortiz a favor for services rendered—meaning he was given one of those babies."

"Very likely, or do you know that for a fact?"

"It doesn't matter. That's why we're making a pact. You have to choose your words with great care when you're telling one of those stolen children the truth: that's something we Mothers of the Plaza de Mayo insist on. When you are told, as an adult, that not only are your mother and father not your biological parents, but that they were associated either directly or indirectly with the disappearance of the woman who gave birth to you, it can have terrible consequences. It's a difficult and traumatic process. We're fighting to expose the truth and give the victims of the junta their true identities back, but the last thing we want is to destroy the lives of innocent people.

"I'll tell you everything I know and can find out about Ortiz. As for you, you'll talk to me—and only to me—if you find out anything about his children. I want you to swear to me that you won't publish anything on the subject without my permission."

"I don't understand."

"There are truths that need time to be revealed. What if you were Ortiz's 'adopted' child? Would you want to find out all of a sudden that your birth parents were murdered, that your life has been one big web of deceit and that your entire identity, right down to your name, is false? Would you want to discover all of that just because you happened to open a newspaper? Have you ever thought about the consequences a newspaper article can have for the lives of the people involved?"

Andrew got the unpleasant feeling that Capetta's shadow was lurking in the room.

"But let's not get too carried away," Luisa said. "We have no proof that Ortiz adopted one of those stolen babies. But just in case he did, I prefer to warn you and make sure we're both on the same page."

"I promise I won't publish anything without asking you first, even though I suspect you're not telling me everything."

"We'll come to the rest of it when the time is right. Meanwhile, you should watch your step. Febres was among the cruelest of the lot. He picked 'Jungle' as his code name during the war because he boasted he was more ferocious than all the predators combined. The stories told by the few people who survived his treatment are horrifying."

"Is Febres still alive?"

"No, unfortunately."

"Why unfortunately?"

"After benefiting from the amnesty law, he spent most of the rest of his life as a free man. It was only in 2007 that he was finally brought to trial, for just four of the four hundred crimes he'd been accused of. Everyone was waiting for the verdict. This was the man who'd strapped a fifteen-month-old child to its father's chest before flicking the switch on the electric chair to make his victim talk. A few days before his trial—and by the way, he was given special treatment in prison, where he lived in princely conditions—he was found dead in his cell. Cyanide poisoning. The military were too scared he'd talk. Justice was never done. For the families of his victims, it is as if the torture continues."

Luisa spat on the floor, then continued: "The only problem is, Febres took everything he knew about the identities of the five hundred babies and children he kidnapped with him to the grave. His death has made things harder for us, but we've carried on with untiring faith and determination. This is all my way of telling you to be careful. Most of Febres's men are still alive and free, and they're prepared to go to any lengths to silence anyone who takes an interest in them. Ortiz is one of them."

"How can I prove that Ortiz is the man hiding behind Ortega?"

"Comparing photos is always useful—we'll see what's left on Marisa's film roll. But there's a difference of more than thirty years between the arrogant-looking major in my album and the 74-year-old salesman he's now become. And a mere likeness won't be enough for the courts. The best way to get what we want, though it seems impossible to me, would be to unmask him and make him confess. How? I have no idea."

"If I start investigating Ortega's past, we'll see soon enough if it stands up to scrutiny."

"You really are incredibly naive! Believe me, if Ortiz changed his identity, he didn't do it without help. His existence as Ortega will be perfectly documented, from the school where he supposedly studied to his college degree and all his jobs, including a fake army job."

Luisa stood up.

"Marisa, come and give me a hand in the kitchen," she ordered.

Left on his own in the living room, Andrew leafed through the file Luisa had left out. Each page had the photo of a soldier, his rank, the unit to which he belonged, the list of crimes he had committed and—in some cases—the real identity of the child or children he had been given. At the back of the album was a list of five hundred babies whose birth parents had disappeared. Only fifty of the names had the word "identified" next to them.

Andrew reflected that Luisa would have made a wonderful grandmother if the junta hadn't deprived her of the possibility of having grandchildren.

Luisa and Marisa reappeared a few moments later. Marisa hinted to Andrew that her aunt was tired and that it would be a good time for them to leave.

Andrew thanked Luisa for seeing him and promised to let her know if he found out anything.

Marisa was tight-lipped when they got back in the car. He could tell from the way she was driving that she was on edge. At a crossroads where a truck refused to give her the right of way, she leaned on the horn and let loose a stream of invective that even Andrew, who spoke fluent Spanish, didn't fully understand.

"Did I say something to annoy you?" he asked politely.

"There's no need to use that tone with me, Mr. Stilman. I work at a bar. I prefer when people tell things to me straight."

"What did your aunt want to tell you without me hearing?"

"I don't know what you're talking about," Marisa answered.

"She didn't ask you to follow her into the kitchen to help her clear away the glasses of lemonade. You left them on the table, and when you came back your hands were empty."

"She told me to watch out for you. She said you knew more than you were letting on, and if you were hiding things from her it meant you couldn't be fully trusted. You didn't run into me at the bar by chance, did you? You better not lie to me, unless you want to take a taxi back to the hotel and forget about me helping you anymore."

"You're right. I knew your aunt was one of the Mothers of the Plaza de Mayo, and that I'd be able to meet her through you."

"So I guess you used me as bait. That's nice to know. How did you find me?"

"Your name was in the file I was given, and the place where you work."

"Why was my name in that file?"

"I don't know any more than you do. A few months ago, my editor Olivia Stern was sent an envelope containing information about Ortiz and a couple of people who had been disappeared. There was a letter accusing Ortiz of taking part in their murder. Your name was there too, and your relationship to Luisa, with a note saying you were someone who could be trusted. Olivia was fascinated by the whole thing. She asked me to track down Ortiz and use his story to expose the dark years of the junta. It'll be the fortieth anniversary next year—a tragic landmark—and all the newspapers will be picking up on the story. Olivia likes to stay ahead of the competition. I guess that's why she's so keen on this investigation."

"Who sent that envelope to your editor?"

"She told me the information came from an anonymous source, but there was sufficient evidence in it for us to take it seriously. And so far it's all been confirmed. Olivia has her faults, and she can be hard to figure out sometimes, but she takes her job seriously."

"Sounds like the two of you are close."

"Not especially, no."

"I wouldn't call my boss by his first name."

"It's one of the privileges of age!"

"She's younger than you?"

"By a few years."

"Your boss is a woman who's younger than you? Your ego must have taken quite a beating," Marisa said, laughing.

"Could you drive me to the archives your aunt told us about?"

"If you want me to be your personal chauffeur, you're going to have to make it worth my while, Mr. Stilman."

"And I'm supposed to be the one with an ego problem?"

Marisa ground to a halt at a gas station. Her Beetle's exhaust pipe was throwing out a shower of sparks, and the engine had started making deafeningly loud sputtering noises.

While a mechanic tried to do a makeshift repair job on it—Marisa couldn't afford a new car—Andrew moved out of earshot and called the office.

Olivia was in a meeting, but her assistant insisted he hold.

"What's the news?" Olivia asked, sounding out of breath, when she came to the phone.

"Worse than last time."

"What is it? I've come out of a meeting to take your call."

"I need some extra money."

"I'm listening," Olivia said.

"Two thousand dollars."

"Are you kidding me?"

"We've got to grease some palms to get what we need."

"I'll give you half that amount and not one dollar more for the duration of your trip."

"I'll manage," replied Andrew, who hadn't hoped to get even that much.

"Is that all you have to tell me?"

"I'm leaving for Córdoba tomorrow. I have every reason to believe our man's hiding down there."

"Do you have proof that it's really him?"

"I'm following up a very promising lead."

"Call me back as soon as you have anything new—no matter how late it is. Do you have my home number?"

"It's in my notebook somewhere."

Olivia hung up.

Andrew was taken by an overwhelming desire to hear the sound of Valerie's voice, but he didn't want to disturb her at work. He'd call her that evening.

The car was ready to go, the mechanic assured them. It could do at least another few hundred miles thanks to his repair job. He had sealed up all the holes and fixed the muffler with new bolts. As Marisa rummaged in her pockets for money to pay him, Andrew handed him fifty dollars. The mechanic thanked him profusely, and even opened the car door for him.

"You didn't have to do that," Marisa said as she got behind the wheel.

"Let's just call it my contribution to the trip."

"Half that amount would have been enough. You got ripped off."

"Marisa, I really need your help," Andrew replied with a smile.

"Wait, what trip are you talking about?"

"Córdoba."

"You're even more stubborn than I am. Before you set out on that fool's errand, I've got an address for you. It's a lot nearer than Córdoba."

"Where are we going?"

"Well, I'm heading back home to get changed. I'm working

tonight. You're taking a taxi," Marisa answered, handing him a piece of paper. "This is a bar where some former Montoneros hang out. When you get there, act humble."

"What do you mean?"

"You'll see three men sitting in the back of the room playing cards. Their fourth partner never returned from his stay at ESMA. Every evening they play the same game all over again, like a ritual. Ask them politely if you can sit in the empty spot, offer to buy them a drink—only one round—and make sure you lose a little, out of courtesy. If you're too lucky, they'll send you packing. If you play too badly, they'll throw you out, too."

"What do they play?"

"Poker, with several variations that they'll explain to you. When you've won them over, talk to the bald man with a beard. He's called Alberto. He's one of the few survivors of the detention centers and was one of Febres's victims. Like many survivors, he's consumed by guilt, and it's very hard for him to talk about what happened."

"Why does he feel guilty?"

"Because he's alive while most of his friends are dead."

"How do you know him?"

"He's my uncle."

"Luisa's husband?"

"Ex-husband. They haven't spoken for a long time."

"Why?"

"That's none of your business."

"The more I know, the less likely I'll be to make a faux pas," Andrew pointed out.

"She's devoted her life to tracking down the former criminals, and he's chosen to forget the whole business. I respect both their choices."

"So why would he talk to me?"

"Because the same blood flows in our veins, and both of us tend to be very stubborn."

"Where are your parents, Marisa?"

"That's not the right question to ask, Mr. Stilman. The question I ask myself every single day is: who are my real parents? The ones who raised me, or the ones I never knew?"

Marisa pulled up to the curb and leaned across to open Andrew's door.

"You'll find a taxi at that corner over there. If you don't get back too late, stop by and see me at the bar. My shift ends around one in the morning."

* * *

The bar looked exactly as Marisa had described it. The decor was untouched by the passage of time, and several successive coats of paint had given the walls the strangest of textures. The only furniture was a handful of wooden tables and chairs. A photograph of Rodolfo Walsh, the journalist and legendary leader of the Montoneros who had been murdered by the junta, hung on the back wall. Alberto was sitting right beneath it. He was bald, and most of his face was hidden by a thick white beard. When Andrew walked over to the table where he was playing with his friends, Alberto looked up and stared at him briefly before turning wordlessly back to the game.

Andrew followed Marisa's instructions to the letter, and a few moments later the man sitting on Alberto's right invited him to join them. Jorge, the man on Alberto's left, dealt the cards and bet two pesos.

Andrew called and glanced at his hand. Jorge had dealt him three of a kind and Andrew should have raised, but, recalling Marisa's advice, he threw his cards facedown on the table. Alberto smiled.

A new hand was dealt. This time Andrew found he had a royal flush. He folded again and let Alberto take the pot, which amounted to four pesos. The next three rounds went the same way. Alberto suddenly folded before the end of the fourth round, looking Andrew straight in the eye.

"It's okay," he said. "I know who you are, why you're here, and what you want from me. You can stop letting us win by pretending to be an idiot."

His two friends roared with laughter. Alberto gave Andrew back his two pesos.

"Couldn't you tell we were cheating? Did you really think you were that lucky?"

"I was starting to suspect something . . . " Andrew replied.

"He was *starting*!" Alberto exclaimed to his friends. "You served us a glass of friendship and that's all it takes for us to have a conversation, even if we're not friends yet. So you think you can get your hands on Major Ortiz, do you?"

"That's the plan," Andrew said, putting down his glass of Fernet and Coke.

"I'm not too happy you're mixing my niece up in this business. This search you're undertaking is a dangerous one. But she's more stubborn than a mule, and I can't get her to change her mind."

"I won't let her take any risks, I promise you."

"Don't make promises you won't be able to keep. You have no idea what these men are capable of. If he was here," Alberto said, pointing to the portrait on the wall above his head, "he could tell you about it. He was a journalist, like you, but he took risks that put his life in danger. They shot him down like a dog. He stood up to them before their bullets mowed him down."

Andrew looked at the photograph. There was something charismatic about Walsh. He seemed to be gazing off toward the horizon from behind his glasses. He reminded Andrew of his own father.

"Did you know him?" Andrew asked.

"Let the dead rest in peace. Tell me what this article of yours is about."

"I haven't written it yet, and I don't want to make promises I won't be able to keep. Ortiz is the linchpin of my article. My editor finds his life story very intriguing."

Alberto shrugged.

"It's funny how newspapers always find the torturers more interesting than the heroes. I guess the smell of shit sells better than the perfume of roses. As discreet as you've been, he'll be on his guard by now. You'll never catch him in his lair, and he doesn't go anywhere unaccompanied."

"That's not very encouraging."

"We can fix things so you're on equal terms."

"Fix things how?"

"Some of my friends are still in good shape, and they'd love to see Ortiz and his stooges brought to justice."

"Sorry, I haven't come here to orchestrate any settling of scores. I just want to question the man."

"As you wish. I've no doubt he'll welcome you into his living room and serve you tea while telling you all about his past. And he says he won't put my niece at risk!" Alberto guffawed, exchanging a look with his fellow poker players.

He leaned across the table, bringing his face close to Andrew's.

"Listen up if you don't want your trip to be a waste of time for us all, young man. You'll have to be very convincing to get Ortiz to tell you his secrets. I don't mean using excessive force—that won't be necessary. Anyone who did what he did is a coward. When they're not in a pack, their balls shrink to the size of hazelnuts. All you have to do is intimidate him a little, and he'll be spilling his story out between sobs. But if you show him you're scared, he'll kill you without the slightest compunction and throw what's left of you to the dogs."

"I'll keep your advice in mind," Andrew said, preparing to get up.

"Sit down. I haven't finished."

Andrew was annoyed by the imperious way Marisa's uncle was talking to him, but he didn't want to make an enemy of the man, so he obeyed.

"Luck is on your side," Alberto told him.

"Not if the cards are rigged."

"I wasn't talking about our card game. There's a general strike planned on Tuesday, and all flights will be grounded. Ortiz won't have any choice but to drive to Buenos Aires to meet his client."

As he listened to Alberto, Andrew realized Marisa had been reporting every single one of his moves back to Alberto.

"Even if he's traveling with an escort, it's on that road you stand the best chance of trapping him. If, of course, you let us give you a hand."

"It's not that I don't want your help," Andrew said. "But I don't want any violence."

"Who said anything about violence? Funny kind of journalist you are, always thinking with your fists. I think with my head, you know."

Andrew looked at him doubtfully.

"I know Route 8 well," Alberto went on. "I've taken it so many times that I could describe the scenery all the way to Córdoba with my eyes closed. The road goes through miles and miles of featureless landscape, and it's very poorly maintained—there are far too many accidents on it. Marisa's nearly lost her life on it once, and I don't want that happening again. Understand this, Mr. Journalist: that man's friends attacked my niece, and the time when they can get away with something like that is over.

"A few miles from Gahan, the road splits in two around a large crucifix. There are some silos on the right—you can hide behind them while you're waiting. My comrades will arrange for Ortiz's tires to go flat at precisely that spot. With all the junk that falls off passing trucks, they won't be suspicious."

"Okay, what next?"

"There's only ever one spare wheel in a car, and if you find yourself in the middle of the night in a place where you can't get a cell phone signal, what choice do you have apart from walking as far as the nearest village to look for help? Ortiz will send his men and stay in the car."

"How can you be sure of that?"

"A former officer like him never loses his arrogance or the high opinion he has of himself. If he walked through the mud alongside his henchmen, he'd be lowering himself to their level. I could be wrong, but I know a lot of guys like him."

"Fine, so Ortiz is alone in the car. How long do we have before his men come back?"

"Probably a quarter of an hour walking either way, plus the time they'll need to wake up a mechanic in the middle of the night. You'll have all the time you need to grill him."

"Are you sure he'll be traveling at night?"

"Dumesnil is a seven-hour drive from Buenos Aires— another three if there's heavy traffic. Believe me, he'll leave after dinner. One man will drive, another will be his bodyguard and the man you presume to be Ortiz will be sleeping peacefully in the back seat. He'll want to get through the suburbs before daylight, and start driving back as soon as his meeting's over."

"It's a thorough plan, except for one little detail: if all the tires on his car blow simultaneously, it'll go crashing into a wall, with him inside."

"Except that there are no walls in that spot! Only fields and the silos I told you about, but they're too far from the road."

Andrew rubbed his forehead, reflecting on Alberto's proposal. He looked up at the photograph of Walsh and stared at it as if he was trying to read his dead colleague's thoughts.

"Dammit, man, if you want the truth you have to have the courage to go looking for it!" Alberto exhorted.

"Okay, I'm in. But Marisa and I will be the only ones interrogating Ortiz. I want your word that none of your men will use the opportunity to settle their scores with him."

"We survived those barbarians without turning into them. Don't insult the people who are trying to help you."

Andrew got up and held his hand out to Alberto. After a moment's hesitation, Alberto took it.

"How do you like Marisa?" Alberto asked, gathering up his cards.

"I'm not sure I understand your question."

"And I'm sure you do."

"She's a lot like you, Alberto. And you're definitely not my type."

* * *

Back at the hotel, Andrew stopped at the bar. It was packed. Marisa was racing from one end of the bar to the other juggling orders. The open collar of her white shirt showed her cleavage each time she bent down, and the clients on the bar stools were lapping up each glimpse. Andrew studied her for a long moment. He glanced at his watch. It was one in the morning. He sighed and went up to his room.

* * *

There was a stink of stale tobacco and cheap air freshener in the room. Andrew lay down on top of the bedspread. It was late to call Valerie, but he missed her.

"Did I wake you up?" he asked.

"There's no need to whisper, you know. I was about to go to sleep, but I'm glad you called. I was starting to worry."

"It's been a long day," Andrew said.

"Is everything going the way you want?"

"What I want is to be lying there next to you."

"But if you were, you'd be dreaming of being in Argentina."

"Don't say that."

"I miss you."

"I miss you too."

"Is your work going well?"

"I can't really tell. Maybe tomorrow . . . "

"Maybe what tomorrow?"

"Will you come and join me here this weekend?"

"I'd love to, but I don't think the subway stops at Buenos Aires. And anyway, I'm on call this weekend."

"Any chance you could call on me?"

"Are the Argentine girls that gorgeous?"

"I wouldn't know. I don't look at them."

"Liar."

"I miss your smile too."

"Who said I was smiling? Okay, I was smiling. Come back soon."

"I'll let you get back to sleep. I'm sorry I woke you up. I needed to hear your voice."

"Is everything okay, Andrew?"

"Yeah, I think so."

"You can call me back anytime if you can't get to sleep, okay?"

"I know. I love you."

"I love you too."

Valerie hung up. Andrew walked over to the window of his room. He spotted Marisa coming out of the hotel. For some reason he hoped she'd turn around, but Marisa got into her Beetle and drove off.

* * *

Andrew was woken by the telephone ringing. He had no idea where he was or what time it was.

"Don't tell me you were still sleeping at 11 in the morning?" Simon asked.

"No," Andrew lied, rubbing his eyes.

"Were you out partying all night? If you say yes, I'm taking the first flight out."

"I had a bad nightmare and then I couldn't get back to sleep until the early hours."

"Yeah, yeah. I'll believe that when I see it. While you're having a ball down there, I've been busy here in Chicago."

"Shit, I'd forgotten."

"I hadn't. Are you interested in what I have to tell you?"

Andrew was suddenly overtaken by a violent fit of coughing, and found himself gasping for breath. Glancing at the palm of his hand, he was alarmed to see it covered in blood. He managed to apologize to Simon and tell him he'd call back later before rushing into the bathroom.

He was horrified by the sight of his reflection in the mirror. His skin was deathly pale. His face looked drawn, and his sunken eyes made his cheekbones stand out. He felt like he'd aged thirty years in the course of the night. He began coughing again, and saw that were specks of blood on the mirror. Andrew felt dizzy. His legs were turning to jelly. He clutched at the edge of the sink and lowered himself to his knees before toppling to the floor.

The touch of the cold tiles against his cheeks revived him slightly. He managed to turn over on his back and stared up at the flickering ceiling light.

He heard the sound of footsteps in the corridor and hoped it was the maid. Unable to call out for help, he tried to grab hold of the hair dryer cord, dangling a few inches away. He strained towards it with all his might, arm outstretched, and managed to touch it, but the cord slipped out of his fingers, swinging gently to and fro before his helpless gaze.

Someone slid a key into the door of his room. Andrew worried the maid might go away if she thought the room was occupied. He attempted to maneuver himself upright with a hand on the rim of the bathtub, but froze when he heard two men whispering on the other side of the bathroom door.

They were searching his room—he recognized the squeak of the closet door when it was opened. He stretched out a hand again to get hold of the damn hair dryer. It was the only weapon he could think of.

He yanked on the cord and the hair dryer landed on the floor with a thud. The voices immediately went silent. Andrew struggled to a sitting position and leaned against the bathroom door, pressing his feet against the tub and pushing back as hard as he could to make sure the men couldn't open the door.

He was hurled forward as an almighty kick splintered the latch and flung the bathroom door inwards.

A man grabbed him by the shoulders and tried to force him down. Andrew struggled; the dizziness disappeared as fear sharpened his senses. He managed to send a punch flying into his attacker's face. The man wasn't expecting it, and he fell into the tub. Andrew got up and pushed the second man, who was flinging himself at him. He grabbed the bottle of liquid soap sitting on the sink and threw it at the man, who ducked. The bottle shattered on the tiles. Two right hooks to his face sent Andrew flying back against the mirror and split open his eyebrow. Blood spurted from the wound and blurred his vision. It was an unequal fight; Andrew didn't stand a chance. The bigger of the two attackers pushed him face-down on the ground. The other man took a knife out of his pocket and stuck it into Andrew's lower back. Andrew screamed out in pain. With one last effort, he picked up a shard of broken glass from the bottle and cut the arm of the man trying to strangle him.

The man let out a cry of pain. As he moved back, he slipped on the soap that had spilled all over the floor, and his elbow knocked against the fire alarm button. A siren went off with a deafening shriek, and the two men bolted.

Andrew slid down the wall. Sitting on the floor, he touched his back. His hand came away covered in blood. The ceiling light was still flickering when he lost consciousness.

19

I f you were so keen on meeting Antonio, all you had to do was ask," Marisa quipped as she walked into the hospital room. Andrew just stared at her.

"I know, not exactly the time to be making jokes. Sorry," she said. "Wow, those guys really messed you up. But the resident says you were very lucky."

"All depends how you look at it. I had a knife blade miss my kidney by a couple of inches. Strange concept of luck that doctor has."

"The police say you must have been the target of some thieves. The cop I talked to told me it's happening more and more often. They're looking for laptops, passports, and other valuables that tourists leave in their hotel rooms."

"Do you believe that version of events?"

"No."

"That makes two of us."

"Did you have a laptop in your room?"

"I work the old-fashioned way, with notebooks and pens."

"In that case they left empty-handed. I've picked up your stuff. It'll be safe at my place."

"Did you get my notebooks?"

"Yes."

Andrew gave a sigh of relief.

"You'll need your rest if you want to question Ortiz on Tuesday," Marisa said. "Still want to take the civilized approach?"

"I didn't come all the way here to rest," Andrew protested,

trying to sit up. He winced in pain, and felt his head start to spin. Marisa came closer and held him steady. She rearranged his pillows, lowered him into a more comfortable position and poured him a glass of water.

"I already have one in the hospital," she sighed. "I should've been a nurse, not a bartender."

"How's your boyfriend?"

"They're going to operate on him again next week."

"What about me? What do the doctors say?"

"They say you should take it easy for a few days, Mr. Stilman," Dr. Herrera said, coming into the room. "You've had a lucky escape."

He walked over to the bed and peered at Andrew's face.

"You could have lost that eye. Fortunately there was no damage to the crystalline lens or the cornea. You'll get off with a bruise. It'll go away on its own, but you might not be able to open your eye for a few days. We also stitched up a serious cut on your lower back. My colleague has already reassured your friend here about that. You're not dying, but you're also not in the best shape. I'm keeping you here under observation. I want to run a few tests."

"What kind of tests?"

"The kind I think are necessary. I suspect you might have internal bleeding somewhere. How were you feeling before this happened?"

"Not exactly in top form," Andrew admitted.

"Have you had health problems lately?"

Andrew pondered the question. "Lately" wasn't the right word, but he didn't see how he could tell Dr. Herrera that he was suffering the aftereffects of a fatal attack that would only take place in a few weeks' time.

"Mr. Stilman?"

"I've been having fainting fits and excruciating back pain. And I'm cold all the time."

"It could simply be a pinched nerve, though a pinched nerve is never a simple thing to fix. But I'm convinced you're losing blood somewhere, and I'm not letting you leave until I've figured out where."

"I've got to be back on my feet by Monday at the very latest."

"We'll do our best. You almost died. Just be thankful you're still alive, and in one of the best hospitals in Buenos Aires. This afternoon we'll do an abdominal ultrasound. If that doesn't show us anything, I'll send you for a CT scan. Now get some rest. I'll stop by again at the end of my shift."

Dr. Herrera left the room, leaving Andrew and Marisa on their own.

"Have you got my cell phone?" Andrew asked.

She took it out of her pocket and handed it to him.

"You should let your newspaper know," she suggested.

"Definitely not. They'll fly me back. I'd rather not have anyone know what happened."

"The police are already looking into it. They'll want to question you as soon as you're feeling better."

"They won't get very far, so why are they wasting their time?"

"Because it's the law."

"Marisa, I refuse to miss this meeting with Ortiz a second time."

"What do you mean, a second time?"

"Never mind."

"Do what the doctor says: get some rest. Maybe you'll have recovered by the weekend. I'll tell my uncle he'll have to wait for a few days."

* * *

Thursday was a succession of ultrasound exams, X-rays,

Doppler scans, and blood tests, with long stints in the waiting area outside each exam room, where Andrew had to wait his turn alongside the other patients.

He was taken back to his room in the early evening, and though they wouldn't remove the IV, which hurt like hell, he was allowed to eat a normal meal. The medical staff was kind, the nurses considerate and the food decent. He really had nothing to complain about, except that he was losing valuable time.

While he was waiting for his test results, Andrew called Valerie. He didn't say anything to her about what had happened to him. He didn't want to worry her, and he was scared she would insist on him coming home.

Marisa dropped by again on her way to the bar to start her shift. Watching her leave, Andrew felt an urge to go after her. Death had been lurking around him for so long—he was suddenly overcome with the desire to jump-start his life; he wanted to feel euphoric, high, and never come down again.

* * *

Dr. Herrera showed up around noon on Saturday with a group of medical students in tow. Andrew wasn't thrilled about being a guinea pig, but he submitted to the exam.

The cut on his eyebrow had puffed up so much he could only see out of one eye. The doctor assured him the swelling would go down within the next forty-eight hours. The kidney scan had revealed some internal bleeding but all the other results were normal. Herrera was pleased his suspicions were correct: hemorrhagic fever coupled with renal syndrome, most likely caused by a virus. The early symptoms resembled those of the flu, and were followed by headaches, muscle and lower back pain, and bleeding. There was no treatment for the disease. Andrew would recover over time, with no long-term effects.

Dr. Herrera wanted to know if Andrew had been camping in the woods. He said people usually became infected with the disease after breathing in airborne particles from rodent droppings. Andrew, who was very fond of his creature comforts, truthfully replied that it had never occurred to him to do any such thing.

"Any chance you could have hurt yourself with a tool someone might have used in the woods, then? A piece of woodcutting or hunting equipment?"

Andrew immediately thought of Olson, and his fists clenched as a desire to smash his colleague's teeth in overtook him.

"Could be," he replied, keeping his anger in check.

"Well, be more careful next time," the doctor beamed, delighted his students were witnessing this display of his knowledge. "If all goes well, I'll let you leave on Monday afternoon—that's what you wanted, right?"

Andrew nodded.

"But take things easy. The wound on your lower back isn't too serious, but you'll have to give it time to heal and make sure it doesn't get infected. When do you return to the US?"

"I'm supposed to go back at the end of next week," Andrew replied.

"I'd like you to come in for a follow-up before you get on your flight. We'll remove your stitches then. I'll see you on Monday, Mr. Stilman. Have a good weekend," the doctor said. He walked out, the students trailing after him.

* * *

A little later that afternoon, a policeman came in to take a statement from him. When he told Andrew that since there were no surveillance cameras at the hotel there was absolutely no chance the culprits could be caught, Andrew decided not to file a complaint. Relieved he could avoid unnecessary paper-work, the policeman left Andrew to convalesce in peace. In the evening, Marisa came to visit after sitting with her boyfriend all afternoon, and spent an hour at Andrew's bedside.

On Sunday, Luisa, who'd heard what had happened from her niece, came to the hospital carrying a meal she had cooked for Andrew. She spent most of the afternoon with him. He described to her some of the high points of his career as a jour-nalist, and she told him how she had come to be a Mother of the Plaza de Mayo. Then she asked if he'd met Alberto.

Andrew told her about the poker game, and Luisa fumed that all Alberto had done for the past thirty years was play poker and get fat. He was such an intelligent man, and yet he'd given up on his life, not to mention his marriage. It still made her mad.

"If only you knew what a handsome young man he used to be," she sighed. "All the neighborhood girls were after him, but I was the one he picked. I played hard to get. I let him believe he left me cold. And yet each time he talked to me or smiled at me when our paths crossed, I melted like an ice cream in the sun. But I was much too proud to let him see that."

"What made you change your attitude?" Andrew asked, amused.

"One evening . . . " Luisa began. She interrupted herself. "Did the doctor say you can have coffee?" she asked, taking a thermos out of her bag.

"He didn't say anything, but they've only given me disgust-ing herbal tea to drink since I've been here," Andrew said.

"Silence means consent!" Luisa declared. She fished out a cup and poured him some coffee. "As I was saying, one evening Alberto came to my parents' house. He rang the door-bell and asked my father for permission to take me out for a walk. It was a stifling hot December, and the humidity made it even worse. I was hovering on the second floor landing, eaves-dropping on their conversation."

"What did your father say?"

"He refused. He showed Alberto the door, telling him firmly: 'My daughter doesn't want to see you.' I used to get a kick out of wrong-footing my father every chance I got, so I ran down the stairs, threw a shawl over my shoulders—I didn't want to shock Papá *too* much—and followed Alberto out of the house. Looking back, I'm sure they cooked it up between them. My father never wanted to admit it and neither did Alberto, but the way the two of them made fun of me for years afterwards each time someone mentioned my first date with Alberto, I just know they did.

"I didn't expect to enjoy the stroll as much as I did. Alberto didn't flirt with me, not like all the other boys, who only wanted to get the girls into bed as soon as possible. He talked to me about politics, about a new world where everyone would have freedom of speech and no one would be doomed to a life of poverty. Alberto's a humanist. He's idealistic and naive, but he's also extremely generous. There was something reassuring about his deep voice, and the way he looked at me made me feel light-headed.

"We'd been so lost in conversation, we hadn't noticed that the evening had flown by. When we started back, it was well past the curfew my father had given me—he had shouted it out after us repeatedly as we were leaving. I knew Papá would be waiting for us on the doorstep, maybe even with his shot-gun filled with rock salt to fire it at Alberto and teach him a lesson. I didn't want Alberto to get in trouble, so I told him it was better if I went home on my own, but he insisted on escorting me.

"When we got to the corner of my road I asked him to pass me his handkerchief, and tied it around my ankle. Then I leaned on his shoulder and pretended to limp the rest of the way. My father calmed down as soon as he caught sight of me, and began running towards us. I told him I'd sprained my ankle, and it had taken us two hours to walk back because I'd had to stop every few hundred feet to rest. I don't know if Papá believed me, but he thanked Alberto for bringing his daughter back home safe and sound. My honor was intact, too, and that was the main thing. As for me, when I went to bed that night, all I could think of was the way I'd felt when Alberto had put his arm around me, and when my hand had touched his shoulder.

"Six months later, we were married. We didn't have much money and it wasn't easy making ends meet, but we always managed to scrape along somehow. We were happy, genuinely happy. I spent some of the best years of my life with him. We laughed so much together. And then the junta came to power, more terrifying than the previous dictatorships. Our son was twenty when they kidnapped him. We'd only had one child. Alberto never recovered from his disappearance, and neither did our marriage. We survived in our different ways. He chose to forget, and I chose to fight. Our roles were reversed.

"If you see Alberto again, you're not to tell him I talked to you about him. Is that a promise?"

Andrew promised.

"I've had trouble sleeping ever since you came to see me. Ortiz isn't one of the key people in my album. He was just a sidekick, like I told you—an officer with an unremarkable career. But now I can't help wondering if he was the one who flew the plane from which they threw my son into the Río de la Plata. I want you to find him and make him confess. There's nothing more terrible for a mother than losing her child. It's the worst tragedy any human being can suffer, a prospect more terrible than death. You can't imagine the pain of not being able to visit his grave, of never having seen his body. Knowing that the child who called you Mamá, who would run into your arms when he saw you and hug you as tight as he could . . . "

Luisa paused.

"When the child who was the light of your life disappears without a trace, when you know you'll never hear the sound of his voice again, your life becomes a living hell."

Luisa went over to the window, keeping her face averted from Andrew's gaze. She took a deep breath and continued speaking, her gaze lost in the distance.

"Alberto took refuge in oblivion. He was afraid that his suffering would drive him into blindly seeking vengeance. He didn't want to be like them. I wasn't afraid of that. A woman wouldn't have the slightest compunction about killing someone who stole her child. If I'd had the chance to do it, I would have."

Andrew thought fleetingly of Mrs. Capetta. Luisa turned back to him. Her eyes were bloodshot, but her bearing was proud.

"Find him. I'm begging you, from the bottom of my heart . . . or what's left of it."

She returned to his bedside and picked up her bag. Andrew thought as he watched her make her way out of the room that she seemed to have aged in the course of their conversation. He thought about his meeting with Ortiz all night. For the first time, he found himself hoping that Alberto's plan would work.

* * *

Andrew's phone rang in the late afternoon. The pain flared up again as he maneuvered himself around to reach it.

"When you say 'I'll call you back in five,' you . . . "

"I'm at the hospital, Simon," Andrew broke in.

"Are you visiting someone?"

"No, I'm the patient."

Andrew told Simon about the attack, and made him promise he wouldn't breathe a word to Valerie. Simon wanted to get on a flight right away, but Andrew refused to let him. He'd drawn enough attention to himself already, and if Simon came it would only complicate matters.

"I'm guessing this is not a good time to give you my report on Capetta's wife."

"On the contrary—I'm not exactly busy."

"She spends her afternoons knitting in a small park, watching her kid play in the sandbox."

"Did you talk to her?"

"When I said she spent her days knitting, I mean that's literally all she did."

"Nothing else?"

"No, except she's too beautiful to have been married to a guy like that Capetta you told me about. But that's probably just jealousy talking."

"Beautiful in what way?"

"Black hair, eyes as dark as ebony, a steely gaze, and an expression on her face that speaks of loneliness and intense suffering."

"You decided all that just by looking at her?"

"Just because I love all women it doesn't mean that I don't pay attention to individual ones."

"Simon, I know you better than that."

"Oh, all right. She was having coffee at a McDonald's, and her kid was walking back to their table carrying a tray that looked a little too heavy for him. I made it so he bumped into me—I sacrificed a perfectly good pair of jeans for you, by the way. Paolina got up and began apologizing profusely. The kid looked like he was about to burst into tears, so I made a couple of funny faces to make him laugh. I gave him ten dollars to buy himself a Coke and some nuggets, and then I asked if I could use the paper napkins on the table so I had an excuse to sit down with her until her son came back."

"That sounds a lot more like you."

"It really pains me to know that's what you think of me."

"What did she tell you?"

"She said she'd moved to Chicago after her husband died to build a new life for herself and her son."

"A son she's depriving of a father who's alive and well. Some widow!"

"The way her face hardened when she mentioned her husband made my blood run cold. There was something terrifying about her, actually."

"What?"

"I couldn't say exactly. I just felt very uncomfortable around her."

"Did she mention she was going to New York?"

"No, and when I told her as I was leaving that she should call me if she was ever in New York and needed anything at all, she said she was never going back."

"She must have thought you were coming on to her."

"Hey, if I'd come on to her, she'd have changed her mind."

"Obviously!" Andrew said sarcastically.

"Yes, obviously! But seeing as I was on my mission and all, I didn't step out of line. I was merely a businessman visiting Chicago, and a father of three in love with his wife."

"How did it feel to play the good husband and father? Not too exhausted this morning, I hope?"

"I thought I missed you, but on second thought . . . "

"Do you think she's capable of killing someone?"

"She's certainly strong-minded enough, and she lied to me about her life and her plans. There's something genuinely disturbing about her. I wouldn't go so far as to compare her to Jack Nicholson in *The Shining*, but she's got these really scary eyes. Listen, Andrew, what are you wasting your time in Buenos Aires for if you really believe someone's going to try and kill you in a few weeks?"

"I've been offered a second chance, Simon—to protect Valerie from my wandering eye, but also to carry out an investigation that's important, and not just for me. I'm even more aware of that now than I was before."

Andrew asked his friend for one last favor. As soon as he'd hung up, Simon went to buy a bouquet of flowers and had them delivered to Valerie with a note Andrew had dictated.

In his hospital room in Buenos Aires, Andrew thought he could hear a voice whisper in his ear: "If Mrs. Capetta thinks you're responsible for making her lose her daughter, you better watch out for yourself."

* * *

Andrew went through another set of tests on Monday morning, and Dr. Herrera discharged him in the early afternoon.

Marisa was waiting outside in her car. After a brief stop at the hotel they went to the bar, where Alberto was waiting for them.

Andrew went straight to the table at the back of the room. Alberto was sitting alone. He unfolded a large sheet of paper and drew Ortiz's itinerary on it.

"When he leaves Villa Maria, a broken-down truck blocking the road will force him to get off National Route 9. His driver will turn south to pick up Route 8. Meanwhile, you'll be driving to Gahan. When you reach the crucifix memorial— you'll recognize it easily, it's a statue of the Virgin Mary under a small glass pyramid, well lit, perfect for our purposes—you'll see three grain silos to your right, about fifty yards from the road. There's a small dirt track leading to them. Hide the car behind the silos and turn off the lights. You and Marisa can take turns sleeping while you're waiting.

"If Ortiz leaves Dumesnil at about 9 P.M., he'll reach Gahan around four in the morning. We'll have taken care of things by then. The road will be strewn with pieces of scrap metal. If the car keeps going after the memorial, it'll be on wheel rims."

"What if his car isn't the first one to come by?"

"There won't be anyone else on the road at that time of night."

"How can you be absolutely sure of that?"

"Our friends will be watching the exits leading out of Olivia, Chazon, Arias, Santa Émilia, Colón, and Rojas. We'll know where he is a quarter of an hour ahead of time, and we'll only booby-trap the road when we're sure he's approaching the memorial."

"There's a town called Olivia in those parts?" Andrew asked.

"Yes, why?" Alberto asked.

"No reason."

"Once his car's out of action, stay hidden until his men have started out for Gahan. You'll be no match for them if it's three against one. I'm told you had a run-in with them recently, and if the state of your face is anything to go by, I don't think you'd come out the winner in a fight."

"How do you know that both men will go for help?"

"It's better to be in company if you're going to wake a farmer up in the middle of the night. Especially around these parts. Whereas Ortiz has nothing to fear sitting in a big car by the side of an empty road."

What about me?" Marisa asked.

"You do the driving, and then you stay put in the car. I forbid you to get out of the vehicle, even if our brave journalist here gets himself shot. Do you understand that, Marisa? I mean it! If anything happened to you, your aunt would come over here and gun me down in broad daylight."

"She won't get out of the car," Andrew promised, earning himself a kick in the shin from Marisa.

"You should leave as soon as possible. Gahan is at least a two-hour drive from here, and you'll need time to scope out the area, find the hiding place and make sure you can't be seen. Ricardo's fixed you something to eat on the way. He's waiting for you in the kitchen, Marisa. Go on. I have a couple things I need to say to Mr. Stilman."

Marisa obeyed her uncle.

"Can you see this mission through?"

"We'll know that tomorrow," Andrew replied lightly.

Alberto gripped his forearm.

"I've rallied a lot of friends to make sure this operation is a success. It's not just my credibility that's at stake. My niece's safety is too."

"She's a grown woman, she knows what she's doing. But it's not too late to demand she stay behind. If I have a good road map, I shouldn't have too much trouble finding the place."

"She won't listen to me. I don't have that kind of authority over her anymore."

"I'll do my best, Alberto. And you do what you can to make sure this mission, as you call it, doesn't turn into a tragedy. Will you give me your word that none of your men will try to get even with Ortiz?"

"I already have!"

"Then it should all go smoothly."

"Take this," Alberto said, placing a gun on Andrew's knees. "You never know."

Andrew gave it back to Alberto.

"I don't think that'll keep Marisa any safer. I've never used a gun. Contrary to popular belief, not all Americans are cowboys."

Andrew made as if to get up, but Alberto signaled that the conversation wasn't over.

"Did Luisa come to see you in the hospital?"

"Who told you that?"

"I was keeping an eye on your recovery, just in case Ortiz's men had the bright idea to finish the job."

"Then you already know the answer to your question."

"Did she say anything about me?"

Andrew looked at Alberto and got up.

"We'll talk about it tomorrow, when I'm back from Gahan. Have a good evening, Alberto."

* * *

Andrew looked around for Marisa's Beetle when he came out of the bar. He heard a car horn honking and turned to see Marisa sticking her head out of the window of a Peugeot 406.

"Shall we go?" she called. "Or have you changed your mind?"

Andrew got in the car.

"My uncle thought my car wasn't sturdy enough," she explained.

"I can't imagine why he should think such a thing," Andrew replied.

"This is his car. That should tell you how much he cares about the success of our mission."

"Stop using that ridiculous word! We're not on a mission, and I work for a renowned newspaper, not the secret service. I'm going to question this Ortega and try to make him confess he's Ortiz—if he *is* Ortiz, that is."

"If you're only going to talk nonsense, then maybe you should keep your mouth shut," Marisa rejoined.

For the hundred-odd miles to Gahan, they hardly said a word to each other. Marisa was concentrating on the road. As her uncle had warned, it was in very bad condition, and there was very little light. They reached the memorial and the fork in the road towards midnight. Marisa stopped the car behind the memorial, flicked on a flashlight and swept its beam over the surroundings.

"If the tires blow out at this spot," she told Andrew, "the car will end up in that field. See? Nothing to worry about. My uncle knows what he's talking about."

Andrew got out to inspect the road, wondering when Alberto's men would step in.

"Get back in the car," Marisa ordered. "There's the dirt track leading to the silos. We should get to our hiding place. We've a long wait ahead of us, so we might as well eat something now."

She started the car up again and drove along the track that wound its way behind the silos. She parked between two of the grain stores and turned off the car lights. When his eyes grew accustomed to the darkness, Andrew realized that while they had a perfect view of the lighted area where the operation was to take place, it would be impossible for anyone to see them from the road.

"Your uncle really hasn't left anything to chance."

"Alberto was a Montonero. He fought those bastards in the days when they didn't hesitate to shoot on sight. Let's just say he's experienced. If he was your age, he'd be the one sitting in this car, not you."

"I'm not his henchman, Marisa. Get that straight once and for all."

"You've repeated that often enough. I got you loud and clear. Are you hungry?"

"Not really, no."

"Eat something anyway," she said, handing him a sandwich. "You're going to need all your strength."

She switched on the ceiling light and looked at Andrew, smiling.

"What? What's so funny?"

"You are."

"What's so funny about me?"

"From the left, you're kinda cute. But your right side looks like the Elephant Man."

"Thanks for the compliment."

"It was only half a compliment. Depends on which side you're sitting on."

"I could sit behind the wheel if you prefer."

"No way. Not that I don't like your disfigured war hero look though. It's more my style."

"I bet Antonio would be happy to hear that."

"Antonio's not handsome. But he's a good guy."

"That's really none of my business."

"What about you? Is your wife pretty?"

"That's really none of your business either."

"We're going to be spending most of the night in this car. What do you want to talk about? The weather?"

"Valerie's very pretty."

"I'd have been surprised if that wasn't the case."

"Why?"

"Because I think you're the kind of guy who's proud of walking around with a beautiful woman on his arm."

"You're wrong. When we met each other in junior high, I was no ladies' man. I was shy, and I had no idea how to flirt with girls. I still don't."

Marisa's cell vibrated in her pocket. She took it out and read the text message she'd just received.

"The truck ploy at the Villa Maria exit worked. Ortiz's car is heading for Route 8. They'll be here in four hours, tops."

"I thought you couldn't get a cell phone signal here?"

"When it's time, I won't. The only exchange in the region is twelve miles away, and once the power's been cut off, the phones will stop working."

Andrew smiled.

"Maybe you were right. This evening *is* feeling more and more like a mission."

"Doesn't sound like that bothers you too much."

"Give me that sandwich. And stop making fun of me all the time, unless you want me to start finding you attractive."

Marisa twisted around and reached into the back seat. Andrew couldn't help but admire her butt.

"Here, have some coffee," she said, handing him a paper cup.

An hour later, they heard the noise of an engine in the distance. Marisa switched off the light.

"It's too early for it to be Ortiz," Andrew murmured.

She burst out laughing.

"You're right to whisper, can't be too careful. We're only fifty yards from the road and they might hear us . . . No, that can't be Ortiz."

"So why did you turn off the light?"

Before Andrew could figure out what was happening, Marisa had swung her legs over the gearshift and straddled him. She stroked his lips with her fingertips, and then she kissed him.

"Ssssh," she whispered. "You're getting married, and so am I. There's no danger of us falling in love."

"You're pretty talkative for someone who's telling *me* to shut up."

Marisa kissed Andrew again. They clambered into the back seat and slid into each other's arms in the silence of the night.

* * *

Marisa reopened her eyes, glanced at her watch and dug her elbow into Andrew's ribs.

"Wake up and get dressed, it's three in the morning!"

Andrew started. Marisa whipped her cell out of her pocket. There were six new text messages, each announcing the name of a village Ortiz had passed through. She looked at the screen again and scrambled into the front seat.

"I can't get a signal anymore: they've already cut off the power supply to the exchange. Ortiz can't be far now. Hurry up!"

Andrew pulled on his pants and sweater and climbed back into the passenger seat. They sat there in total silence. He turned his head to look at Marisa. She was staring intently at the road.

"Look at the road, that's where it'll all be happening!"

"What about what happened in the back seat?" Andrew asked.

"Nothing happened. It was just two consenting adults having a good time."

"How good?" Andrew asked, smiling.

Marisa gave him a poke with her elbow.

"Do you think your uncle's friends saw us when they came to sprinkle that scrap metal over the road?"

"Let's hope they didn't—it wouldn't be good for either of us. Now just pray we haven't missed Ortiz."

"If his car had already gone past it'd be there in the middle of the road, wouldn't it? Do you see a car?"

Marisa didn't answer. They heard the sound of an approaching engine. Andrew could feel his heart beating faster.

"What if it isn't them?" he croaked.

"Collateral damage. Unfortunate, but sometimes inevitable."

As Andrew sat there fretting, a black sedan sped toward the crucifix memorial. As it approached, three of its tires blew out. The driver tried to hold a straight course, but the car swerved sharply and started weaving before landing on its side. It slid forward until the front fender got stuck in a pothole. The back of the car lifted and the sedan flipped over several times with a deafening crash of metal. The windscreen shattered as the front passenger went right through it. The upside-down car continued its crazy forward skid, shooting out a trail of sparks, and finally shuddered to a stop on the edge of a field.

The cacophony of the crash was replaced by a deathly silence.

"It was all supposed to go smoothly," Andrew said angrily, starting to get out of the station wagon.

Marisa grabbed hold of his arm and forced him to sit down again. The look on her face was hard, determined. She turned the key in the ignition and drove down the dirt track. She stopped on the side of the road and turned on the headlights, revealing a scene of total devastation. A man was lying a few yards from the wreck. Andrew ran towards him. He was badly injured, but he was still breathing. Marisa walked over to the smashed car. The driver was unconscious, his face covered in blood. In the back, trapped in the wreckage of the car, a dazed man lay groaning.

Andrew joined Marisa and leaned into what was left of the car.

"Give me a hand," he told Marisa. "We have to get him out of there before the car goes up in flames."

Marisa crouched down and stared coldly at the wounded man.

"Did you hear that? The car's going to start burning. We've got some questions to ask you. You better answer them quick if you don't want to be roasted like a pig in there."

"Who are you? What do you want from me?" the man moaned.

"We're asking the questions. You just answer them."

"For Chrissake, Marisa, stop that bullshit and help me, there's been enough damage already," Andrew shouted, trying to pull the wounded man out of the wreck.

"Leave him right there until he starts talking. What's your name?" she asked.

"Miguel Ortega."

"Yeah, and I'm Evita Perón! I'm going to give you one more chance," she said, putting a cigarette between her lips. She took a box of matches out of her pocket, struck one and moved the flame close to Ortega's face.

"My name's Miguel Ortega!" he shouted. "You're crazy! Get me out of here!"

"Try harder. It's really starting to stink of gas in here," she said.

Andrew was trying with all his might to pull Ortega out, but the old man's legs were trapped under the driver's seat. He couldn't do it without Marisa's help.

"Come on, we're getting out of here," Marisa said, letting her match drop inside the car. The flame flickered and went out. Marisa lit another match and set the box on fire, holding it with her fingertips.

Ortiz looked at the flames dancing above his head.

"Ortiz," he said. "My name's Felipe Ortiz. Put that out, I beg you. I have a family. Don't do it!"

Marisa flung the matchbox into the distance, then turned back and spat on Major Ortiz's face.

Andrew was fuming. Marisa slipped inside the car and pushed at the driver's seat. Andrew managed to pull Ortiz free. He dragged him a little way up the road, away from the car.

"We have to get the driver out," he said.

As he was walking back towards the sedan, sparks started shooting out from under the hood. The next moment, the car was ablaze. He saw the flames licking at the driver's body and caught a glimpse of his distorted face before a cloud of smoke obscured the nightmarish scene.

Andrew clutched his head and dropped to his knees. He threw up. When he had stopped shaking, he got up and walked back to where Ortiz was lying on the shoulder. Marisa was crouched next to him, smoking.

"We're taking him to the hospital," Andrew ordered. "The other man, too."

"Nope," Marisa said, swinging the station wagon keys. "And if you get any closer, I'll chuck these into the field."

"Isn't one death enough for you?"

"One? Compared to three thousand? No, it's not enough. The game has run into overtime, and now I'm ahead. If this sonofabitch wants to stay alive, he's going to have to talk. Get out your notebook and pen, Mr. Journalist. This is your moment of glory!"

"Take me to the hospital," Ortiz begged. "Please, I'll tell you whatever you want to know on the way."

Marisa got up and walked over to the station wagon. She opened the glove compartment and came back with Alberto's revolver. She pressed the barrel against Ortiz's temple and cocked the hammer.

"Shall we start the interview?" she asked Andrew. "See all that blood pouring out of his leg? I wouldn't waste any more time if I were you."

"Are you going to shoot me if I refuse to go along with this crap?" Andrew snapped.

"No, I like you too much to do that, but I'd have no problem at all taking him out. In fact I'd probably enjoy it."

Andrew knelt down next to Ortiz.

"Let's get this over with as soon as possible so I can take you to the hospital. I'm sorry. I didn't want it to happen this way."

"Do you think he was sorry when he had the brake lines cut on Antonio's car? Or when he sent his goons to your hotel room?"

"You were in my world and you were asking everyone questions," Ortiz protested. "We only wanted to dissuade you, give you a scare, not hurt you."

"Yeah, sure," Marisa scoffed. "You can tell that to Antonio

when you're lying next to him in the hospital. We wanted to give you a scare too, so I guess we're even. Take a look at my friend here. See how your men rearranged his face? So we're not even after all."

"I had nothing to do with that. I don't even know who you are."

Andrew was convinced Ortiz was being sincere; he genuinely didn't seem to know who he was.

"My name's Andrew Stilman, and I'm a reporter with *The New York Times*. I'm investigating the career of a pilot and certain things he did during the junta. Are you Major Ortiz, who served as a coast guard pilot from 1977 to 1983?"

"To November 29, 1979," Ortiz corrected him. "I never flew a plane again after that date."

"Why?"

"Because I could no longer stomach what I was being ordered to do."

"What kind of missions did you fly, Major Ortiz?"

Ortiz sighed. "It's been a long time since anyone called me 'Major.'"

Marisa pressed the revolver against his cheek.

"We don't give a shit about your nostalgia. Just answer the question."

"I flew surveillance flights along the border with Uruguay."

Marisa slid the revolver down Ortiz's body and stroked the gaping wound on his leg with the barrel. Ortiz screamed out in pain. His leg was broken. Andrew shoved her out of the way.

"You do that one more time and I'll leave you here on your own; you'll have to walk all the way back to Buenos Aires," he said icily. "Is that clear?"

"My, my. How unfriendly we're being, Mr. Stilman," she pouted, giving him a flirty look.

"Take me to the hospital," Ortiz begged.

Andrew got out his notebook and pen.

"Did you take part in the death flights, Major Ortiz?"

"Yes," he whispered.

"How many of those flights did you make?"

"Thirty-seven," he murmured.

"If you count twenty passengers per flight, that's over seven hundred people this bastard tossed into the Río de la Plata," Marisa said.

"I couldn't see what was going on in the back from my place in the cockpit, but I knew. Whenever the plane suddenly got lighter and started to climb, I knew what had happened. I just obeyed orders. I'd have been shot if I refused. What would you have done in my place?"

"I would have died rather than be part of anything so horrific," said Marisa.

"You're young. You don't know what you're taking about. You don't understand the meaning of authority. I was a career soldier, programmed to serve my country and obey without question. You don't know what it was like in those days."

"You piece of shit. My real parents were among the people you tortured and murdered."

"I never tortured anyone. They were dead or dying by the time they were put on my plane. And if I'd tried to play the hero, I'd have been executed, my family would have been arrested, and another pilot would have taken my place."

"So why did you stop flying in 1979?" Andrew asked.

"I couldn't do it anymore. I was only an ordinary soldier, a normal man, and not an especially courageous one at that. I wasn't capable of openly defying my superiors. I was too scared of the consequences for my family.

"One evening, I tried to nosedive my plane into the river, with its cargo and the three officers on board. It was night, and we were flying at a very low altitude with all our lights out. I only had to push the joystick forward. But my copilot managed to wrest back control at the last minute. When we returned to base, he reported me. I was put under arrest and court-martialed. A military doctor saved me from the firing squad. He testified that I was no longer in my right mind, and therefore couldn't be held responsible for what I'd done. Luckily I was on Febres's good side. And I wasn't the only soldier who'd started cracking up. He was afraid that if he had me shot it would encourage others to desert, but showing mercy to an officer who had served his country would earn him the sympathy of his men. I was discharged and told I could return to civilian life."

"You took part in the murder of more than seven hundred people, remember? You hardly expect us to feel sympathy for you, do you?" Marisa sneered.

"Not in the least. Those unseen faces have haunted me for the past thirty years."

"How did you build yourself a new identity? How have you managed to remain anonymous for all these years?" Andrew asked.

"The army protected itself by protecting the men who'd served it. After the dirty war ended, Febres helped us. We were given new papers, a reconstituted past, and a piece of land or a small business to start over."

"Land and businesses that were stolen from their rightful owners!" Marisa shouted.

"You're Alberto's niece, aren't you?" Ortiz asked.

"Well, you may be a civilian, but it seems your intelligence service is as good as ever."

"I don't have access to any intelligence. I'm just a humble businessman with a small tannery. I guessed who you were the minute I saw you snooping around Dumensil. You look like him, you talk like him . . . That crafty fox has been tracking me for a long, long time, but he's become too old to do the job himself."

"That'll do for now," Andrew said, putting his notebook away. "Go get the car, Marisa. We're taking him with us, and the

248 - MARC LEVY

other one too—let's hope he's still alive. And hurry up unless you want to get left behind."

Marisa shrugged, put her gun away and strolled towards the station wagon with her hands in her pockets.

"I didn't send those men to your hotel," Ortiz said as soon as he was alone with Andrew. "I'm sure it was Alberto. That man is a lot more deceitful than you think. He's been manipulating you from the start, to get you to do what he couldn't. He was the one who set up this ambush, wasn't he? You're only a pawn in his game."

"Shut up, Ortiz! You don't know what you're talking about. It wasn't Alberto who made me come to Argentina. I've been on your trail for weeks, ever since I was given this story."

"Why were you on my trail and not somebody else's?"

"Chance. Your name was mentioned in the tip we got at the newspaper."

"And who sent you that file, Mr. Stilman? I'm seventy-seven years old, my health is failing. It wouldn't bother me at all to spend the last few years of my life in prison; the penance would almost come as a relief. But I have two daughters, Mr. Stilman. They've done nothing wrong, and the younger one knows absolutely nothing about my past. If you reveal my identity it's not me you'll be punishing, it's her. Tell the story of the despicable Major Ortiz if you must, but I beg you not to quote me. And if it's revenge you want, leave me here on this roadside to bleed to death. It'll be a release. You don't know how heavy a price one pays for contributing to destroying innocent lives. It's not too late for you."

Andrew took his notebook out again and flipped through the pages until he found the photograph he'd tucked in there. He showed it to Ortiz.

"Do you recognize this little girl?"

Ortiz peered at the face of the two-year-old child in the photograph and his eyes filled with tears.

"Yes. I raised her."

* * *

The car sped along Route 7. Ortiz had fainted when Andrew and Marisa laid him out in the back of the station wagon, and his bodyguard wasn't holding up well either.

"How far is the nearest hospital?" Andrew asked, glancing back at their two wounded passengers.

"There's one in San Andrés de Giles, twenty-five miles away. We'll be there in half an hour."

"You'll have to get us there quicker if you want them to still be alive."

Marisa stepped hard on the gas pedal.

"It'd be nice if the two of us were alive too," said Andrew, clutching his seat.

"Don't worry. Now that he's confessed I don't want him to die anymore. He'll stand trial and pay for his crimes."

"I'd be very surprised if that happened."

"Why?"

"What do you think you're going to tell the judge? That you got Ortiz to confess by holding a gun to his head? And will you say that before or after you reveal that we deliberately caused an accident that led to a man's death? But maybe the judge will take a lenient view. We could always ask him to put us in the same cell as Ortiz so we can continue our interrogation."

"What are you talking about?"

"That you've gotten so used to cheating, you and your uncle, you've forgotten that in the world outside that crummy bar of his, there are laws you can't flout. We're responsible for a murder, possibly two, if we don't get to the hospital in time. I don't even know if I'll be able to publish my article!"

"It was a car accident and we had nothing to do with it. We

were passing by and we helped these two men. That's the only story you'll be telling."

"That's the story we'll tell when we get to the emergency room. Unless of course Ortiz comes to and denounces us before we've had time to escape."

"Are you giving up?"

"How am I supposed to justify the way I obtained my information? You want me to tell the editorial board that I was part of a premeditated massacre? They'll love that; it'll be great for the newspaper's reputation. You and your uncle have gotten me into deep trouble. Not to mention weeks of work down the drain."

Marisa braked as hard as she could. The tires squealed, and the car swerved to a stop across the middle of the road.

"You can't give up."

"What else do you want me to do? Spend ten years in an Argentine prison waiting for justice to be done? Just start driving before I really lose my temper, throw you out of this car and leave you behind. Get moving!"

Marisa shifted into first gear and the car moved forward. Ortiz had started moaning in back.

"That's all we need," Andrew sighed. "Give me that gun of yours."

"Are you going to bump him off?"

"No. Will you give me a break and stop talking bullshit?"

"In the glove box."

Andrew picked up the gun and turned around with every intention of knocking Ortiz out cold. He slowly lowered his arm.

"I can't do it."

"Hit him, for Chrissake. If he breathes a word, we're screwed."

"We should have thought about that earlier. In any case, he'll denounce us as soon as he's regained consciousness."

"At least that'll give you enough time to leave the country. You can get on the first flight back to New York."

"What about you? He knows who you are."

"I'll figure something out."

"No, it's out of the question. We got into this madness together, and we'll get out of it together."

Andrew put the gun back in the glove box.

"I think I have an idea. Step on it. And don't talk. I need to think."

By the time the station wagon screeched to a halt in front of the hospital, Ortiz had passed out again. Marisa blew the horn and yelled at the two nurses who came running out of the double doors to bring another stretcher. She told the doctor on duty that they had come upon an accident scene in the vicinity of Gahan. She and her friend had managed to pull these two men out of the car, but the driver had died in the fire. The doctor asked a nurse to call the police. He gave orders for the accident victims to be wheeled into the operating room, and told Marisa to wait until he returned. Marisa assured him she'd be back as soon as she had parked the car.

* * *

"What do we do now?" she asked as they swung back onto the road.

"Now we wait."

"Sounds like a brilliant idea."

"We don't want him to tell our story, and he doesn't want us to tell his. A policeman friend of mine once said to me that if you've arrested your culprit but you haven't understood his motives, your job's only half done. If Ortiz denounces us he'll have to explain why we set that trap for him. We're bound to him by our shared secret. As soon as he's on the way to recovery, I'll go back and make a deal with him."

"So he's going to get away with it, just like that?"

"We'll see who has the last word. Your uncle's not the only one who likes playing games."

20

I t was early morning by the time Marisa dropped Andrew off at his hotel.

"I'm going to return the car to Alberto," she said. "See you later."

"Is it really his car?"

"What difference does it make?"

"If there was a surveillance camera at that hospital, he'd be well advised to get rid of it and report it stolen as soon as possible."

"Don't worry, our rural hospitals are too poor to afford cameras. But I'll tell him."

Andrew got out and leaned down to the window.

"Marisa, I know you won't listen to me, but don't tell your uncle just yet that I've found a way to make Ortiz keep his mouth shut."

"What are you scared of?"

"It's the two of us who are on the front line. Alberto was hiding in his bar the whole time. Trust me, just this once."

Marisa roared off. He stood there and watched until the station wagon disappeared.

* * *

Andrew asked for his room key at reception. The manager came out to apologize personally, assuring him nothing of the kind had ever happened before in his hotel. Security measures were being put in place to ensure it would never happen again. He begged Andrew's forgiveness, and informed him he'd had his things moved to a junior suite on the top floor.

It was hardly comparable to a suite in a luxury hotel, but it had a small living room, and a nicer view of the street. The bathroom taps weren't leaking, and the bed was a lot more comfortable. Andrew opened his suitcase to make sure nothing was missing. As he rifled through the contents, he felt a small bump in the side pocket. He opened the zipper and found a miniature steam engine inside—the one he'd hankered after at the antique shop in Williamsburg. There was a rolled-up bit of paper sticking out of the smokestack. He extracted it and smoothed it out.

I miss you. I love you. Valerie.

Andrew lay down on the bed, placed the engine on the pillow next to him and fell asleep looking at it.

* * *

He was woken in the early afternoon by someone knocking on his door. He went to open it and found Alberto standing outside.

"I didn't think you ever left that bar of yours," Andrew said.

"Only on special occasions," Alberto replied.

"Ortiz accuses you of sending those goons to my hotel room."

Alberto's eyes narrowed. "Get dressed, I'm taking you out to lunch."

Out on the street, Andrew smiled when he saw Alberto's car—a Japanese make, not the station wagon.

"I took your advice," said Alberto. "Anyway, that old car had clocked up more than 120,000 miles. It was about time I got a new one."

"I hope you didn't come here just to show me your new car."

"Oh, this one's borrowed. I came to apologize to you. The last thing I wanted was for a man to lose his life."

"I warned you."

"I know. You should leave Argentina before the police catch up with you. I told Marisa to lay low in the countryside until things blow over."

"Did she agree?"

"No, she doesn't want to lose her job. If it becomes really necessary, I'll write to her aunt to ask her to intervene. Marisa will listen to her. It's different for you—you're a foreigner, and it'll be more complicated for you to flee the country later. There's no point taking risks."

Alberto parked in front of a bookshop.

"I thought we were going out to lunch."

"We are. There's a restaurant in the back. This place belongs to a friend of mine so we'll be able to talk in peace."

The bookshop was a charming place. A long corridor lined with bookshelves led to a patio where a few tables were laid out. The owner was serving meals to a handful of regulars who sat surrounded by hundreds of books. Alberto greeted his friend, found a table and motioned to Andrew to sit down across from him.

"Luisa and I separated because I'm a coward, Mr. Stilman. It was my fault our son . . . disappeared. I was an activist during the Dirty War. I didn't do anything particularly heroic. I merely contributed to putting together an underground opposition newspaper. We had hardly any money, just determination and a copy machine—not much, you see, but we felt we were doing what we could to resist. The military managed to flush out a few of my comrades. They were arrested, tortured, and disappeared. Those who fell into their hands never talked."

"Do you remember if one of them was named Rafael?" Andrew asked.

Alberto stared at Andrew before replying.

"Maybe. I don't know. It was forty years ago, and we didn't all know each other."

"What about his wife, Isabel?"

"I told you, I don't remember," Alberto repeated, his voice rising briefly. "I've done my best to forget. My son Manuel was kidnapped shortly after the raids that decimated our ranks. He had nothing to do with any of it. He was just an ordinary mechanical engineering student. Febres wanted to get at me through him. That's what Luisa thinks, anyway. Febres must have believed I'd give myself up to get Manuel out. I didn't."

"Not even to save your son?"

"No. I had to save my friends. I knew I wouldn't be strong enough not to give up their names if I was tortured a second time. And in any case, they wouldn't have freed Manuel. They never released any of their prisoners. Luisa's never forgiven me for it."

"Did she know about the newspaper?"

"She used to write most of the articles in it."

Alberto fell silent.

"Did you send those men, Alberto?"

The old man didn't look up. He took out his wallet, extracted a yellowing photo of a young man and handed it to Andrew.

"Luisa's child was stolen from her. The whole world is guilty in her opinion. See what a handsome boy Manuel was? He was brave and generous, and so funny. He loved his mother more than anything. I know he didn't talk either . . . he wanted to protect her. He knew about her activities. You should have seen the two of them together. We had a more distant relationship, my son and I, but he was the person I loved most in the world, even though I never knew how to show it. I wish I could have seen him again one last time. I would have told him how proud I was of him, how happy he'd made me as a father, how much his absence has weighed on me since he left us.

"My life stopped the day they took him away from us. Luisa

has no tears left. As for me, my tears flow each time I see a boy his age in the street. More than once I've followed a young man who looked like him in the hope that he'd turn around and call me Papá. Sadness can drive you insane, Mr. Stilman, and it's only now I realize that I never should have done what I did. Manuel won't ever come back. I dug a hole in the courtyard of our house and buried his things in it—his schoolbooks, pencils and novels; the sheets he slept in his last night at home. Every Sunday I wait for the lights to go out in Luisa's room and I go to the foot of that big jacaranda tree to mourn for him. I know my wife's hiding behind her curtains and looking out at me. I know she's praying for him too. Maybe it's all for the best that we never saw his body."

Andrew reached out and covered Alberto's hand with his own. Alberto looked up and smiled sadly.

"Maybe I don't look my age, but I'm going to be 80 next year, and I'm still hoping death will give me a chance to meet my son again. I suppose living to such an old age is my penance."

"I'm sorry, Alberto."

"And so am I. Because of me, Ortiz will get off lightly. When he recovers, he'll go back to his life as if nothing had happened. And yet we were so close."

"Would you lend me your car until tomorrow evening?"

"Where do you need to go?"

"We'll talk about it later."

"Drop me off at the bar, and then you can keep it."

"Where can I find Marisa right now?"

"At her place, I suppose. She works nights and sleeps all day. What a life!"

Andrew handed his notebook and pen to Alberto.

"Write down her address for me, please. But don't let her know I'm coming."

Alberto looked at him questioningly.

"It's your turn to trust me," Andrew said.

* * *

After dropping Alberto at the bar, Andrew followed his directions to Marisa's place in the Palermo Viejo neighborhood. He climbed the stairs to the third story of the small building on Calle Malabia. Marisa looked taken aback to see him when she opened the door, dressed only in a towel.

"What are *you* doing here? I was expecting a girlfriend."

"Call her and cancel, then get dressed. Or the other way around if you prefer."

"Just because we slept together once doesn't mean you can order me around."

"It's got nothing to do with that."

"I'll tell my friend it's off. We can stay here if you like," Marisa said, dropping her towel. She looked even sexier than Andrew remembered. He knelt to pick up the towel and wound it around her shoulders.

"Sometimes the second time's not as good as the first. Go get dressed. We've got important things to do."

She stalked away, slamming the bathroom door behind her.

Andrew looked around Marisa's studio apartment. The living room doubled as a bedroom. The bed was unmade, but the rumpled white sheets looked clean and inviting. Books were in precarious piles against one wall, and brightly colored cushions were scattered around a low table in the middle of the room. Shelves groaned under the weight of more books on another wall, between two windows that let the light flood in. The place was as messy and attractive as the woman who lived in it.

Marisa reappeared wearing a pair of jeans that were ripped at the knee and a tank top that hugged her breasts revealingly.

"Where are we going?" she demanded, hunting for her keys.

"To see your aunt."

Marisa stopped short.

"Why didn't you say so?" she grumbled.

She went and pulled a pair of black corduroy pants and an old T-shirt out of a pile of clothes on the floor. She slipped off her jeans, yanked her top over her head and got changed in front of Andrew.

* * *

Andrew drove. Marisa lit a cigarette and opened the window.

"What do you want from Luisa?"

"I need to ask her a question to wind up my investigation. And I also want to ask her to stop treating me like an idiot."

"Why do you say that?"

"Because she and your uncle still see each other, despite their claims to the contrary."

"I find that hard to believe. What business it is of yours, anyway?"

"You'll understand later."

* * *

Luisa didn't seem surprised when she opened the door and found Andrew and her niece standing there. She showed them into the living room.

"What can I do for you?" she asked.

"Tell me everything you really know about Major Ortiz."

"I've already told you, I don't know much about him. Before I met you, he was just one of many photos in my album."

"Can I see your album again, please? Not the one with the photos of the torturers—the one with the pictures of their victims."

"Of course."

Luisa opened the sideboard drawer and handed Andrew the album. He flicked through every last page.

"Don't you have any photos of Isabel and Rafael Cruz?" he asked Luisa, staring at her intently.

"Sorry, but those names don't mean anything to me. I don't have photos of every single one of the thirty thousand people who were disappeared—only the five hundred or so whose children were stolen."

"They had a daughter called María Luz. She was two when her parents were killed. Have you overlooked her story, then?"

"You don't intimidate me, Mr. Stilman, nor does your impertinence. You know very little about the work we've accomplished. Since we began our battle to expose the truth, we've only managed to establish the true identities of ten percent of the stolen children. We still have a long way to go. Considering my age, I'll probably never see us attain our goal. Why are you so interested in this little girl's fate?"

"Major Ortiz adopted her. Quite a coincidence, don't you think?"

"What do you mean, 'coincidence'?"

"There was a photo of María Luz in the file that put us on Ortiz's trail, without any explanation of the connection between the two."

"It would seem your informer, whoever he is, wanted to steer you in a certain direction."

"He . . . or she?"

"I'm tired, Marisa. You need to take your friend home; it's time for my siesta."

Marisa gestured to Andrew to get up. As she kissed her aunt goodbye, she murmured into her ear that she was sorry.

"Don't be," Luisa whispered back. "He's not bad looking, and life's too short."

On their way down the front steps, Andrew asked Marisa to

wait in the courtyard for a moment; he'd left his pen on the dining room table.

Luisa frowned when she saw him return.

"Have you forgotten something, Mr. Stilman?"

"Please call me Andrew. I'd be delighted if you would. I just had one last thing to say before I let you get your rest: I'm glad you and Alberto have made up."

"What are you talking about?"

"Considering your age you should be past seeing men in secret. Don't you agree?"

Luisa didn't reply.

"The jacket hanging up in your lobby is the one Alberto was wearing when I met him in the bar. Have a nice siesta, Luisa. You don't mind me calling you Luisa, do you?"

* * *

"What on earth were you doing?" Marisa asked when Andrew joined her in the courtyard.

"I did explain before we left your place, but you don't pay any attention to what I say. Are you working tonight?"

"Yes."

"Tell your boss you won't be able to. Just say you're ill. One more lie won't make any difference."

"And why wouldn't I be going to work?"

"I promised you yesterday that we'd finish what we'd started together, and that's exactly what we're going to do. Can you tell me where there's a gas station? I need to fill up the car."

"Where are you taking me?"

"San Andrés de Giles."

* * *

They reached the edge of the village in two hours' time.

Andrew pulled over to ask a passerby where the police station was, then set off in the direction he'd been given.

"Why are we going to the cops?" Marisa inquired.

"You aren't. Just stay in the car and wait for me."

Andrew walked in and asked if he could speak to a detective. The officer at the front desk replied that the only detective had already gone home. Andrew grabbed a notepad from the counter and scribbled down his cell phone number and hotel address.

"Last night I drove past the scene of an accident that claimed a life, over near Gahan. I drove two injured people to the hospital. I don't have much else to say, but if you need a statement, here's how to get in touch with me."

"I know about it," the officer said, getting up from his chair. "The doctor we spoke to said you'd left without leaving your contact details."

"I waited in the car park for quite some time, but I had to get to an important meeting in Buenos Aires, so I decided I'd come back as soon as I could. And I have, as you can see."

The officer offered to take his statement which he could give to the detective. He sat down at a typewriter and tapped out what Andrew had to say. Nine lines and not a word more. Andrew signed the piece of paper, humbly accepted the officer's congratulations for saving two lives, and went back out to the car.

"Would you mind telling me what you've been doing in the police station all this time?" Marisa asked.

"I've removed one of Ortiz's pieces from the chessboard. I'll explain later. Right now we need to get over to the hospital as fast as possible."

* * *

"How are the accident victims that were brought in last

night doing?" Andrew asked. "We wanted to check in on them before we head back to Buenos Aires."

"You've come back!" said the doctor, seeing Marisa with Andrew in the lobby. "We couldn't find you last night, so I thought you must be guilty of something and had run off."

"We couldn't wait, and you didn't give us a sense of when they'd be out of surgery," Andrew said.

"How could I have known?"

"That's what we thought, and we weren't about to spend the night in the car park. We've just been to the police station and given a statement."

"Whom did you speak to?"

"An Officer Guartez. Nice guy with a deep voice and big glasses."

The doctor nodded. The description matched Guartez, one of only three policemen in the village.

"They were lucky—very lucky—that you drove past at the right time. The patient with the worst injuries was transferred to the capital early this morning. We're a very small hospital and not equipped to deal with such serious cases. Mr. Ortega only had a deep wound, broken bones and muscle laceration. We've operated on him. He's resting in a room down the hall. Would you like to see him?"

"I don't want to tire him out unnecessarily," Andrew answered.

"I'm sure he'll be delighted to have the chance to thank his rescuers. I've got to go and do my rounds. You can find your own way: it's just down there at the end of the corridor. But don't stay too long—he does need to get his strength back."

The doctor said goodbye and informed the nurse on duty that they could go and see the patient.

When they got to the room, Andrew drew the curtain

closed around Ortiz's bed, even though the neighboring bed was empty.

Ortiz was asleep. Marisa shook his shoulder.

"You again!" he said, opening his eyes.

"How are you feeling?" Andrew asked.

"Better since they gave me some painkillers. What do you want from me now?"

"To give you a second chance."

"And what second chance might that be?"

"You've been admitted under the name of Ortega, if I'm not mistaken."

"That's the name on my papers," the ex-major replied, looking down.

"You could leave here under the same name and return home as normal."

"Until you publish your article?"

"I'd like to make a deal with you."

"I'm listening."

"Answer my questions honestly, and I'll just tell Major Ortiz's story without revealing his new identity."

"What proof do I have that you'll keep your promise?"

"I can only offer you my word."

Ortiz stared at Andrew for a long time.

"What about her? Will she be capable of holding her tongue?"

"Yes. As capable as she was of holding a gun to your head last night. I don't think she wants me to expose you. Her future depends on it, doesn't it?"

Ortiz said nothing, his face fraught with tension. His gaze came to rest on the IV bag sending fluid into his veins.

"All right, then," he whispered.

"What were the circumstances in which you adopted María Luz?"

The question hit a nerve. Ortiz turned to Andrew and didn't take his eyes off him again.

"When I was discharged, Febres wanted to make sure I wouldn't talk. He took me to a secret orphanage. Most of the children were babies only a few weeks old. He ordered me to choose one, explaining it'd be the best way for me to regain a sense of reality. He told me that I, too, had helped save this innocent soul by flying the plane from which her parents had been thrown into the sea."

"And had you flown it?"

"I had no idea. No more than he did. I wasn't the only one piloting those flights, as you can imagine. But it was a possibility. I was a newlywed back then. María Luz was the oldest baby there. I told myself it would be easier having a two-year-old."

"But she was a stolen child!" Marisa protested. "And your wife agreed to take part in this monstrous act?"

"My wife knew nothing about it. Right up to her death, she believed what I'd told her: that María Luz was the child of soldiers killed by the Montoneros, and that it was our duty to help her. Febres gave us a birth certificate in her name. I explained to my wife that it'd be easier for María Luz to live her life to the fullest if she knew nothing about the tragedy which left her an innocent victim. We loved her as if we'd given birth to her ourselves. María Luz was twelve when my wife died, and she cried for her like any girl who had just lost her mother. I brought her up on my own. I worked like a maniac so I could pay for her to study languages and arts at the university. I gave her everything she wanted."

"I can't listen to this," Marisa objected, jumping up.

Andrew shot her a furious look and she sat down again, straddling her chair with her back to Ortiz.

"Does María Luz still live in Dumesnil?" Andrew asked.

"No, she left a long time ago. The Mothers of the Plaza de Mayo found her when she was twenty. She used to spend her weekends in Buenos Aires. She was a political activist and she never missed an opportunity to go to demonstrations for what she called 'social progress,' all the budding trade unionists she'd met at college had put those ideas into her head. Quite the opposite of the education we'd given her."

"Yet in line with her real parents' ideals," Marisa interrupted. "It wasn't your blood flowing through her veins. It seems the apple doesn't fall far from the tree."

"So you think leftism is hereditary? Perhaps. Plenty of other defects are passed on that way," Ortiz jeered.

"I don't know about 'leftism,' as you call it so contemptuously. But humanity—very likely!"

Ortiz turned to Andrew.

"If she interrupts one more time, I won't tell you another thing."

At that, Marisa exited the curtain, giving Major Ortiz the finger as she went.

"The Mothers of the Plaza de Mayo spotted María Luz during one of the many demonstrations she went on. It took them several months to actually approach her. When my daughter discovered the truth, she asked to change her name. She left the house the same day, without saying a word, without even looking at me."

"Do you know where she went?"

"I haven't the faintest idea."

"Did you try to find her?"

"I went to Buenos Aires whenever there was a march. I would walk up and down, scouring the parade of people in the hope of catching a glimpse of her. I did, once. I went up to her and begged her to spare me a moment so we could talk. She refused. All I could see in her eyes was hatred. I was scared she'd denounce me, but she didn't. After she got her degree, she left the country, and I never heard anything about her again. You can write your article, Mr. Stilman, but I hope you'll keep your word. I'm not asking that for myself, but for my other daughter. She only knows that her sister was adopted."

Andrew put his pen and notebook away. He stood up and left without saying goodbye to Ortiz.

Marisa was waiting for him behind the curtain, scowling.

* * *

"Don't tell me that bastard's getting off just like that!" Marisa yelled, climbing into the car.

"I'm a man of my word."

"You're as bad as him!"

Andrew looked at her, a smile playing on his lips. He started the engine and steered the car onto the road.

"You're very sexy when you're angry," he said, putting his hand on Marisa's knee.

"Don't touch me," she replied, pushing it away.

"I pledged not to reveal his identity in my article, but I didn't promise anything else, as far as I know."

"What do you mean?"

"There's nothing stopping me from printing a photo to illustrate my article! If somebody recognizes Ortega in Ortiz's face, that's not my problem. Direct me to that photographer friend of yours who developed your film. Let's hope it isn't grainy. I really don't want to have to come back here tomorrow."

Marisa looked at Andrew, took his hand and put it back on her thigh.

* * *

It was a beautiful day. A few wispy clouds streaked across the azure sky above Buenos Aires. Andrew spent his last few hours in Argentina visiting the city. Marisa showed him around La Recoleta cemetery. Andrew looked in amazement at the mausoleums containing coffins laid out on shelves, not buried beneath the ground.

"That's how it is here," Marisa said. "People spend a fortune on getting their final dwelling place built. A roof, four walls, an iron gate to let the light in. Eventually the entire family ends up reunited here for all eternity. I'd certainly prefer to watch the sun rise," she added, "than rot at the bottom of a hole. I also find it a cheerful idea that people can still call on you in your 'home.'"

"You're right," Andrew said, suddenly consumed by the dark thoughts he'd almost completely pushed from his mind since he'd arrived in Argentina.

"We've got time; we're still young."

"Yes . . . At least you've got time," Andrew sighed. "Can we go now? Let's go somewhere more lively, please."

"I'll take you to my neighborhood," Marisa said. "It's full of life and color, and there is music playing on every street corner. I couldn't live anyplace else."

"I think we've finally found something in common!"

She took him to dinner in a little restaurant in Palermo. The owner seemed to know her well. Although lots of other customers were waiting in line for a table, Andrew and Marisa were the first to be seated.

They continued their evening in a jazz club, where Marisa swayed her hips rhythmically on the dance floor. She tried several times to drag Andrew onto it with her, but he preferred to stay put on his stool, leaning on the bar as he watched her dance.

At around one in the morning, they went for a stroll through the still-bustling narrow streets.

"When are you going to publish your article?"

"In a few weeks."

"When it comes out, Alberto will identify Ortega from the photo of Ortiz. He'll press charges. He's determined to. I'm sure he's been hoping to do it for a long time."

"Other witness statements will be needed in order to expose him."

"Don't worry—Luisa and her network will do what's necessary. Ortiz will answer for his crimes in a court of law."

"She's a hell of a woman, your aunt."

"You were right about Alberto and her, you know. They meet on a bench in the Plaza de Mayo once a week. They sit next to each other for an hour, often barely exchanging a word. Then each leaves in a different direction."

"Why do they do that?"

"Because they need to meet, to be the parents of a son whose memory they want to keep alive. There's no grave for them to go and meditate by."

"Do you think they'll live together as husband and wife again?"

"No. What they've been through was too much."

Marisa remained silent for a few seconds, then added: "Luisa really likes you, you know."

"I hadn't realized."

"I had. She thinks you're attractive, and she's a woman with good taste."

"I'll take that as a compliment, then," Andrew said, smiling.

"I've left a small gift for you in your things."

"What is it?"

"You'll find out when you get to New York. Don't open it before then, though. Promise me. It's a surprise."

"I promise."

"My place is only a short walk away," she told him. "Come on, follow me."

Andrew accompanied Marisa to the foot of her apartment building, stopping at the door.

"Don't you want to come up?"

"No, I don't want to come up."

"Don't you like me anymore?"

"That's just it—I like you a bit too much. It was different in the car—it wasn't part of the plan. We were in a dangerous situation. I said to myself that life was short and I had to live for the moment . . . Actually, I said nothing of the sort. I just wanted you, and— "

"And now you think that life will be long, and you feel guilty you cheated on your fiancée."

"I don't know whether life will be long, Marisa. But yes, I do feel guilty."

"You're a better guy than I thought, Andrew Stilman. Go back to her. What happened in the car doesn't count. I don't love you, you don't love me—it was just sex. Good sex, but nothing else."

Andrew leaned over and kissed her on the cheek.

"It makes you look old when you do that," she said. "Now get out of here before I have my wicked way with you right here on the sidewalk!" Andrew turned to go. "Wait. Can I ask you one last question? When I collected your notebooks from the hotel, I saw you'd written *What if I could replay my life?* on the first page of one of them. What did you mean by that?"

"It's a long story . . . Goodbye, Marisa."

"Goodbye, Andrew Stilman. I don't think we'll ever see each other again and I wish you a wonderful life. I'll always have fond memories of you."

Andrew walked away without turning back. At the intersection, he jumped into a taxi.

Marisa ran up the stairs, opened her apartment door and let fall the tears she'd been holding back.

21

The plane landed at JFK late in the afternoon. Andrew had fallen asleep immediately after takeoff and only woke up when the wheels touched the ground again.

To his surprise, he found Valerie waiting for him behind the sliding doors once he'd gone through customs. She wrapped her arms around him and told him how much she'd missed him.

"I almost got into a fight with Simon because he wanted to come and pick you up!"

"I'm happy you won," Andrew replied, kissing her.

"I have to say you hardly ever called me."

"I was working night and day. It wasn't easy."

"But you finished your investigation?"

"Yes."

"So it was worth me pining for you all this time."

"You moped around the whole time?"

"I wouldn't go that far. I've never worked so hard before in my life. I've been coming home in the evenings and literally collapsing into bed—I couldn't even gather the energy to eat dinner. I missed you terribly."

"It was about time I came back, then. I missed you too," Andrew said, leading her to the taxi stand.

* * *

The doorbell rang several times. Andrew jumped out of

bed, slipped on a shirt and crossed the living room to the front door.

"So how was Buenos Aires?" Simon asked.

"Keep your voice down. Valerie's still asleep."

"She's had you to herself all weekend. *I* didn't even get a phone call."

"We hadn't seen each other for ten days, so you do understand we . . . "

"Okay, okay—no need to give me the details. Get some pants on. I'm taking you out to breakfast."

"And hello to you too."

Andrew got dressed quickly. He wrote a little note to Valerie and stuck it on the fridge door, then joined Simon outside the front of the building.

"You could've called me yesterday, you know. So how was the trip?"

"Intense."

They walked into the café on the street corner and sat down at Simon's favorite table.

"Did everything go according to plan out there?"

"For my article, yes. But as for the other thing, we can forget the Argentina lead."

"How can you be so sure?"

"Ortiz can't possibly be aware that I'm going to publish his photo. I'll explain everything another time, but we need to look elsewhere, Simon."

"That only leaves Mrs. Capetta, your colleague Olson, and . . . "

"Valerie?"

"You said it, not me. There is actually another person to add to the list. While you were frolicking around in South America, I had several phone conversations with your inspector friend."

"What about?"

"You're not going to believe this: as crazy as it sounds, Olson may be right about that serial killer."

"You're not serious."

"I try my best not to be . . . But the NYPD is starting to take it seriously. Same weapon and approach, and theft wasn't the motive for the attack on the jeweler we visited in Lenox Hill Hospital."

"That's not what the guy told us."

"He was trying to con his insurance company. He must have woken up in the hospital and hit on the idea of saying he'd been on his way to see a customer. Actually, he was just walking home from work through the park. An assessor from the insurance company saw through him before you could say 'fraud.' There was no such customer, and on the claim form the idiot listed two supposedly stolen necklaces that he'd already claimed in a previous burglary. The attack on him was just a random thing."

"I find it hard to believe Olson could've stumbled on such a big story."

"Listen, just so we're clear about this: are you absolutely sure you're not threatened by Olson? Professionally, I mean?"

Andrew looked away.

"Yeah, sure. Completely sure."

"Okay, back to business. The police are asking questions. And we can hardly go and tell them that a fourth victim may be added to the serial killer's list in early July."

"If it really is a madman who killed me," Andrew said pensively, "we're done for."

"You always need to make a big deal out of things."

"By 'things,' do you mean my death? So sorry for making a big deal out of it. You're right—what was I thinking?"

"That's not what I meant. And anyway, there's nothing to prove your story's linked to that case. We've still got four weeks to go."

"We may have."

"What do you mean?"

"In Argentina, nothing happened exactly as it did the first time round."

"You mean you experienced new things?"

"The order of events was different. And, yes, some things were new."

"Maybe you'd just forgotten them?"

"I doubt that very much."

"What are you hiding from me?"

"I had sex with the bartender who helped me track down Ortiz. That didn't happen before."

"I knew I should have come along!" Simon exclaimed, thumping his fist on the table.

"To stop me from doing stupid things?"

"No, you do what you like. Then again, if I'd been there, I'm the one who'd have slept with her. You're not going to tell me you're feeling guilty, are you?"

"Of course I feel guilty."

"You really are incredible, Andrew. You're convinced someone's going to murder you in a month, and you're feeling guilty about a minor tryst? What's done is done. Just don't say anything to Valerie, and focus on the coming days, okay? Let's change the subject," Simon quickly added, looking out of the window.

Valerie walked into the café.

"I knew I'd find you in here," she said. "The look on your faces! Have you had an argument?"

Simon stood up and kissed Valerie.

"We never argue. I'll leave you two lovebirds on your own—a customer's waiting for me. Andrew, come and see me at the garage if you can, so we can finish our discussion."

Valerie waited until Simon had left, then sat down in his place.

"Sometimes I get the impression he's jealous of me," she said, amused.

"You might be right. Simon is a bit possessive."

"What were you talking about? There was tension, don't deny it."

"About the bachelor party he wants to organize for me."

"I fear the worst!"

"Me too. I told him so, and he took it badly," Andrew replied.

First lie to Valerie since I've been back, he reflected.

* * *

Andrew went straight to his editor's office when he got to work. Olivia Stern hung up her phone and asked him to sit down. Andrew told her about his trip, the circumstances in which he'd assembled the facts, and the deal he'd had to strike with Ortiz.

"You want us to publish it without mentioning his assumed name? You're asking a lot of me, Andrew. Your article will lose credibility. You'll defeat the whole purpose of it."

"I thought the idea was to tell the life story of an ordinary man who became an accessory to atrocities. What purpose are you talking about?"

"Denouncing a war criminal! If we're not doing that, I don't see how we can put it on the front page."

"Were you really planning to make it the lead article?" Andrew asked.

"I was hoping to, but you're going to have to choose between personal glory and keeping your word. Only you can make that decision."

"There are other ways of denouncing him," he said, getting an envelope out of his pocket and placing it on the desk.

Olivia opened it. The expression on her face changed when she saw the photos of Major Ortiz that Marisa had taken.

"He looks older than I pictured him," she murmured.

"He looked even worse in his hospital bed," Andrew replied.

"You're a funny guy, Andrew."

"I know—I've already been told that this morning. So, do you have what you need now?"

"Write up your article. It's your top priority. I'm giving you three weeks. If your text is up to par, I'll ask the editorial board for a lead paragraph on the front page and a double-page spread inside."

Andrew asked to have the photos back, but Olivia put them away in her drawer, promising she'd return them to him as soon as they'd been scanned.

Andrew left her office and went straight to see Freddy.

"Back already, Stilman?"

"Looks like it, Olson."

"You look awful. Was Brazil that bad?"

"Argentina, Freddy."

"Oh, yeah. South America is all the same—let's not argue."

"What about you? Everything going well at work?"

"Couldn't be better," Freddy answered. "But don't expect me to say anything more than that."

"I've got a cop friend. He's retired, but he can still pull strings. You only need to ask."

Freddy looked at Andrew distrustfully.

"What are you plotting, Stilman?"

"Nothing, Freddy. I'm not plotting anything. I'm tired of our petty squabbling. If you really are on the trail of a serial killer and I can give you a hand, then I'll be happy to—that's all."

"Why would you help me?"

"To stop him from committing another crime. Does that seem like a good enough reason to you?"

"You really make me laugh, Stilman. You've sensed I'm on to something big. Do you want co-author credits while you're at it?"

"No, that hadn't crossed my mind. But now that you mention it, you've given me an idea. Instead of turning our backs on each other, what if we were to publish a report together one day? I know someone who'd be thrilled."

"Oh yeah? Who?"

"My most loyal reader, Spooky Kid! I can just imagine how happy that'd make him. We could even dedicate it to him."

Andrew walked back to his desk, leaving Freddy, whose cheeks had flushed red, to reflect on his proposal.

A text message from Valerie reminded him to drop by the tailor's to get his wedding suit altered. He turned on his computer and began working.

* * *

Andrew spent the whole week on his article. He'd started having nightmares again since he'd returned from Buenos Aires. He dreamt the same scenario each time: he was running along the Hudson River footpath with Freddy on his heels. Freddy always caught up with him and stabbed him under Valerie's amused, conspiratorial gaze. Sometimes, just before he died, he'd recognize Inspector Pilguez, Marisa, Alberto, Luisa, even Simon among the group of joggers. Each time, Andrew woke up suffocating, frozen to the bone and dripping in sweat, with the excruciating lower back pain that now never completely went away.

Wednesday, Andrew left his office a little earlier than usual; he'd promised Valerie he'd be on time for dinner with their maid of honor and best man.

On Thursday, the air-conditioning in Andrew's apartment gave up the ghost, and Valerie, who was woken each night by

Andrew's cries, decided they'd move then and there into her East Village apartment.

Andrew felt increasingly exhausted. His back pains got so bad he sometimes had to lie down on the floor by his desk, much to the amusement of Freddy on his trips to and from the bathroom.

When Andrew left for work on Friday, he swore to Valerie he wouldn't let Simon take him to a strip club. In fact, Simon took him to the last place he'd expected.

* * *

Novecento was jam-packed. Simon elbowed them to the bar. Andrew ordered a Fernet with Coke.

"What's that?"

"You won't like it. Don't bother trying it."

Simon grabbed the glass, took a swig, made a face and ordered a glass of red wine instead.

"Why did you bring me here?" Andrew asked.

"Hey, I didn't force you to come. If I recall your story correctly, tonight's the night you fell head over heels, isn't it?"

"I don't find that at all funny, Simon."

"Just as well. I wasn't trying to be funny. What time did the fateful encounter that screwed up your marriage take place?"

"You don't like Valerie, Simon, any more than you like that we've decided to get married. You've brought me here so I make the same mistakes again. Is that the best you could come up with to 'screw up' my marriage, as you put it?"

"You must really be at the end of your rope if you're getting so aggressive. You've got it all wrong—I brought you here to help you see your fantasy for what it really is. For your information, I like Valerie, and I like the thought that you'll be happy together even more!"

Simon spotted a Bond girl lookalike with legs up to her armpits walking across the room. He stood up and wandered off without a word, leaving Andrew alone at the bar.

A woman sat down on the bar stool next to Andrew and flashed him a smile as he ordered a second Fernet and Coke.

"It's quite unusual for an American to like that drink," she said, staring him in the eye.

Andrew stared back at her. The sensuality she exuded took his breath away. She had a startlingly naughty glint in her eye. Her long, black hair fell elegantly down the back of her neck. He could hardly tear his eyes away from the sheer beauty of her face.

"It's the only unusual thing about me," he said, standing up.

Outside Novecento, Andrew inhaled the night air deeply. He took out his phone and called Simon.

"I'm outside. You do what you want. I'm going home."

"Wait for me; I'm coming," Simon replied.

* * *

"Why the long face?" Simon said as he joined Andrew out on the sidewalk.

"I just want to go home."

"Don't tell me you fell in love at first sight again."

"No, I won't. You wouldn't understand."

"Name me one single thing I haven't understood about you in the past ten years."

Andrew thrust his hands into his pockets and started walking up West Broadway. Simon followed close on his heels.

"I felt the same as I did the first time around."

"So why didn't you stay?"

"Because I've caused enough harm as it is."

"I'm sure you won't even remember what she looks like in the morning."

"That's what you thought last time, but events proved you wrong. There'll be no more lies—I've learned my lesson. I'll probably think of her sometimes, sure, but I've made my choice. True love is the love you have, not dream of. I hope you find it one day, Simon."

* * *

When Andrew walked into his apartment, he found Valerie doing leg lifts in the middle of the living room dressed only in her bra and underwear.

"Aren't you asleep?" he asked as he took off his jacket.

"Yes, of course I am—with my feet in the air and my hands under my butt. It's early. Did Simon fall crazy in love with some stripper and desert you? I can add a setting at the wedding table if things get serious between them."

"No, Simon didn't meet anyone," Andrew replied, lying down next to Valerie. He lifted his legs and began copying her exercises in time with her.

"Was the evening a washout?"

"My stag night was great," Andrew answered. "Much better than I'd thought it'd be."

22

T he next day, Andrew dropped by Mr. Zanetti's for his wedding suit fitting. The tailor asked him to step up onto a low box. He surveyed Andrew and lifted the right jacket shoulder.

"It's not your fault, Mr. Zanetti; I've got one arm longer than the other."

"Yes, I can see that," the tailor replied, pinning the fabric.

"I know you wouldn't want anyone to accuse you of doing a bad alteration, but I've got an important article to finish."

"And you're in a hurry. Is that it?"

"A bit, yes."

"So, did you go back there?" Mr. Zanetti asked, not taking his eyes off his work.

"Where?" Andrew replied.

"That bar, of course. That's where your troubles started, isn't it?"

"How do you know about that?" Andrew exclaimed, stunned.

Zanetti gave him a broad smile.

"Do you think you're the only person to have been treated to a second chance? You're very self-centered, my dear Mr. Stilman. And naïve."

"So you too . . . "

"That stranger in the bar—have you seen her again?" Zanetti interrupted. "Of course you've seen her. You look even more awful than last time. But I suppose if we're hemming your pants, that means you've decided to get married. Funny—I'd have guessed the opposite."

"Why . . . Why did it happen to you?" Andrew quizzed, his voice trembling.

"The only question that should concern you, Mr. Stilman, is why did it happen to *you*. If you don't make it more of a concern, you're going to die soon. Do you really think you'll have a third chance? That'd be taking it a bit far, don't you agree? Stop trembling or I'll end up pricking you."

Zanetti stepped back and examined Andrew's suit from top to bottom.

"It's not quite right yet, but it's better than it was. A quick tuck below the shoulder and it should be perfect. I love perfection, and old habits die hard at my age. If I told you my age, you'd be amazed," Zanetti added, bursting out laughing.

Andrew went to step down from the box, but Zanetti held him by the arm with surprising strength.

"And where do you think you're going in this outfit? So, you chose your teenage love? Wise decision. Take it from someone who knows. I've been married four times, and it's wrecked me. But you probably won't have time to worry about that if you still haven't found your murderer. I don't mean to ramble on, but it's something you really need to think about."

Zanetti walked behind Andrew and gently pulled at the bottom of his jacket.

"You really are oddly proportioned. Stand up straight, please. It's difficult enough as it is. Where was I? Oh yes, talking about your killer. Do you have any idea who it is?" Zanetti asked, bringing his face up close to the back of Andrew's neck. "Is it your future wife? Your colleague? That mysterious serial killer? That mother whose adopted daughter was taken away because of you? Your editor?"

Andrew suddenly felt an intense tearing in his back. The pain took his breath away.

"Or me?" Zanetti sniggered.

Andrew looked at himself in the mirror opposite. His face was frighteningly pale. He saw Zanetti behind him with a long, blood-spattered needle in his hand. Andrew's legs gave way and he fell to his knees on the box. A bloodstain spread across his shirtfront. As he collapsed face-first onto the ground, Mr. Zanetti's insane laughter echoed around the room.

Everything went dark.

* * *

Andrew woke up drenched in sweat with Valerie shaking him vigorously.

"If getting married is stressing you out that much, there's still time to put if off, Andrew. Tomorrow it'll be too late."

"Tomorrow?" he asked, sitting up in bed. "What day is it?"

"It's Saturday. Two in the morning. Saturday the 30th," Valerie replied, looking at the alarm clock. "Actually, our wedding is today."

Andrew jumped out of bed and rushed into the living room. Valerie pushed back the sheets and followed him.

"What's up? You look terrified."

Andrew glanced around the room, and threw himself onto his bag, which he'd spotted on the floor next to the sofa. He opened it frantically and took out a thick file.

"My article! If it's already the 30th, I haven't finished my article on time."

Valerie walked over and hugged him.

"You sent it to your editor by e-mail earlier tonight. Calm down! I thought it was excellent. She'll think it's fantastic too. Please, Andrew, come back to bed. You're going to look terrible in the wedding photos. I will too if you keep me awake."

"It can't be the 30th already," Andrew muttered. "It's impossible."

"Do you want to cancel our wedding, Andrew?" Valerie asked, looking him hard in the eye.

"No, of course not. It's got nothing to do with that."

"What doesn't have anything to do with that? What are you hiding from me, Andrew? What's scaring you? You can tell me everything."

"If only I could."

23.

J ust before the ceremony started, Valerie's mother came up to Andrew, patted him on the shoulder and leaned forward to whisper something in his ear. Andrew pushed her gently away.

"You thought I'd never marry your daughter, didn't you? I understand why. The idea of having you as a mother-in-law probably put quite a few suitors off. But here we all are in church!" he replied sardonically.

"What's gotten into you? I never thought anything of the sort!" Mrs. Ramsay protested.

"And a liar to boot!" Andrew chuckled, walking into the church.

Valerie had never looked lovelier. She was wearing a simple, elegant white dress. Her hair was tied up and topped with a small white hat. The priest's sermon was perfect, and Andrew was even more moved than at his wedding the first time round.

After the ceremony, the little procession left the Church of St Luke in the Fields and walked down the path through the garden. Andrew was surprised to see his editor, Olivia Stern, among the guests.

"I didn't want our wedding night to be spoiled, waiting for her feedback on your article," Valerie whispered in her husband's ear. "While you were at home sweating blood over your work yesterday, I took the initiative of phoning her at the paper and inviting her along. She is your boss, after all."

Andrew smiled and kissed his wife.

Olivia Stern wandered up to them.

"It was a beautiful ceremony, and you both look stunning. Your dress suits you to perfection," she told the bride. "I'd never seen you in a suit before, Andrew. You should wear one more often. May I borrow your husband for a minute or two, Valerie?"

Valerie left them and joined her parents, who were walking ahead.

"Your article is outstanding, Andrew. I don't want to bother you on your wedding day, so I hope you won't mind if I sneak off—it's for a good reason. I'll send you my notes tonight. Sorry to make you work the day after your wedding, but I need you to write me a few more pages. I'm publishing your piece on Tuesday. I've bagged the front page and three inside pages. You're going to be famous!" Olivia said, tapping him on the shoulder.

"So you don't want to wait?" Andrew asked in a daze.

"Why postpone an article this important, and one that'll make our competitors green with envy? You've done a great job. See you on Monday. Have a lovely evening."

Olivia kissed him on the cheek and said goodbye to Valerie as she left.

"She seemed very pleased. It's the first time I've seen you smile all day. You can relax at last."

Valerie was happy, and Andrew felt good, exceptionally good. Until, as they came out on Hudson Street, he glimpsed a black SUV with its windows closed stopped at a red light. Andrew felt a lump in his throat.

"What's that look on your face for?" Simon said, joining Andrew. "Have you seen a ghost?"

The light turned green and the SUV drove off.

"I've jumped forward two weeks, Simon."

"You've done what?"

"They've vanished into thin air. I was at Zanetti's getting my suit tailored the day after you took me to Novecento and he told me the same thing had happened to him. He knew my whole story. I don't know what happened. It was a nightmare, and when I woke up, it was two weeks later. I've jumped through time again, but into the future this time. I don't know what's happening anymore."

"That makes two of us, if that's any reassurance. You're not making any sense at all. What are you talking about, Andrew?" Simon asked, seriously worried.

"About what's going to happen to me! About us, Pilguez, Mrs. Capetta . . . I've only got eight days left! I'm terrified."

"Who are Pilguez and Mrs. Capetta?" Simon quizzed, more and more intrigued.

Andrew stared at Simon for a long time and sighed.

"I've lost you and Pilguez by jumping through time. You don't have the slightest idea what I'm talking about, do you?"

Simon shook his head and put his hands on Andrew's shoulders.

"I knew marriage caused side effects, but you're taking it a bit far!"

Valerie walked over and put her arm around her husband's waist.

"You won't be cross with me if I keep him to myself on our wedding day, will you Simon?"

"Keep him for the whole week. Until the end of the summer if you like. But give him back to me mentally and physically sound, because right now he's off his rocker."

Valerie led Andrew to one side.

"I wish the day was over so I could be alone at home with you," Andrew sighed.

"You took the words right out of my mouth," Valerie replied.

* * *

They spent Sunday at Valerie's apartment. It was pouring rain; one of those summer storms that drenched the city.

After lunch, Andrew immersed himself in reworking parts of his article based on Olivia's notes. Valerie took the opportunity to write up some surgery reports. Late in the afternoon, they went for a short stroll to the grocery store, walking huddled against each other under their umbrella.

"The East Village isn't bad either," Andrew said, surveying his surroundings.

"Would you change neighborhood, then?"

"I didn't say that. But if you heard of a nice three-room apartment going, I wouldn't be against seeing it."

Back at Valerie's place, Andrew carried on working while she read.

"This isn't exactly a great honeymoon," he said, looking up. "You deserve better."

"Depends how you look at it . . . But you're the love of my life."

Andrew finished his article as the sun set. It was past nine o'clock. Valerie proofread it and clicked "send" on the computer.

Andrew was shuffling his rough drafts together when Valerie took them out of his hands.

"Go lie down on the sofa and let me put this stuff away."

Andrew willingly accepted. His back was hurting and the idea of lying down for a moment was very welcome.

"Who's Marisa?" Valerie asked a short while later.

"My contact in Buenos Aires. Why?"

"Because I've just found a small envelope with a note to you on the front."

Andrew held his breath as Valerie read it to him.

For you, Andrew,
A gift borrowed from Luisa.
In memory of Isabel and Rafael.
Thank you on their behalf.
Marisa

Andrew jumped up off the sofa and grabbed the envelope out of Valerie's hand. He opened it and found a small black and white photo inside. Two smiling faces were frozen in the paleness of time.

"Is it them?" Valerie asked.

"Yes, it's Isabel and Rafael," Andrew replied, moved.

"It's weird," Valerie said. "I don't know if it's from knowing their story or from reading your article, but her face looks familiar."

Andrew peered more closely at the photograph.

"It's got nothing to do with my article," he replied, astonished. "I know this face too; much better than you'd imagine."

"What do you mean?" Valerie asked.

"I'd thought of everything—except this. I'm a complete and utter fool."

* * *

Before entering the doors of 620 Eighth Avenue, Andrew glanced up at the black lettering emblazoned across the façade of *The New York Times*. He hurried through the lobby, got into the elevator and went straight to his editor's office.

He sat down in a chair opposite Olivia without waiting to be asked. She looked at him, intrigued.

"Have you read the end of my article?"

"It's exactly what I expected of you. I've sent the text to be laid out. Unless something major happens today, it'll be on tomorrow's front page."

Andrew pulled his chair up to the desk.

"Did you know there's a village with the same name as you close to where Ortiz lives? Strange to think there's a place in the middle of nowhere called 'Olivia,' isn't it?"

"If you say so."

"You don't seem to find it strange. Perhaps if it was called 'María Luz,' you'd have found it stranger—a village with the exact same name as yours."

Andrew took the small envelope out of his pocket, pulled out the photograph and put it down in front of his editor. She stared at it at length, then put it back down without saying a word.

"Do you recognize that couple?" Andrew asked.

"I know who they are, but I never knew them," Olivia sighed.

"The woman in the photo looks so much like you that for a moment I thought it *was* you. You've known since the day Luisa revealed your true identity to you, haven't you, María Luz?"

Olivia stood up and walked over to the window.

"It happened in a café where we university students used to hang out after class. Luisa went there many times, but she never approached me. She would sit on her own in the corner of the room and watch me. And then one day she came over and asked if she could sit down at my table. She had important things to tell me—things that would be hard for me to hear, but that I had to know. My life was turned upside down when she told me the story of Isabel and Rafael, my real parents. I didn't want to believe her. You can't imagine what it was like finding out that twenty years of my life had been one big lie, that I didn't know anything about my roots, that I loved a father who was partially responsible for their fate, and mine. Accepting the truth was a terrible ordeal. I'm not complaining—I got a chance that others haven't, or haven't yet: to rebuild my life.

"I left the house I'd grown up in that very same day, without saying a word to the man who'd brought me up. I moved in with my boyfriend at the time and applied for a scholarship to Yale. I became a dedicated student. Life gave me the opportunity to come out of this dreadful experience a stronger person, to pay tribute to my parents, to make them triumph over those who wanted them wiped out forever. Later on, with the help of my professors at Yale, I acquired American citizenship. When I'd finished my studies I joined *The New York Times* as an intern, and worked my way up."

Andrew picked up the photograph of Isabel and Rafael, and looked at it again.

"Did my investigation in China give you the idea? Did you say to yourself: he's managed to track down stolen children before, he could do the same thing in Argentina? Was it Luisa or Alberto who sent you the file?"

"Both of them. I've never lost touch with them. Luisa's like a godmother to me."

"You sent me after Ortiz the way a hunter would send a dog to drive a wild animal out of its lair."

"I was able to hate him, but not to denounce him. He brought me up. He loved me. It's much more complicated than you imagine. I needed you."

"You do realize that if we publish this article, he'll probably be arrested and condemned to spend the rest of his life in prison?"

"I do this job because of my love for truth. It was the only way I could survive. I turned my back on him a long time ago."

"You've got real nerve talking to me about truth. You've manipulated me since the start! Everything was fixed: Marisa, Alberto, Luisa; Ortiz supposedly spotted visiting a customer. You already knew everything, but you wanted me to find it out. You needed a journalist, an outsider in the whole affair, to put the pieces of the puzzle together for you. You've used me and this paper to carry out a personal investigation."

"Stop the histrionics, Stilman. I handed you the best assignment of your career. When it's published, your China exposé will be nothing more than a dim and distant memory. This report will make you famous. You know that as well as I do. But if you want us to be totally truthful . . . "

"No, that's not what I want, I assure you. And what about your sister? Ortiz told me his second daughter knows nothing about his past. Are you planning to tell her about this or let her find out for herself when she reads the paper? You probably believe it's none of my business, but think carefully. I know what I'm talking about, even if I can't tell you what to do."

"My sister has known the truth for a long time. I told her everything before I left Argentina. I even suggested she join me in the States, but she never wanted to. It was different for her; she's his legitimate daughter. I can't blame her, and neither do I resent her for disowning me for the choices I've made in life."

Andrew scrutinized Olivia's face.

"Who does your sister look like?"

"Her mother. Anna's breathtakingly beautiful. I have a photo of her taken on her twentieth birthday," María Luz said.

She turned round, picked up the photo frame sitting on her desk and held it out to Andrew.

"Luisa sent it to me. I've never found out how she got hold of it."

Andrew turned pale when he saw the portrait of the young woman. He jumped up and rushed over to the door. Before leaving, he turned around. "Olivia, promise me that, whatever happens, you'll print my article."

"Why do you say that?"

Andrew didn't reply. Olivia watched him run down the corridor towards the elevators.

* * *

Andrew left the paper, his thoughts going wild.

A clamor drew his gaze towards a group of joggers trotting down Eighth Avenue towards him. His senses were on alert. Something was wrong.

"It's too early. It isn't the day. Not yet," he muttered as the first runners jostled their way past him.

Panic-stricken, Andrew tried to retrace his steps so he could take cover inside the building, but there were too many runners blocking the way back to the door.

Andrew suddenly recognized a face in the crowd. The stranger from Novecento was walking towards him. She had an elevator slipped up her sleeve, and the blade was shining in the palm of her hand.

"It's too late," Andrew called to Anna. "There's no point anymore. Whatever happens to me, the article will be printed."

"My poor Andrew. You're the one it's too late for," she replied.

"No!" Andrew shouted as she came closer. "Don't do it!"

"But I've already done it, Andrew. Look around you. This is all in your mind. You're already dying, Andrew. What did you think? That you'd risen from the dead? That life really had given you a second chance by sending you back to the past? You make a pitiful sight. All those dizzy spells and nightmares, that shooting pain in your back, that cold feeling that never goes away, those electric shocks bringing you back to life every time your heart stops . . . You've been fighting for your life in this ambulance since I stabbed you. You're being drained of your blood like a slaughtered animal. You've fought all this time, reexamining your memories, reconstructing your past, on the lookout for the tiniest detail that could have escaped you—because you wanted to understand. And you finally remembered that photograph you'd seen so many times behind María Luz's desk. Congratulations. I didn't think you'd figure it out.

"I have nothing personal against you, but without realizing it you became an instrument of my half-sister's machinations. She's an ungrateful coward. My father gave her everything. He loved her as much as he loved me, and she betrayed us. Did that bitch truly think I was going to let her destroy us? I've been on her trail for weeks—since you left Buenos Aires. I hunted you down like you hunted down my father. Over and over again, I practiced the gesture that would silence you. I waited patiently for the right moment to attack. It was perfect—nobody saw me; nobody will remember anything. The hospital isn't much further. I have to say you've survived longer than I thought you would. But now you understand, you can give up, Andrew. You have no reason to fight anymore."

"Yes, I do," Andrew murmured as the last of his strength ebbed away.

"Don't tell me you're thinking about your wife. After what you did to her? Andrew, you left her on your wedding night, remember? You fell madly in love with me. Believe me—you can let go of her. Your death will delight her as much as it does me. Farewell, Andrew. Your eyes are closing. I'll let you live your final moments in peace."

24

The ambulance transporting Andrew Stilman arrived at the emergency room at 7:42 A.M. The traffic hadn't been as slow as usual that morning. A team of doctors and nurses busied themselves around his stretcher as soon as it appeared.

"Thirty-nine-year-old male stabbed in the base of the back half an hour ago. Severe hemorrhaging. Three cardiac arrests. Resuscitated each time, but his pulse is very weak and his body temperature has dropped significantly. He's in your hands now," said the emergency doctor, handing the admission form over to the surgeon.

Andrew opened his eyes. As he was being wheeled into surgery, the neon strip lights formed a broken white line above his head.

He attempted to speak, but the intern leaned over and told him to reserve his strength for the operation.

"I'm sorry . . . Valerie . . . Tell her . . . ," he whispered, then lost consciousness.

* * *

A police car stopped outside, its sirens wailing. A woman got out and ran into the hospital. She hurried across the lobby and caught up with the nurses pushing Andrew's stretcher.

A nurse grabbed her around the waist to stop her from going any further.

"I'm his wife!" she screamed. "Please tell me he's alive!"

"You've got to let us operate on him, ma'am. Every minute counts. We'll let you know as soon as we can."

Valerie watched Andrew disappear through the doors to the operating room. She stood rooted to the spot, stunned. Seeing that she was in shock, a nurse led her to the waiting room.

"The surgeons on duty this morning are the best I know. He couldn't be in better hands," she assured Valerie.

Simon arrived a few moments later. He rushed towards the reception desk and spotted Valerie sobbing in the waiting room. She stood up when she saw him and collapsed into his arms.

"It'll be okay, you'll see," Simon said through his tears.

"Tell me he'll get through this, Simon."

"I promise you he will. I know him: he's a fighter. He loves you, Valerie. He was telling me yesterday, over and over again. He was so angry at himself. Who could have done this? Why?"

"The police officer who drove me here told me that nobody saw anything," Valerie said, choking back a sob.

"Maybe Andrew saw something . . . "

Simon and Valerie sat next to each other, waiting as the hours ticked by, their eyes riveted to the closed doors leading to the operating room.

* * *

In the afternoon, a surgeon came to find Valerie and Simon in the waiting room. They held their breath as they listened to his report.

Half an hour had passed between Andrew being stabbed and arriving at the hospital. His heart had stopped beating several times in the ambulance. The first responders had brought him back to life each time, but they had nearly lost him.

The operation had gone as well as the doctors could have hoped. The weapon had caused severe, deep lesions, and he'd lost a lot of blood—far too much blood. He was alive but his prognosis was critical and would remain so for at least the next forty-eight hours.

That was all the surgeon could tell them. As he left he added that Valerie and Simon should keep their hopes up; in life, anything was possible.

On Tuesday, July 10, Andrew Stilman's article appeared on the front page of *The New York Times*. Valerie read it out loud to Andrew on his hospital bed. He still hadn't regained consciousness.

THANKS TO

Pauline, Louis, and Georges.
Raymond, Danièle, and Lorraine.

Susanna Lea.
Emmanuelle Hardouin.
Nicole Lattès, Leonello Brandolini, Antoine Caro.
Elisabeth Villeneuve, Anne-Marie Lenfant, Arié Sberro, Sylvie Bardeau, Lydie Leroy, and all the staff at Editions Robert Laffont.
Pauline Normand, Marie-Ève Provost.
Léonard Anthony, Sébastien Canot, Romain Ruetsch, Danielle Melconian, Naja Baldwin, Mark Kessler, Stéphanie Charrier, Katrin Hodapp, Laura Mamelok, Kerry Glencorse, Julia Wagner, Aline Grond.
Brigitte and Sarah Forissier.

Mary's Fish Camp.

And a big thank you to Victoria Donda, whose life and writings have informed this story.

ABOUT THE AUTHOR

Marc Levy's novels have sold over thirty million copies and been translated into over 40 languages, making him today's most widely read French author. His English language debut, *If Only It Were True*, sold almost half a million copies and was made into a film starring Reese Witherspoon and Mark Ruffalo. Levy lives with his family in New York.